DUSK *to* DAWN SERIES

# COME AND GET ME

## TINA MARIE NICHOLS

DP DIVERSIFIED
244 5th Ave Ste G-200
NY, NY 10001

Come and Get Me, Book 2
Dusk to Dawn Series

Published by
DP Diversified
*a division of DocUmeant Publishing*
244 5th Avenue, Suite G-200
NY, NY 10001
Phone: 6462334366

http://www.DocUmeantPublishing.com

For permission contact the publisher at:
publisher@DocUmeantPublishing.com

Disclaimer: All characters appearing in this work are fictitious. Any resemblance to real persons, living or dead, is purely coincidental.

Editor: Philip S. Marks

Cover Design and Layout: Ginger Marks, DocUmeantDesigns.com

Library of Congress Control Number: 2023936526
ISBN: 9781950075973 (pbk)
ISBN: 9781950075980 (digital)

To my wonderful family,
I love you for your never-ending love,
confidence, and support.

# ACKNOWLEDGMENTS

**I'VE HEARD IT** said that it takes a village to raise a child. Well, it definitely takes one to publish a book. My sincerest gratitude belong to my Publishing Village and my designer, Ginger Marks of DocUmeant Designs. Without you this book wouldn't be a reality.

# CHAPTER ONE

**BENEATH A HEAVY** cocoon of blankets, Raine Andrews tossed restlessly, the ever-occurring nightmare drawing her deeper into its fog-shrouded grasp. There was a face, too, that kept fading in and out of the swirling fog. It belonged to her evil husband.

Sheer terror gripped her as she stared in horror when the heavy curtain of fog parted revealing the living, breathing monster that pursued her in both waking and sleeping moments. In one hand he held his favorite weapon—a leather belt folded in half that cracked like a bullwhip each time he snapped it together. It was the weapon he'd used to inflict terrible agony on her in the past and, heaven help her, he was about to do it again.

The thought had barely formed when the strap tore into her tender flesh. In that instant she emitted a shrill scream that jerked her awake. Her heart was pounding like a jackhammer as she switched on the bedside lamp, still fully expecting to see Addison in the flesh. He wasn't there. The cracking noise in her nightmare was a tree branch rapping sharply against a windowpane that was eerily echoing the belt's snapping.

Easing from the bed she noted her slumbering four-year-old hadn't budged despite all the thrashing about. Katy-bug could sleep through anything. Just then the rapping came again. "And that," she muttered under her breath, "has definitely got to go!"

Any further sleeping was definitely not an option, so she padded quiet as a mouse to the kitchen. There was no sense dragging Cora from her bed. It was bad enough that she was up before the neighbors' rooster started crowing. After setting a pot of coffee on to brew, Raine took a well-needed shower. As the hot water cascaded over her, memories of the mess she'd fled from nearly four months ago played through her mind. That mess being the culmination of mental cruelty and physical abuse that ended violently on a sweltering September night. Fueled by the combination of alcohol and cocaine, her once loving husband had jumped off the cliff of no return. After nearly beating her to death, he tried to shoot her. If not for a guardian angel protecting her, he might have succeeded.

Cold shivers raced up her spine as the image of Addison waving the gun filled her head and the ensuing struggle, the weapon ending up between them. When it went off with a deafening explosion, she'd waited for pain and death, positive he'd accomplished his mission. Only neither came. Instead, it was Addison who'd collapsed to the floor.

A perverse chuckle mingled with the spray from her shower. Talk about karma! Served him right to be on the receiving end, or should it be the deserving end, of the gun. During all the past times he'd gotten physical she'd never wanted him dead, but this was the final straw that broke the camel's back. For so long he'd controlled her, made her life a living hell, and in that moment standing over his still form she'd had a debate with her conscience whether to let him die, or save his sorry hide.

Though eventually opting to save him, all she'd gotten in return was more damn trouble from the ungrateful S.O.B. While the EMTs were treating him he'd regained consciousness and had the gall to accuse *her* of trying to murder him. But for all Addison's pity-crying, his accusations fell on unsympathetic ears. No one believed him, plus it didn't take a rocket scientist to figure out what had really happened, especially given the shape she was in — bloody, battered, and barely clothed. Still, the police investigation was done by the book, including testing the gun for fingerprints. In the end the sweetest icing on the great big celebration cake was her fingerprints were *not* on the gun and off to the pokey he'd gone! The image of Addison wearing jailhouse orange so brightened her spirits she did a happy dance right there in the shower.

A few minutes later, snug in a plush red robe, she was ready for the coffee that beckoned her with waves of delicious aroma. Filling a mug, she inhaled deeply before taking a sip. It was liquid silk sliding down her throat. Curling up in the butter-soft leather recliner, the quiet of the early morning stole over her. During those tumultuous times this had always been her favorite part of the day. Katy would still be sleeping, and Addison would have left for a jobsite taking with him the turmoil of their relationship. Before leaving Phoenix she couldn't remember the last time she'd truly relaxed. It seemed she'd been walking on eggshells forever. But the eggshell-walking and the knocking-around had come to an abrupt halt.

Her stomach knotted as more memories from that night vividly replayed through her mind. She'd been on the receiving end of Addison's temper many times but that had been the worst. It was as if a demon had slipped inside him turning Addison into a monster, one controlled by drugs and alcohol. She would always be thankful that Katy had been at Cora's and not been part of what happened.

Addison, already indulging in his favorite pastime of cocaine and alcohol, had become enraged finding she wasn't wearing the dress he'd specifically picked for her to wear to the party being thrown in his honor. Too angry to accept her explanation of losing weight and the dress being too big, he'd accused her of defying him. As if. Addison had controlled her like Geppetto controlled Pinocchio's strings. Going on the attack, from the first blow to the last, there wasn't a place left untouched, except her face. Not stupid, Addison couldn't very well have her looking like a Mack truck had run over her then backed up for good measure. Not wanting anyone to know his dirty secrets, he never touched her face.

When he'd finished meting out her punishment, and not caring that she could barely move, he'd ordered her to get cleaned up and better damn well be wearing the dress he'd picked out when she walked out the front door. If not, he'd give her more of what he'd just done.

Picking her battles, she'd put herself back together, put on the dress, at least it had covered the bruises marking her arms, and went to the party, his warning ringing in her ears. She'd wanted to scream her head off but in order to avoid more of his wrath, she'd kept her mouth shut and not one soul even guessed they were not the happily married couple behind the facade.

The only thing that kept her going was *her* secret; that come Monday morning as soon as Addison's taillights faded, she was going to make her escape. Obviously that hadn't happened. Again, she pondered her decisions during that time. Had she told anyone about Addison's abuse, especially her best friend Molly, would things have turned out differently? That was something she'd never know, and thinking about "what-ifs" got her nowhere. Besides, fate had stepped in that night sending her life in a totally different direction.

On the drive home from the party Addison accused her of flirting with their host. Though not true, there'd been no convincing him otherwise and from that point on everything went way beyond hell-in-a-hand-basket. She'd ended up severely beaten and Addison shot. Both ended up in the hospital, but she got to go home while Addison went to jail.

Though he'd stuck to his innocent victim story, there'd been no denying the proof that her fingerprints weren't on the gun and she sure as heck hadn't beaten herself up. For the first time in a long time Raine had the hammer and used it. Addison deserved to rot in hell for what he'd done, so she refused to drop the charges, as did the state. On top of that she filed for divorce, demanding sole custody of their daughter.

Furious to the very marrow of his bones that no one believed him, Addison screamed revenge to anyone who would listen. That didn't sit well with her attorney, or the detectives working the case for there wasn't a doubt in their minds he'd make good on his threat, or have someone else do it. So, they advised her to leave town for a while.

Their concerns were justified given her in-laws, especially her mother-in-law, hated her and would do anything to hurt her. Though leaving felt like Addison was winning, wisely she'd heeded their advice and once able to travel loaded up Katy and Cora, her neighbor, who'd refused to let them go off alone, and departed for parts unknown.

With no particular destination in mind, they'd driven the old Route 66 Highway. Of course, they'd run into plenty of dead-ends and had to backtrack. They laughed hilariously over those incidents, and the further away from Addison she got, the more layers of stress peeled away. She thought of the endless ribbons of asphalt they'd traveled, their journey taking them through charming towns that enticed them to stay, but Addison had seemed too close. It was while driving through the rolling, green hills of Missouri that a warm feeling enveloped her and she took it as a sign they could stop for more than just a day.

For nearly a week they called a cozy, family-style resort near Meramec Caverns, home. And with the mantle of worry not so heavy, Raine found enjoyment in exploring her surroundings, including a walking tour of the caverns that the infamous outlaw Jesse James supposedly used as a hideout. Katy, knowing about Jesse James from watching old western movies, half-expected the outlaw to jump from the shadows of the cave.

Further exploring led them along rural back roads and to one in particular that steered them to their final destination. Thinking of the rickety, one-lane-bridge they'd crept over made her stomach pitch. She'd thought sure they'd plunge over the side into the deep green water flowing below. And once off it, they'd come face-to-face with a solid rock bluff. That's when fate forced them to make a decision — turn left, or right?

Savoring another sip, Raine pondered where they'd be had they taken the right turn. Opting for left had led them to a chance meeting with a complete stranger named Inez McCullen and an end to their aimless wandering. Sardonically, she guessed Katy deserved credit for meeting Inez. The only reason they'd stopped in the first place was Katy insisting she *had* to go potty. And maybe she had, but for certain it was the giant revolving hamburger perched atop the building that had snagged her attention.

Still looking a hot mess from Addison's handiwork, everyone in the place stared at her when she walked in, and especially Inez McCullen. Thanks to her four-year-old social butterfly waving constantly at her, Inez took it as an open invitation to enter their lives. It didn't take long to learn the woman was a force to be reckoned with, either. In minutes she'd gleaned the whole sordid story out of Raine like milk pouring from a jug. When Inez McCullen set her mind to something she'd give a dog digging for a bone competition, refusing to quit until she had it between her teeth.

After hearing Raine's story Inez had set her sights on a huge bone, which was — a place for her new-found friends to stay. With grit and determination, and a bit of embellishing the truth, she'd gotten her way. Without a doubt, getting Jess Harper to let them have one of his cabins had been a major feat and the wily woman had resorted to major duplicity. Playing on his sympathy, there'd been no way he would refuse. But talk about riled up when he realized he'd been duped! The man was worse than a snarly old bear with its winter snooze interrupted. Blazing furious, Raine thought the surrounding woods would go up in a firestorm. And though he hadn't outright accused her of being Inez's cohort, his gnarly attitude had made it crystal clear he preferred they would hot-foot it on down the road.

Admittedly, she'd been amused, and a bit ticked-off, too, at his stinky attitude, especially when he'd crossed his muscular arms over a broad chest and spouted with a curled lip, "I've no use for needy females and don't want you underfoot all the time! Save for something to do with the cabin, you leave me be!" Well, that silly demand went right out the window with the washwater given Katy already had a mad crush on him. "She 'wu'ved' Mr. Jess."

At the time Raine had no clue about the story Inez had spun but apparently the cunning woman was quite adept at skimming

6

the truth to get her way. Inez's less than stellar story of an older woman needing a place to hide from her mean-as-a-snake husband had snagged Jess Harper hook, line, and sinker. At least the mean-as-a-snake husband was true.

But to give the man his due, he wasn't the only one hood-winked. Inez had let Raine believe Jess Harper a grizzled-face, smelly old hermit living out in the sticks. One glance at his rug-ged good looks and hard muscled body and she'd turned into a drooling teenager. Katy wasn't the only one who'd fallen for the hunky cranky-pants man.

At least the cozy cabin nestled in the secluded woods would more than make up for his cranky attitude. The serene ambiance was exactly what Raine needed—its owner, not so much! Bull-headed and contrary to the bone, it took a while for him to get over being duped by one of his so-called friends.

Every time Raine thought of that explosive first meeting, amusement filled her. Jess had been pricklier than a porcupine but that hadn't stopped her from falling for this hard-headed man. Oh, there'd been a cage-match between her heart and her head. One insisted she take another chance on love while the other screamed she needed love like she needed a toothache. Wisely, she'd followed her heart.

As for Jess, he'd fallen for her, too, which sent him spinning. A confirmed bachelor, he wanted no permanent female fixtures especially one that was totally forbidden—a married woman. It was just one of his steadfast moral rules. You don't mess around with a married woman.

Ironically, while *they'd* abided his orders to stay away, it was Mr. Cranky-Pants Harper who couldn't keep his distance which led him to his getting mad at himself and taking it out on her. He'd become a freaking baboon! Infuriated, she'd nicknamed him Mr. Cranky-Pants and lost count of the times she wanted to dropkick his cranky-pants behind into the next universe. In fact, only a few days ago, her belly full of his snotty attitude, she'd decided it was time to move on down the road. After everything she'd gone through with Addison no way was she taking any guff from Jess Harper. But the leaving hadn't happened.

Refilling her mug, Raine stared out the window into the growing dawn. Suddenly the image of a dark-haired woman popped into her head right along with a spark of green-eyed jealousy. Her grip on the handle tightened as she swore if she ever saw the curly-topped troll again she'd punch her lights out! That'd teach her to mess with her man! Jess Harper was off-limits! And as a reminder to him, she'd punch the living daylights out of him, too.

Just then she'd have sworn a cackle of laughter sounded from the direction of her right shoulder and she instinctively glanced around, half-way expecting to see the elfin, green-eyed monster. It popped up every time she thought of the troll. Well, he'd be laughing even harder if she ever saw her again! He'd have a front row seat to watch those bouncy curls yanked right off her head! Then Raine scolded herself. Get a grip, girl. You and Jess are together and there'll be no more curly-mopped-troll-trouble and no nightmares are going to control you. Instead use them as an incentive to bring Addison to his knees.

For now, the coke-head was behind bars and as for the curly-haired troll, she was in Jess's past. The future looked rosy and that reminded her of something special happening that no troll or Addison would ruin. Kids from the county orphanage were spending the holidays with them and that trumped Addison and the troll hands down!

Lost in thought, she nearly jumped out of her skin when a little voice asked. "Mommy, is the girl coming today?"

"Good morning, Pumpkin! You're up early, and yes, the little girl will be here today." Her mini-me cutie-pie was referring to the lone girl from the orphanage.

"Yippee! I gotta' get dressed!" She dashed away only to return pulling a robe on over her reindeer pajamas. At least she'd put on her snow boots. "Okay. I'm ready."

A swell of emotion squeezed Raine's heart, thankful the turmoil surrounding them hadn't affected Katy. She'd worked hard to shield her from Addison's bouts of rage but, as they'd escalated, she admitted a time might come when she couldn't protect her, so leaving again was the only option. She'd tried once and put her trust in the wrong people. From then on, she'd never trusted her in-laws and of course she'd paid dearly for that folly and heeded Addison's threats until his escalating behavior convinced her to try again before one of them ended up dead.

A chill raced up her spine as she remembered how close that had actually come to fruition. Katy left to the mercies of a drugged-out, alcohol-swilling father was unthinkable. Perhaps she should have chanced leaving sooner. It wasn't like Addison had locked a GPS around her ankle monitoring her every move. He hadn't needed to. Instead, he used an invisible leash to keep her steadfastly in her place — his threats to disappear with Katy. So, she stayed, enduring his bouts of hellacious temper until fearing he'd either kill her or turn his wrath on Katy, he'd forced her hand again. She put her ducks in a row preparing to leave the Monday after Addison's party. All she'd needed was to get through the weekend then as soon as he left for work, she and Katy would disappear.

Unfortunately, everything blew up in her face. Her well-laid plans went straight to hell. However, good or bad, she firmly believed things happened for a reason. Point being, had Addison not gone off the deep-end she wouldn't be here today — free of him and in love with Jess.

But a little voice whispered in her ear. "You're not free of Addison and won't be until you completely dispose of him." She knew in her heart that the voice was right. Addison would never leave her alone. It was up to her to end it. How, was the tricky part but she'd figure it out. Until then she'd bait him in the text-taunting game he loved playing. Warned not to have any contact with her, somehow, he'd gotten hold of a phone and continued. She could have turned him in, but she wanted ammunition for the future should things get ugly again. Until then she'd do her part to drive him crazy. The image of Addison in a straitjacket made her chuckle and with that she shoved him to the back of her mind. With an appraising eye she said. "Katy-bug, I don't think you really want to meet her wearing your pajamas. Go change while I start breakfast."

"Okay, but can we have the widd'le pancakes? You know the ones that are for widd'le kids."

"Yes, sweetie-pie . . ." Her words fell on empty space for Katy had dashed off again.

# Chapter Two

**LATER, KATY'S EXUBERANT** laughter, coupled with Jess's surprised yelp, interrupted Raine as she cut out gingerbread cookies. She and Cora were in the midst of baking dozens of assorted cookies for the new arrivals. Dropping a spoonful of chocolate chip dough onto a baking sheet, Cora gave her a dubious look. "Wonder what the two kids are up to. You might better check on the big one. The little one's liable to have him trussed up like a Christmas tree with those lights they're stringing."

Cora was probably right but shrugging into her coat, Raine feigned insult. "My sweet little munchkin would never do that." Cora's doubt-filled "un-huh" followed her out the door into the brisk air. Just then Katy's mischievous laughter rang out again, a dead giveaway she *was* the culprit and Jess her innocent victim. Following the trilling sound, she found both sprawled in the inches deep snow, fanning their arms and legs making snow-angels.

"Look mommy! I'm making an angel." As if Raine couldn't figure that out for herself. "Mr. Jess showed me how and I hit him with a snow ball, too." Proud glee filled her tone.

"You certainly did. Katy, I believe you've got the makings of a baseball player." Jess decreed while bestowing his most angelic look—actually it was more a rakish one, on her mommy. "Come on, mommy, you make an angel, too."

"Nope!" She shook her head emphatically. "No way am I lying down in that wet stuff. You two are doing just fine without me, but I thought you were stringing lights up in the trees."

"We were but we've been working really hard and needed a snow-angel break." Getting to his feet, he brushed clinging white puffs from his coveralls then helped the little half-pint up, doing the same to her cotton-candy pink snowsuit. Giving the angels an appraising look, he said. "Katy-bug, we made awesome angels. I'm thinking we ought to show the new kids how to make them." His imprint was three times the size of Katy's.

"When are they getting here?" This was about the tenth time she had asked in the last thirty minutes.

"Soon," Raine checked her watch. "You better hurry up or you'll still be stringing lights when they get here."

That lit a fire under Katy. "Come on, Mr. Jess! Hurry up!"

Jess gave Raine a keen-eyed look. "I'll be right there, Katy-bug. I want to talk to your mommy for a minute." The woman had a way of making his blood run hotter than an Arkansas spring. Had Katy not been around he *would* have talked her into making snow-angels. Hmm . . . maybe later they could sneak away to the backside of property? Oh, who was he kidding? There'd be too many people around. Another cold shower was in his future.

"So big guy, what's on your mind?" Though from the heat in his eyes she could just about guess. She guessed wrong.

"You and those dark circles under your eyes." He gave her a pointed look.

"I don't know what you're talking about!" She denied pertly. Frowning, he opened his mouth to argue but she pressed a firm finger against it. "I know what you're going say, but for the next few days let's just focus on having a wonderful Christmas."

Anger glittered in his dark eyes. He'd never met her ex, only seen his leftover handiwork, but it was enough to want him to suffer more than just a few months behind bars. His vote — the scumbag should be eating dirt! For about the millionth time Jess wondered how someone could viciously hurt the person you swore to love and protect? The bastard didn't deserve to breathe another breath! He opened his mouth to vent.

"No . . ." She said firmly, knowing what was coming.

"Damnation! I hate it when you do that. You always know what I'm thinking."

"Only when it comes to Addison, then you're an open book. It doesn't take a rocket scientist to know what you want to do," she patted his cheek, "and no, you are not doing away with him. I deserve the honor should that happen."

"But I get to help," he sulked, tucking a silky strand of hair behind her ear. "I guess since offing him isn't on the table, we'd better make plans just in case he does show up." And he would, Jess was certain of that. "You're the only one who knows how his mind works and you believe he'll hunt you down. You bested him and you can bet that twenty-five-pound turkey we're having for Christmas dinner it's eating him alive. In his irrational mind he believes he has a score to settle with you."

"You're right on every point. I know exactly how he thinks. And of course I'm worried. I'd be crazy not to be. Heaven knows, I've been on the receiving end of his temper more times than I care to count. but I refuse to let him intrude on this special time. So for the next few days we're going to forget he even exists. Addison can go to the devil until after the holidays."

Jess's concern made her love him even more. Leaning closer, her intent was to sneak a kiss but over his shoulder she caught her sly scamp climbing the ladder propped against the cabin. "Katy Andrews, get off that ladder . . ." She yelled. The words were barely out before Jess was there sweeping the pint-sized daredevil onto his broad shoulders, her trilling laughter filling the air.

Watching them, apprehension filled her. She talked big but she *was* terrified of Addison finding her. He could make off with Katy and wouldn't care that he'd be kidnapping her having signed away his parental rights. She hadn't thought he'd agree but it was just further proof which priorities came first in his life. Goosebumps suddenly pebbled her flesh that had nothing to do with the cold. She had the eeriest feeling of being watched. Not for the first time she wondered if Addison might already know her whereabouts. Although behind bars, he had a stable of minions to do his bidding and of course, the dear old in-laws would do anything for their precious boy.

Casually glancing around, all she saw was the snowy landscape. Her gaze returned to watch Jess patiently help Katy wind a strand of garland around a railing. Those two were her world. She'd do anything to keep them safe. Before Addison, she'd never thought of resorting to violence . . . but now? Where he was involved, she could. "Addison," she whispered, "you'll never get the better of me again." He'd been the puppet-master pulling the strings making her dance to his every tune, but no more. One way or another she was going to be the string-puller. Her life was wonderful, and Addison wasn't ruining it! If she had one wish for Christmas it would be for him to drop off the face of the earth. Unfortunately, she knew that there was one more chapter to their story—the ending coming with the showdown looming on the horizon.

Sensing her stare, Jess looked up. Though she smiled, something set his insides to skittering. Instinct said she was up to something,—or keeping something from him, something involving her ex-husband. A constant rage simmered inside Jess. He ached to get his hands on the vindictive S.O.B. He'd make damn sure he was never heard from again! At least, he reflected, securing the garland, the scumbag was locked up until spring. Time enough for enlisting some very capable people without Raine knowing it. That was a sticking point between them. Miss Hard-Head was adamant no one else be involved. Well, what the stubborn woman didn't know wouldn't rile her up!

Back inside, the stubborn woman picked up where she'd left off, rolling, cutting, then placing the shapes on the cookie sheets and thinking of the past months and the changes since that harrowing night back in Phoenix. Had anyone told her then that she would fall madly in love right away, and with a stone-stubborn Marine, she'd have pushed them into the icy Big River that flowed nearby.

Not that the cantankerous man had made it easy. From the get-go they'd butted heads, and the road to happiness had been full of potholes, some so deep they'd swallow a semi. Each had done, and said, some atrocious things and only a few days ago she'd been on the point of leaving. Fortunately, Cora had stepped in with a much need wake-up call, shoving them together for an honest-to-goodness conversation instead of tearing each other apart with appalling assumptions and silly misunderstandings. Now, they were on the same page, their future shiny as a new copper penny.

Unfortunately, that shiny penny was quickly tarnishing, for obscured behind a thick stand of cedar trees across the road a hooded figure was snapping pictures of Raine and Jess while debating taking pictures of the kid. His conscious said leave her alone, that she'd suffer enough heartache down the line if her father got his way. *And you could put a stop to it,* shouted the pesky voice of his conscious.

Not and live to see another day. He'd die either by Andrews' hand, or by the holder of his markers.

# CHAPTER THREE

**AS JESS STRUNG** garland, he couldn't shake the feeling the tricky little blond was concocting some trouble. He thought about confronting her right then but there wasn't time. The kids were due soon but at the first opportunity he was going to find out, even if, a gleam entering his eyes, he had to kiss a confession out of her. In the meantime, he'd keep a sharp eye on her.

Thinking of the kids stirred memories of Jess being an orphan himself. He remembered what it was to be in the system, how lonely it could be, especially this time of year. Been there, done that. It was bad enough the rest of year, but the holidays were the pits. This should be a time for Christmas cheer and breathless anticipation of what Santa would bring them. A child didn't decide on its own to be in that situation. Circumstances beyond their control dictated it, so he was going to do his level best to make this a Christmas they'd remember forever.

From the corner of his eye he caught Katy sneaking toward the ladder again. "Young lady!" He called sternly.

Giggling, she raced to him, throwing her arms around his legs. "I love you, Mr. Jess."

"I love you, too, Katy-bug." Swooping her up, he kissed her rosy-red cheek while berating her father. The jerk didn't deserve to call himself father to this sweet child. But, he thought with a secret smile, one of these days Katy would have *him* as her daddy. "Come on, Katy-girl, I think we're all done. Let's have some hot chocolate." Suddenly, he sniffed the air and swore he smelled cigarette smoke, which was ridiculous since no one on the place smoked. Blaming his imagination, that still didn't stop him from doing a cursory glance around.

Taking a final drag off his cigarette, Robert Ford exhaled, a steady stream of blue-gray smoke filling the air. A moment later he saw Jess sniff the air and do a slow circle. Surely, he hadn't smelled the cigarette smoke from there. The man must have a bloodhound's nose! He'd better be more careful from now on. Tucking the smokes in a pocket he high-tailed it to his vehicle and was in time to see a blue multi-passenger van pull through the gate. What the heck was going on? He got his answer as the van barely stopped before its doors opened and bunch of rambunctious boys tumbled out followed by one petite blond girl dressed in jeans and purple puffer coat. Great! A complication he hadn't expected. All it took was one nosy brat discovering him and he'd be toast.

Excited chatter filled the air while the lone girl quietly looked around with apprehensive blue eyes before spying Katy and rushing to her. In moments they were best buds. Seeing the delight shining on both faces, Raine's heart filled with joy. This was definitely going to be a Christmas to remember.

Once settled in, they gathered back at Raine's for lunch. The boys, anxious to explore, quickly scarfed up their lunches, and when Jess told them about the horses, the stable was the first place they headed. At dinner time they gathered back at Raine's for a steaming pot of chili, cornbread, and all the condiments imaginable. When Raine filled her bowl, added corn chips and Longhorn cheese chunks, so did Kathy. And Jess, having never tried it that way, followed suit. Taking a bite, he declared he'd be eating chili this way from now on. The hero worship already started; the boys enthusiastically went right along with Jess. Their excited chatter stirred old memories for Raine, too, since like Jess, she'd also been an orphan. A newborn left on the steps of a church, her only belongings a doll-sized suitcase and a redacted birth certificate with only the name Raine Elizabeth Danvers. With no birthdate, the nuns had chosen the date she'd been found. Raine had no idea who her parents were, or why they'd abandoned her. Had they been young and unable to keep her? It was a mystery never to be solved. At least they'd left her someplace she was sure to be found.

From across the room Jess saw her blink away tears and knew she was thinking of her own parentless past. At least he had some memories of his mom and dad. She had nothing save that battered suitcase and altered birth certificate. He longed to find her long-lost parents, but attempts had been made years ago and they'd come up empty-handed. It was as if they'd never existed.

At bedtime Raine tucked the sleepy girls into bed while Jess and Cora tidied up. He was pouring glasses of wine when she joined them. "They're tucked in but too keyed up to sleep yet." Smiling at him, she accepted a glass. "It was an exciting day for them. I'm glad Katy has a friend her own age. She's never had that." At their curious looks, she explained. "I couldn't have someone's child around in case Addison had one of his fits."

"Addison would give the devil a fitting run for his money, and I'd bet next month's retirement check he'd win, too." Cora retorted, lifting her glass. "Here's to a wonderful Christmas for those kids," which led to discussing Christmas presents for the kids. New territory for Jess, he paid attention to their suggestions, but nothing really appealed to the little boy inside him. This was going to take some thinking. He had six days until Christmas Eve. Surely, he'd come up with something by then.

Voices from the bedroom snagged their attention. They heard Katy tell Kathy not to worry, that Santa Claus would find her. But it was Kathy's plaintive, "But he doesn't know what I want 'cause I haven't got to see him," that had the eavesdroppers vowing Kathy would see Santa if they had to kidnap him and bring him to her.

Gradually, they quieted down and taking their cue, Cora went to bed. Finally alone, Jess gave into temptation and kissed Raine deeply and thoroughly. Though Katy adored him, he was wary of her reaction to seeing someone besides her daddy kissing mommy, even if it had been a long time since daddy had kissed mommy. Just being near Raine awakened an intense yearning to whisk her away and make love to her, but, he thought sagely, that wasn't happening anytime soon. Instead, he settled for a bit of cuddling in front of the fireplace before calling it a night himself.

A while later, Raine started to turn off the bedside lamp but just couldn't resist checking the number of text messages Addison had sent that day. The phone had vibrated non-stop all day. She counted twenty-six. Oops! Twenty-seven . . . another popped up. He was definitely furious at being ignored. Maybe tomorrow she'd respond—or maybe not. And on that thought, she snapped off the lamp.

However, Addison kept texting his scathing messages detailing exactly what he would do to her. Tired of being locked up, he was ready to punish the bitch!

# Chapter Four

**TOTALLY CAUGHT UP** in having fun, Raine realized Christmas was only three days away and she still had shopping to do. Still, she wouldn't have traded the precious moments for anything in the world. Of course, there'd been some not so precious moments she'd never forget. The girls, now joined at the hip, copied everything the boys did, and it didn't take long to learn the dainty little girls could turn into scrapping tomboys at the drop of a hat. If the boys climbed the old oaks around the house, then the girls did too. Catching sight of her child dangling from a frozen tree branch nearly drove her to a heart attack as she reached her just before Katy let go. While her mother's knees shook, Katy clamored to do it again.

Learning Raine and Cora were going shopping, the little girls wanted to go along. "We have to get presents for Mr. Jess!" Katy declared firmly.

When Kathy informed the boys they couldn't hang out with them, it was all the adults could do not to collapse with hilarity at the sheer relief on the boys' faces. Obviously, they were in dire need of some freedom from females.

The shopping also provided Jess an opportunity to put his idea into action without a certain female knowing about it. Had Raine even suspected what he was up to she'd unload buckshot into him with both barrels. So, smart man that he considered himself to be, he didn't share his secret. What she didn't know wouldn't get him shot.

After securing the girls in their car-seats Jess moved to the driver's open window and automatically ducked his head to kiss Raine. Immediately, girlish giggles erupted from the back seat. "Uh oh . . ." He murmured against her lips, "I just messed up. We're busted." Until that moment they'd been careful, but his mind had taken a short vacation, an occurrence that happened quite often since she'd driven into his world.

Scrambling from her seat and out of the vehicle, Katy stared up at him with serious eyes. "You kissed my mommy."

Jess couldn't tell if she was upset. Squatting to her level, he clasped her pudgy hands. "Yes, I did, Katy-bug. That's because I love your mommy, and she loves me. Do you mind?" *Please let her be okay with it, he prayed fervently.*

For the longest moment those intense blue eyes just like her mother's studied him intently. A sinking feeling filled his stomach, then in a solemn voice she asked. "Do you love me, too?"

Swallowing past the boulder in his throat, Jess assured her. "Oh yes, Katy-bug, I love you, too."

Instantly, little arms wrapped his neck in a stranglehold. "I love you, too, Mr. Jess, and it's okay if you kiss mommy." And such was the simplicity of a child's world. "Okay, fasten me back in. We're going shopping. I'll bring you some'fing back."

"I'd love that, Katy-bug." Having this little girl for his daughter would be wonderful. Grinning proudly at Raine, he said, "You be very careful. You're carrying some mighty precious cargo."

As they drove out of sight Jess thought life couldn't get any better, well . . . except for the pesky ex-husband. The guy had to disappear. As he headed back to his place, a scrap of guilt crept over him that he was going behind Raine's back. But, he rationalized, he was protecting her the best way he knew shy of shooting Addison the second he stepped out of jail, which he was sorely tempted to do. Not that he didn't fully expect a royal hissy fit from the little spitfire when she did find out, but by then it'd be too late. His new motto where Raine was concerned

... "What she didn't know can't rile her up." He'd been on the receiving end of those fits. They sure as hell weren't pleasant!

Sitting at his desk and drumming his fingers, he pondered the get-out-of-jail-early card Andrews had finagled. Under the plea agreement he should've been locked up for years. He'd bet there'd been some palm-greasing with a slick judge that didn't give a damn about collateral damage. If only there was a way to prove his theory he'd be on the next plane and take matters into his hands. Booting up his laptop, he started searching for more information on Addison Andrews. So far all he had was a folder containing scant notes of things Raine had imparted, and some outdated newspaper articles. There were bound to be things he'd kept her in the dark about.

A couple of hours later he raked his fingers through his hair in frustration. His search revealed nothing new. The dirty stuff must be buried deeper. Momentarily he wished he'd told her his plan to enlist his friends to help fend off Addison. It would have served two purposes. They could use her input, plus it would be a good time for them to meet. Actually, he considered Cooper, Belle, and Cory the family he never had. And, he thought with a sardonic grin, thankfully he'd cleared up the calamity involving, Belle. That could have turned into a really hot mess.

Since strategizing called for munching, he checked the supply of sandwich fixings, grabbed a beer, and headed for the front porch swing. It creaked as he set it in a gentle to-and-fro motion. Gazing at the snow-covered landscape, he thought of the witless stunt involving Belle, just one of many he'd pulled since Raine arrived on his doorstep. This particular instance Cooper had duty, so he'd taken Belle to dinner to discuss their helping with the foster kids when Raine had walked into the restaurant. A wave of shame rippled through him now, but at the time revenge had overruled shame. Not thinking straight, in that moment he'd gotten the bright-eyed idea of pretending he was on a date with Belle. His acting skills must have been superbly convincing given the stricken look on Raine's face. But the look lasted barely a nanosecond before anger replaced it with scorching glares so fierce he'd felt their searing heat clear across the room. Then, like flipping a switch, the fiery glares turned to icy disdain and she'd left the restaurant without a backward glance.

Feeling lower than a chigger's butt, he'd wanted to chase after her, but she'd have probably run over him then backed up for good measure. Instead, he'd endured a well-deserved tongue-lashing from an irate Belle who'd barely restrained herself from beating the crap out of him right there in the middle of the restaurant. She might have restrained herself from physically smacking him but in no uncertain terms she unloaded on him to quit acting like a jackass and get his act together before he lost the best thing to ever happen to him. Of course, it had taken more than Belle's dressing down before he came to his senses. A truth-filled heart-to-heart with Cora who'd imparted Raine was leaving finally straightened him out. Now things were great, and smug in the knowledge he was in the clear over that stunt, he pondered Christmas gifts for the kids.

# CHAPTER FIVE

**WHILE RAINE WAS** having fun Christmas shopping, in a tiny country jail, Private Investigator Robert Ford watched his client stroll into the visitor's room. He marveled at the man's self-assured swagger. It seemed he hadn't a care in the world and where confinement should have broken his spirit, instead he'd become master of it, reveling in the power he wielded over the jailors jockeying favor with him. Most men would've been beaten down, but not Addison Andrews. Freshly groomed, hair neatly trimmed, smelling of expensive cologne, save for the jailhouse garb, he looked ready for a date.

Of all the clients he'd ever represented, Addison Andrews was the slimiest. Just being locked behind iron bars would have taken the wind out of most men's sails, but Andrews acted as though he'd done nothing wrong. There wasn't one remorseful bone in his hard-muscled body. Again, Robert Ford's conscious screamed to walk away and though he tried masking his distaste, he wasn't successful. The minute Addison stepped into the room Addison homed in on his feelings.

Straddling a putty colored metal chair, Addison Andrews rested thick-muscled arms along its back. In the corner of his mouth a wooden toothpick resided. Studying the PI with all-knowing eyes, Addison decided this relationship wasn't working. The guy had a squeamish conscious and could rat him out then that pretty little plea deal would be shot to hell. Unfortunately, for now, he had no choice but pray he'd keep his mouth shut. Why his father had chosen him he hadn't a clue.

The guy was as useless as a car with flat tires. Despite all the tailing of the bitch he'd come up empty-handed. Even when he'd tailed her from Missouri to Phoenix and back, he'd gotten zero, zilch, on why she'd made the trip. *Any idiot could do that.* When the idiot opened his briefcase and extracted a manila envelope from it, suddenly, a burst of hope percolated through Addison. Maybe the guy might finally be earning his keep.

Well, well, was this the proof of his wife's cheating ways? Divorced or no, as far as he was concerned Raine would always be his wife. After all, hadn't they vowed "till death do us part" in front of God? Well, when he finally got his hands on her she'd wish she were dead. That little whipping he'd given her was nothing compared to what he'd do next time. And, he vowed darkly, there would be a next time. Raine would pay dearly for everything she'd put him through.

"I believe this is what you've been wanting." Even as Robert Ford shoved the envelope across the table his conscious ate at him like a rat gnawing garbage to chuck the whole rotten business. But he couldn't. Not while he owed money to the bookies. Caught between a rock and a hard place, if he didn't pay up, they'd come after him, and if he skipped out on Andrews, he'd do the same. Talk about bad choices. If he had do-overs, he'd stay away from the gambling *and* this crazy nutcase. But he didn't, so all he wanted was to get down to business then get the hell out of there.

Robert Ford's nerves jangled as Addison contemplated the envelope for several moments as though getting the measure of an adversary. It was all he could do not to yell at him to open the damn thing! Then as if reading his mind, Addison slid the contents out. Instantly, a white roaring filled his head, his soaring blood pressure turned his face a florid red. Instinctively Robert Ford shrank back against Addison's imminent explosion at seeing the intimate images of his ex-wife with another man.

Addison didn't explode. Other than a visible tic in his cheek throbbing double-time, he remained deceptively calm. When he finally spoke his voice belied no fury, but Robert Ford wasn't fooled. If Raine Andrews had been within striking distance, she'd be dead. Feeling the hate emanating from Addison's burning eyes, he could only imagine the fiendish tortures he dreamed of inflicting on his unsuspecting ex-wife. Again, his conscious screamed to warn her.

Addison returned the photos to the envelope. "Don't let these out of your sight. I'll need them when I get out. My lovely little wife is going to pay dearly for cheating on me." Not trusting the little weasel, Addison licked and sealed the glue-edged flap. "On second thought take them to my secretary. Tell her it pertains to my case and no one's to open it, including her, since it's not company related."

Masking his feelings, Robert Ford cringed inwardly at the idea of going near Addison's office. Again, if he didn't need the money so badly, he'd walk out, tip off the authorities, and disappear. But that wasn't an option. He didn't need the Vegas factions coming after him, nor Andrews when he was free.

Studying Robert Ford's telltale expression, Addison again zeroed in on his qualms. His instincts were spot-on not to trust him. A strong case of conscious was eating him alive. Addison couldn't have that. Sometime in the near future Robert Ford would have to be eliminated. Changing the subject before he reached across the table and strangled the bum, Addison asked. "Have you seen my baby girl since you've been tailing her mother? She must be missing her daddy something fierce, especially since mommy's otherwise occupied."

Mulling over how best to answer, Robert Ford decided to lie. Nor was he mentioning the older woman's presence. Andrews might go after her just because she was helping his ex. "No, but remember, it's colder than well digger's ass right now. I doubt her mother would want her getting sick."

The answer seemed to pacify Addison. "You're probably right. I'll give Raine credit for that. She's a good mother. She'd never hurt Katy for anything in the world." No matter what she'd done to him, he could never fault her as a mother. From some place within his burned out mind came a taunting voice.

*"And this mess is your fault, not hers. She's got every right to
do whatever she wants. You wanted the booze and drugs more
than you wanted your family, so you can take credit for tearing it
apart."*

The whispery voice maddened him. None of this was his
fault! Suddenly, it occurred to him Raine had someone with
her given Katy wasn't in that car wreck a few weeks back. Not
to worry. His first priority was the bitch then he'd take care of
whoever was with her. He turned his attention back to what
Robert Ford was saying, " . . . hell, I've nearly frozen to death
sitting out in those woods, so I understand if she's not letting the
kid outside. And to give credit where credit's due, if not for that
snowstorm you might never have found her."

"Fate is wonderful." Addison smirked. "You know when I'm
sprung from here I'm treating myself to a vacation. A hunting
one, and," he snapped his fingers, "I know the perfect place.
I understand Missouri's got good hunting."

No surprise there. "When are you supposed to get out?" The
sooner he washed his hands of this whole nasty business the
better.

"May," Addison replied. "And between now and then I'm
going to be a good little boy, minding my p's and q's." And
wasn't that a big fat lie, thinking of the taunting text messages he
was sending the bitch. "I don't plan on staying in this hole any
longer than necessary. Although, it's not as bad as it could be, if
you know what I mean." Addison winked conspiratorially.

Of course, he knew exactly what Addison meant. With
unlimited funds all Addison Andrews had to do was snap his
fingers and anything he wanted magically appeared, including
the white lines of powder. And he'd probably procured the early
release by monetary means, too. No doubt some judge's re-
election coffers were over flowing, but he wasn't going there. He
wasn't about to stir up another hornet's nest.

At last, able to make his escape, Robert Ford practically ran
from the building. Never in a million years would he get used
to the metallic sound of those iron doors clanging shut. He

breathed deeply of the fresh air, cleansing the jailhouse stench from his lungs while vowing never to take on another job for the crazy man. Sliding behind the wheel, another rush of guilty conscious assailed him. He'd just given Addison more ammunition to take down his unsuspecting ex-wife. Should he listen to his screaming conscious? Should he cut his losses and tip off the authorities? Take his chances disappearing? Caught between two minds, he pulled out of the parking lot.

# Chapter Six

**DUSK WAS CHASING** away daylight when Jess's friends eagerly converged on him. Knowing he needed help it was a no-brainer they'd jumped into the thick of things. Plus, it was an opportunity for some well-deserved razzing considering each of them had been on the receiving end of his relentless harassment when they'd done something ludicrous. And, lo and behold, he'd jumped right into the ludicrous pool with them, making a complete jackass of himself. That was bad enough, but even worse was dragging Belle into the brainless scheme. He was just asking for payback and the woman could hardly wait.

She and Cooper were the first to arrive. Stopping in the driveway, he watched his wife rubbing her hands in gleeful anticipation and scowled. "You're really looking forward to this, aren't you?"

Sassy green eyes flashed with retribution. "You're darn tootin' I am! Jess Harper deserves everything he's got coming to him." Shaking his head in sympathy for his friend, Cooper got out in time to see Cory Dugan whip into the driveway. Now Jess has double-the-trouble. *Maybe he should give him a bullet-proof vest.*

Cory, youngest of Inez and Hank McCullen's four children, had gleaned the horrible details of Raine's marriage from her mother and would definitely help. Cory also knew firsthand what an angry man was capable of when out of control and had scars no one knew about to prove it. She'd endured a living hell at the hands of her abusive ex-husband. But, she gloated in satisfaction, her daddy's shotgun had convinced him to leave her alone.

"Hey girlfriend," Cory stepped alongside Belle. Well aware of Jess's crazy escapade, she barely contained her own glee. "I can't wait to see the fireworks. This is going to be fun."

Earlier in the week they'd met for lunch and Belle had told her of the crazy stunt Jess had pulled. The man, nowadays their favorite topic of conversation, was crabby as hell and his horrible attitude made both women want to smack him. Believing Raine still married, and reconciling with the abusive man when he was released, he'd gone over the edge resorting to the harebrained idea involving Belle. "I could've cheerfully kicked him off his chair."

"Sounds like the feisty Ms. Andrews did it without even lifting a foot. I don't even know her, but I'm tickled she isn't taking any guff off the cantankerous man."

"Oh, he was cantankerous all right, and he looked like a guilty hound dog with his tail tucked between his legs when she walked out without a backward glance. I wish I'd recorded it."

"I'd have loved to have seen that. Man, the love-bug sure did take a mighty big chunk out of Jess. And him always bragging there wasn't a female worth her salt would ever set a permanent foot on the place!" She'd affected a mimicking deep voice. "Well now that he's come to his senses, he needs to pop the question and get some little Harper off-shoots started."

Now Belle whispered gleefully, "And the fun begins."

Watching from the porch, Jess sighed in resignation. From the expressions on their faces, he was in deep doo-doo. What on earth had ever possessed him to use Belle to make Raine jealous? It had to be the stupidest stunt he'd ever pulled and given the sparks shooting from Belle's vibrant green eyes he was about to pay hell to the curly-haired piper.

Cooper shot him a pitying look. "Sorry ole buddy." The poor schmuck should've known better than to mess with Belle. Since meeting Raine Andrews the steady-as-a-rock man had been knocked off kilter. But, Cooper had to admit, it was an experience he was thoroughly enjoying and with Belle primed to unload both barrels full of grief at him, let the fun begin!

Nailing Jess with a scorching look Belle didn't disappoint either. Emerald green eyes flashed retribution—and mischief. He rolled his eyes. Yep! He *was* in deep doo-doo. The petite package with a sassy mouth and mass of dark curls tumbling down her back had blood in her eyes. He threw up his hands in surrender. "Okay, okay. Get it over with. Rake me over the coals for being a jackass." The second she opened her mouth he knew he'd been spot-on.

"Jackass is right, Jess Harper! You should be ashamed of yourself pretending we were on a date so you could make her jealous! I should've dumped your plate on your head! It would've served you right. Actually, *she* should've done it. And when she did, I would have cheered her on with great big pom-poms." Glancing at the other two, Belle smirked. "You should have seen the hang-dogged look on Mr. Macho's face when the lady left without a backward glance. I half-expected him to run after her whining and licking those shiny black boots she had on." Jess narrowed his eyes as she continued dishing more grief. "I was beginning to wonder about you. Pretty face, supreme bod, but nothing up here." She thumped his head like a watermelon.

"Let me tell you, buddy-boy, I could've drop-kicked you into the next universe and I'd bet she wanted to do more than that, so you deserve a lot more than just a little ragging. You should be ashamed of yourself using me like that." This time she punched him on the shoulder. He winced. Damn! For a little thing she packed one hell of a wallop. A skeptical brow lifted. "And, you nut-head, please tell me you cleared up the mess you created? I'd hate for her to come after me."

This time it was Jess who did the head-thumping on hers. "Don't worry, Miss Smarty-Pants, you've nothing to worry about. She knows you were an innocent party to my shenanigans. Raine Andrews is the sweetest, most forgiving woman I've ever met, and, luckily for me, there's not one spiteful bone in her gorgeous body." Instantly he wanted to cut out his tongue for he'd handed them more ammunition and it started firing immediately.

"And just how do you know her body's gorgeous?" Cooper waggled his brows wickedly, getting in on the fun and receiving a dirty look for it.

"Shut up, Cooper! You're not helping here. Don't encourage these two troublemakers."

"Troublemakers!" Cory sputtered as they walked inside. "Jess Harper, we didn't start this, you did. And you must really have been bonkers to pretend Belle was your girlfriend."

Giving Belle a mock salute, she continued, "You have my utmost admiration. You're my idol, girlfriend. I admit it. You're more woman than I am. Taking care of one gorgeous husband while you have another hunk on the side? Sister, you must be exhausted!"

"That's it! If you two don't stop, I'll toss your skinny butts out in the snow!" He took a threatening step, "and don't think I won't!"

Cory cocked her head at Belle. "Think he's serious? Think he'd really throw two helpless females out in the snow?"

Jess snorted. "Helpless my backside; and you bet I will!" He opened the door at the same time.

Belle chimed in, "I have to think about it." Looking from him to the open door, she knew he wouldn't hesitate to follow through on his threat. "I . . . oh, all right. But you really are an idiot. It's too bad she's not here or I'd tell her so."

"She already knows it." He commented dryly, shutting the door. "She's had first-hand experience with me in that department."

"Haven't we all!" Belle quipped, shrugging out of her coat. "Now where is she? What little I saw the other night she looked nice."

"Mom thought so, and you know my mom, her opinions are usually spot-on. From the first time they met, she liked her. Said she looked like she'd gone twenty rounds in a boxing match, but she didn't even try to hide it, either. And of course, you know mom, if there's a story to be had, she's going to sniff it out." Heaping chips and dip onto a saucer, she continued. "Mom said her little girl's so adorable, she had everyone in the place practically eating out of her hand."

"Katy-bug is a sweetie." Jess agreed, his expression softening. They noted it. For a man who shied away from permanent bindings, this was a grand change. "And she's pretty, just like her momma. As for your mother," he glared at Cory, "she pulled a fast one to get me to let them stay. And," he turned that glare on Belle, "I did set the record straight about the other night."

Suddenly a flicker of uncertainty wended through him. Surely, he'd explained it was a ruse with Belle. If not, both were going to put a flaming torch to his backside. "Okay, I'm sorry for using you to make her jealous, but if it helps you to know, it was a spur of the moment thing. Apparently, she'd tried explaining that her divorce was final, but being the jerk that I am, I wouldn't let her talk."

Cooper jumped in again. "So then old buddy, just what did you let her do if it wasn't talk?" Cooper loved yanking Jess's chain every chance he got. After all, he'd suffered through his own barrage of potshots from Jess over his dust-up with Belle. "Is that when you discovered her gorgeous body?"

"Yeah Jess, just what were the two of you doing, if not talking?" Both women asked in unison then burst into hearty gales of laughter at his exasperated expression.

Heat scorching his face, he retorted. "*That* is none of your damn business!"

Seeing the flush, Cooper realized it must have been damn difficult for this man with such strong moral convictions to be in love with a married woman. Guilt driving him crazy, and fighting those feelings, it was no wonder he'd pulled that crazy stunt. Fortunately, Cooper reckoned, all the misunderstandings were straightened out and it'd be smooth sailing from here on out — save for the ex-husband, that is.

He gave Jess a sympathetic look. "Never mind those two. You should've known you were asking for trouble getting them together. They've been chomping at the bit for days to get at you." Belle stuck her tongue out at him. "Nice. But save it for later, honey." He grunted at the sharp jab in the ribs she gave him.

Belle crossed her arms. "Okay, hot shot, I accept your apology. But," she had to get one last zinger in, "you must have really been desperate to pick me. Weren't you afraid I'd get my evens? You've seen firsthand how vindictive I can get."

Shuddering, Jess knew exactly what Belle was capable of, but in that moment retaliations hadn't occurred to him. "Obviously I wasn't thinking. Do I need to watch out for paybacks?"

Winking at Cory, she answered. "No, you get a free pass this time, but if you do one more stupid thing where she's concerned that pass is gone and you'll be sleeping with one eye open for the rest of your life." *Should he be grateful*, he wondered. "And we'll try not to remind you too often what an idiot you can be. Now, bring us up to speed on everything you know about her ex-husband. And where is she?" Belle asked again. "We thought she'd want to be in on this gathering."

"Christmas shopping and I didn't mention asking for your help. She'd just pitch a fit."

"That's just ridiculous! She can pitch a fit until hell freezes over. We're still helping. Refusing's not on the table." When Belle dug her heels in, she was as stubborn as any flipped-eared mule.

"She's right," Cory dipped a corn chip in the French Onion dip. "I'm helping, that's for darn sure. Otherwise, mom would skin me alive and I'd rather face a pack of angry dogs than my mother when she's on the warpath. Speaking of warpath, I'm surprised she hasn't already formed her own welcoming committee should the ex-husband show up." No one in his right mind would cross the formidable Inez McCullin when she was up in arms. "It just makes me so damn mad when we arrest the bad guy and put him behind bars, only to have some bleeding-heart idiot let him loose." An ember popped loud in the fireplace as if in agreement.

"I'm more inclined to believe it was a money-grubbing judge instead of a bleeding-heart idiot who was bought off." Belle intoned. "It burns me up every time a slime-ball gets turned loose, especially when the victim isn't notified." She spoke from a very bad personal experience. "At least we've a general idea when he's getting out. Best case scenario — he'd never set foot in this direction."

"Don't bet on it." Jess scoffed. "You'd lose. If he had any sense he'd get on with his life, but according to Raine you can carve it in stone he'll start looking for her the second he walks free and won't care who he plows through to get her."

"Then we'll just be prepared." Fire burned in Cooper as he reached for Belle's hand, squeezing it, and thinking of her attacker. "It'd give me the greatest pleasure taking someone like him out. Now, tell us everything you know about this *character*."

Seated around the knotty-pine table, Jess passed each a manila folder containing copies of notes he'd been keeping along with articles he found while surfing the internet. Several pertained to the Andrews' Construction Company's success along with a few pictures of Addison and Raine together at various functions. As much as he hated admitting it, they made a striking couple. Just goes to show, he supposed, fingering one of the pictures, you never know what goes on behind closed doors.

For the next hour they went over everything Jess had put together and he answered their questions as best he could. Ideas were bounced around on how best to locate, recognize, and eliminate Addison. Their favorite was stopping him dead in his tracks with one clean shot. Of course, that led to a good-natured debate on who got the honors of pulling the trigger. In the end they all agreed it should be Raine. Again, in hindsight he wished he'd told her about the meeting and dealt with the fallout, but it was too late. When she did find out, he was going to be neck deep in hot water that no amount of kissing would get him out of.

# Chapter Seven

**WHILE THEY STRATEGIZED,** an exhausted Raine was trying to remember when she'd had so much fun with the little shop-a-holics. Traipsing all over the mall searching for the perfect gifts for "Mr. Jess", was priceless. Not surprisingly, Kathy had slipped into the role of protective older sister. Though only five, for one so young, she possessed a weary wisdom from having experienced too much heartbreak. Raine didn't know much about her background except neither parent was in the picture. What she did know was the child was starved for affection. Even at bedtime that first night when she'd kissed Katy goodnight it was obvious that Kathy wanted to be kissed, too. If only she could keep her forever. *How wonderful it would be to have two dainty little girls to love!*

On the drive home, total silence emanated from the back seat. Both girls had conked out and were missing all the pretty Christmas lights that were decorating the little village of Vail. Raine's favorite place — the sprawling three story log home to her left was brightly lit from top to bottom. No doubt the three children living there were as anxious for Santa as her girls were. Driving a little further on, a darkened driveway off to the right led to another log home. This one was at the opposite end of the spectrum. Abandoned, it was held captive by the overgrowth claiming it. Raine thought, *with a lot of tender loving care it would gleam like a shiny new diamond.* Raine's heart leapt at the thought of being the one to make it sparkle!

Once the girls were tucked into bed, Cora, with a bliss-filled sigh, dropped like a rock into the recliner and kicked off her shoes. Wiggling her toes, she sighed with delicious abandon. "Those Christmas presents are staying put tonight. I may never leave this chair ever again. I've walked so much today I don't think I'll ever want to see the inside of a mall—until next Christmas. Wiggling her toes again she continued, "if my feet could talk, they'd be giving me the silent treatment."

"I know what you mean," Raine commiserated. Thirsty, she fetched two ice-cold sodas from the fridge, handing one to Cora. Taking a long drink, the sweet fizziness slid down her parched throat. "Who'd have thought two short-legged girls could walk so much. They certainly put a new spin on shop-until-you-drop. I lost count of how many times we ran back and forth across the mall searching for the perfect presents for "Mr. Jess".

"I'm thinking "Mr. Jess," Cora air-quoted, "is going to look quite dashing in that god-awful Santa Claus sweater. And you know he'll be right proud of those reindeer ears and elf slippers." She chortled.

"There was no talking them out of it, either, especially after Katy's "but he loves me mommy, he gots to have them." Raine mimicked again as a mischievous grin lit up her face. "I'm thinking "Mr. Jess" should model his new outfit. And we'll need pictures, too! Why should we deny his friends the opportunity to see him all decked out."

"You're one evil woman, Raine Andrews, but I'll make sure my camera's handy!" Cora chuckled in gleeful relish. "This will be a Christmas he won't forget for a long time."

"And we're going to make absolutely sure of that!" Stepping to the window overlooking his place she saw lights. One look at Cora and her knowing smile was all she needed. "I won't be long."

"Don't hurry back. The girls are down for the count and I'm not far behind."

Giddy with anticipation, she fairly floated down the stone path on the chilly night breeze. Finally, everything was turning out great and the icing on the cake was getting a second chance at love. Feeling like superwoman, there wasn't anything she couldn't handle now. But she wrong, with a big fat "W" for in the blink of an eye she wasn't soaring like superwoman but plunging back to earth like a rocket with the heart-stopping crash eminent. Staring in disbelief in the cabin's window, her temper began boiling hotter than lava spewing from an erupting volcano. Jess had company! Female company! With curly black hair! What the hell was the curly-mopped troll doing in his house! Oh, don't be stupid! The answer was obvious!

With blood in her eyes she marched closer vowing with each step to teach the cheating rat a lesson he'd never forget! How dare he lead her on! How dare he bring that . . . that curly-mopped floozy into his home! Especially after professing to love her! Then, the second I'm out of sight he's tom-catting around! Talk about a gullible fool wearing rose-colored sunglasses. She'd believed every lying word, thought he wanted the same things she did—marriage, kids, the little white picket-fence, or in this case the white stables. Obviously, he'd been lying through his pearly whites and that . . . floozy was making herself right at home!

Stomping a boot-shod foot, she wanted vengeance *and* she'd begin by kicking Jess Harper so hard it'd take him weeks to walk properly. Actually, he was behind a solid wall so she kicked the next best thing. Rearing back to give herself momentum, with a mighty swing, her foot connected solidly with the plastic Santa statue standing sentry beside the back door. It landed with a loud clatter. Still outraged, she kicked it a second time sending it skittering across the porch. The third sent it sailing into the snow-covered yard.

# CHAPTER EIGHT

**THE SUDDEN RACKET** startled everyone inside the cabin putting them on instant high alert. Not knowing what they were facing, Cooper and Cory drew their weapons as Jess jerked open the door. What they weren't expecting was a raging mad woman. Jess swore the fiery sparks shooting from her eyes singed him. Instinctively he took a step backwards, but in the next moment he was on the attack.

"What the hell's wrong with you? Are you trying to get shot? And what the hell did you do to my Santa Claus?" He demanded, catching sight of the plastic statue lying in the snow-covered yard. Something had riled her up, but it damn well wasn't him. He'd done nothing wrong and now *he* was getting mad.

A derisive snort shot from her. Seriously! Did the jerk really think she was blind as well as stupid? Her fists clinched with rage. The cheating jackass acted all innocent like he hadn't a clue *why* she was furious. Any coherent thought remaining disappeared, as, with rage-filled strength, she shoved him. Hard! Caught off-guard, Jess slammed against the side of the cabin. "Give me a damned gun and I'll shoot *you*! And I kicked your damned Santa because I couldn't kick you, you two-timing jerk!' She sputtered. "But I can now!" The words were barely out when the toe of her boot connected solidly with his right shin. Then, she was off like a fast-moving bullet back up the hill.

Pain exploded through Jess's leg. Ignoring it, he gave chase, a litany of blue curses filling the air. "Hell and damnation woman!

You little hellcat, get your rear back here!" Hearing his pounding steps behind her, she sped up, but he was faster, catching her arm in a tight grip. "Stop!" He yelled, jerking her around. "What the hell are you mad at me for? I haven't done anything wrong."

"Ha! You might not think so, but as far as I'm concerned, you're a two-timing jerk!" She yelled right back.

If she hadn't been so furious it would have been downright hilarious. He'd never had anyone take out Santa Claus because they were pissed at him. But something had seriously jerked her chain. "Just what the hell am I supposed to have done?" He demanded, even as a part of him admired her scrappiness.

"Let me go or I swear I'll punch your lights out!" She brandished a doubled-up fist. "You know what's wrong! That woman you were fawning over the other night is in your house right now. My God! Are you that insatiable? It's only been a few days since we spent the night together." Now she was screeching loud enough for the neighbors to hear.

At her words a humongous light bulb blared in his head and his grip slackened. Oh . . . no, he gave himself an imaginary head-smack, I guess I didn't clear the air about Belle, and given the howling laughter from his three friends who were practically rolling in the snow, they'd heard every word. Now, he wasn't sure who was ticking him off more — Raine for accusing him of something he hadn't done, or his friends' hysterical enjoyment at his dressing down. Actually, both were making him hot under the collar.

Taking advantage of his momentary distraction, Raine broke loose, dashing off only to get a few yards across the snowy ground before he caught her again. Fast as lightening, she kicked him again, this time squarely in the kneecap.

Despite the sharp pain radiating in his knee, Jess still wasn't about to let her get away. But taking a step, the knee buckled and despite fighting to keep his balance, it was a losing battle and down he went, taking her right along with him.

Landing hard, the breath was knocked out of her. Damnation! The big lummox had fallen on her and is going to crush her! Gasping for breath, she thrashed like a wildcat to dislodge him. She didn't care that pain streaked through her still sore ribs, the ones injured in the crash three weeks earlier. "Get off me you big oaf!"

"Enough!" He ground out. "Stop it or I swear to God I'll keep you here until your mouth freezes shut! Now shut up and let me talk!" Panting hard, his breath formed white puffs of steam between them. To get his threat across he bore his weight into her. Big mistake for despite his dander being up, he instantly reacted to her, wanting to kiss her senseless for throwing boulders at his character. On second thought, that probably wasn't such a hot idea. She might bite him. Mad as she was, her mouth freezing shut wasn't such a bad idea, after all. Still, he really ought to get off her, but her frantic bucking kept him anchored on her.

"Let me up, you cheater!" She spat.

Fiery indignation rippled through him that she dare accuse him of cheating on her! That he'd even want another woman after finally winning her heart was downright insulting! In fact, he was sorely tempted to turn her over his sore knee and give her delectable backside a good paddling!

Trapped beneath him, she could only glower at the hard chiseled features above her. He was all angles and shadows and despite her outrage, she yearned to drink in his warmth. Suddenly, a curl of doubt wended through her. Had she jumped to the wrong conclusion? Was he really innocent and she'd just made a colossal fool of herself in front of strangers? But then why was that woman in his house? Oh no! Jess Harper had some explaining to do before the word sorry came out of her mouth!

"Fine, then explain why *that curly-mopped troll,*" and it came out sounding just as snide as she'd meant it to, "is in your house right now. And let me up, you two-timing jerk!"

Bristling again at her name-calling, when Jess spoke his tone held a silken threat. "I don't think so! I don't want you making another break for it. And if you call me a two-timing jerk one more time I'm going to show you what a real jerk I can be!" For

41

good measure he bore his weight into her again, though careful of her tender ribs. He wanted to get his point across—not hurt her.

"Fine!" She spat. "You're not a jerk! I won't run!"

Damn! She was stubborn! But he wasn't stupid. No way in hell would she give up so easily! "Un-uh. You're staying put until you hear me out. Now. Shut. Up." He enunciated each word, his warm breath fanning her face held the scent of mint with a hint of wine. "That curly-mopped troll, as you say so contemptuously, actually is not in my house right now. Those hyena sounds you hear are coming from her." She stiffened against him again. "Easy," he admonished softly, "and those other braying sounds are her husband and Cory Dugan, Inez's daughter. They're my so-called friends and right now they're hysterically rolling in the snow at our little exhibition." He flung a scalding glare in their direction. "I certainly hope you're happy with this little spectacle we're putting on!"

The hysterical laughter finally penetrated her furious mind at the same time his words did but only certain ones registered. The troll's husband was here too, *and* Inez's daughter? Could it get any worse! Talk about two-faced with the holier-than-thou act thinking she was still married when the whole time he's swinging with the curly-headed troll, her husband, and Inez's daughter! They did foursomes! How kinky-sick was that! How could she have been so stupid to fall for a no-morals man? Her temper bubbled hotter than a witch's caldron on Halloween. Good Lord! If this is what they did for entertainment in the sticks she wanted no part of them!

"Her husband's here, too? Are you all part of some swap club? And you're messing around with a married woman? How two-faced can you get Mr. I-Never-Touch-a-Married-Woman? Just how kinky are you all?" Her ear-splitting shrieks were louder than a pair of banshees in mating season and she didn't care if they did hear her, which based on the renewed howls of laughter, they did.

"That's it! I've had all the character assassinations I'm taking from you." Ignoring his throbbing shin and aching knee, Jess struggled to his feet then none-to-gently hauled her up. Keeping a tight grip on her arm, he marched her across the snow-covered yard. With every step she hissed fighting like a wildcat threatening bodily injury. The whole time his so-called friends continued laughing hysterically, which made him even madder.

"Shut up!" He thundered.

"Oh God, Jess," Cooper wheezed, fighting to catch his breath. "This is just too priceless! It's got to be the funniest thing I've ever seen. The guys at the station are going to have a field day with this."

"Cooper Michaels, if one word of this gets out to anybody you'll be damn sorry! And you," he shook a warning finger at Cory, "the same goes for you. You'd better not breathe one word of this to anyone, especially your mother, or so help me I'll tell her you're seeing the fire-chief on the sly and planning to run off with him."

Despite the threats they couldn't stop laughing nor the tears running down their faces. Hearing his threats, a sick sense of dread washed over Raine. Oh no! She really did have it all wrong! Mortification covered her from her boots to the roots of her long blond hair. She wanted to crawl into the deepest snow bank she could find and never come out.

Sensing her urge to turn-tail and run, Jess tightened his grip, again not enough to hurt her, or make her feel afraid. "Oh . . . no . . . you . . . don't!"

Cooper, gasping, was doing a very poor job of trying to stop laughing. "But Jess, honest, you should've heard it from our side. You'd find it just as hilarious." At Jess's black look he finally garnered a modicum of control and turned to Raine. "Let me formally introduce us. I'm Cooper Michaels, Jess's kinky best friend and that wickedly kinky curly-headed troll there," he nodded to the pretty, black-haired woman, "is my wife, Belle, and the other kinky one is Cory Dugan."

Belle swatted Cooper then pushed him aside. "Don't pay him any mind. He's just as sick in the head as Jess. I've been itching to meet the woman who finally broke down the great wall the nut-head erected to protect himself from mercenary females. And I want you to know I had no idea he'd pull that stupid stunt, either. He's been acting like a total jackass lately." At his grunt she sent him a quelling look. "Don't deny it, either!" Turning back to Raine she said, "Jess has a twisted mind when it comes to women, gets some of the craziest ideas. Like the other night wanting you to think we were on a date. I told him he was being a complete jackass and obviously the jackass forgot to tell you it was all a put-on. No wonder you jumped to the wrong conclusion."

"Thank you, Dr. Michaels!" Jess spat with prickly sarcasm. "I needed that bit of psycho-babble!" He shot a glare at Cory. "Well? You haven't taken any potshots." He was the aggrieved party and hadn't done a damned thing wrong! Well . . . unless you count forgetting to clear up the mess involving Belle. He'd had other things on his mind, he reasoned. One thing was for damn sure, he huffed—it'd be an eternity before they let him forget it. Hell would probably freeze over first.

"I'm still mulling it over. It just might be worth mom finding out about the chief and me. You know how she loves playing matchmaker," a knowing grin lit up her face as she added, "that's probably what she had in mind the second she laid eyes on Raine." Then she smacked him on the arm giving him a friendly buss on the mouth, and that's exactly what it was—a friendly gesture that could never be misconstrued as anything else. "Nope, I'm good. Besides, Belle's doing just fine for the both of us. But," she shook her head in amazement, "that show you two put on sure was a hoot. I'm only sorry I didn't film it. Mom would have a field day." Ignoring his threatening scowl, she said to Raine, "We've not met but I feel as though I already know you. My mom is Inez McCullin."

"I love your mom. If not for her there's no telling where we'd be right now." *For sure I wouldn't be here knee-deep in embarrassment*, she reflected. "She's quite the take charge person."

Cory Dugan was a pretty, younger version of her mother. Inez must have been quite a looker at Cory's age, and there was no denying the love she had for her mother. Her expressive brown eyes lit up just talking about her. Cory grinned ruefully. "I'd be more apt to say she's bossy and nosy, but you're right, she's got the biggest, kindest heart of anyone I know. And I'm not just saying it because she's my mom."

"Bossy's putting it mildly." Jess groused, watching Raine interact with his friends, amazed at how she'd transformed from the spitting wildcat kicking the stuffing out of him and Santa to this gracious lady. If not for his throbbing knee and aching shin, *and* Santa laying out in the yard, the whole episode could have been a figment of his imagination. His sense of humor returning, he supposed it did look pretty funny from their view point. Then he looked at Raine. In the glow of the porch light her cheeks still flamed red with embarrassment. Well, she should be embarrassed for casting aspersions on his character!

Sensing his eyes on her she met them sheepishly. "I'm sorry," she mouthed but the impish gleam shining in her eyes had him doubting it. Turning to Belle, she said, "I'm so sorry about the terrible things I said about you." Regret laced her every word.

Expressive green-eyes danced merrily as Belle patted her arm reassuringly. "Don't worry about it. You had no idea Jess would lose his marbles."

At Belle Michaels' forgiving manner Raine didn't feel quite such an idiot and she felt something else, an unexplainable connection. The connection to Cory she understood because of Inez confiding Cory's ex-husband had also been violent.

Belle's impression of Raine was on mark. Not only was she a beauty but a fighter, too. Add to that, she'd stolen Jess's cynical heart endeared her even more. She must really love the lug to throw such a hissy fit Good! He needed someone with that fiery passion to keep him on his toes. He needed this woman to love him. Clasping one of Raine's ice-cold hands, she said. "Let's get you warmed up. You're freezing after rolling around in the snow with the idiot." Her green eyes flashed a mocking glare when they passed him.

Jess threw his hands in surrender. "Okay, blame this idiot for the temper-tantrum, but she didn't have to kick Santa Claus into next year." *Women! He couldn't win for losing.* Hearing Raine's barely concealed snicker, his eyes became tiny slits. When she stepped inside the mudroom to hang up her coat, he was one step behind her. She deserved some retribution, and he knew just the thing. Before she could react, he yanked her into his arms, his mouth devouring hers in a scorching kiss that stole her breath and turned her mind blissfully fuzzy.

"You owed me that," he growled against her mouth when they came up for air. Desire wound its way through him. Given the house full of jokesters, a lot of good it did. "Come on, you need something to warm you up." He thought he heard her mutter, "You're doing a good job of that."

# Chapter Nine

**HIS HEAD WAS** a mite fuzzy from their kiss, but it immediately filled with panic when Raine passed by the kitchen table. Fortunately, she paid no attention to the papers strewn across it or there'd have been another rumble. His knee throbbed in agreement as he got her a glass of Chardonnay.

Cooper and Belle claimed the loveseat, Cory the recliner, so they took the sofa. Still chagrined at the scene she'd caused, Raine took a sip and turned inward. Talk about embarrassing outbursts! Holy smokes! If she'd thrown a fit like that with Addison he'd have beaten the living daylights out of her. In fact, he had done just that.

Belle, homing in on her embarrassment, said. "Don't worry about that little scene. I'd have done the same thing in your shoes. If Cooper had pulled a stunt like Jess did the other night I'd have gone after him with a twelve-gauge shotgun. I'd be so mad I wouldn't give a damn about what I did. We've all been that furious at one point or another. I know I have."

The instant the words were out she could've cut her tongue out with a dull steak knife. It was a given that one of them would jump at the chance to remind her of her own infamous jumping-to-conclusions folly and the sparks firing in Jess's eyes attested to the fact that he wasn't about to miss an opportunity to get his digs in. Sighing in resignation, Belle guessed he deserved to be off the hot seat given he'd been the butt of their fun, thus far.

Jess didn't disappoint her either. Glad to be off the receiving end of the torture, retribution gleamed darkly in his dark eyes. It was Belle's turn to be roasted and he was going to enjoy turning the spit. He loved tormenting and taking potshots at his friends, just as they did to him, and though they could joke about this particular incident now, it had nearly resulted in Belle's death.

With extreme relish, and a wicked grin, he crossed his arms superiorly over his broad chest. "Well now, little miss-trouble-maker, I seem to recall you jumping to some powerful wrong conclusions." He glanced at Raine. "Belle even got so bent out of shape she sabotaged Cooper's truck just because it was parked in front of Lila Coleman's place all night."

Belle shot a pleading look at her husband, but he was no help. "No matter what he says about you, or how bad it is, I'll still love you, babe."

"Thanks!" she snapped, then glared at Jess. "Go ahead. Tell her about my ride on the idiot-go-round!"

And he did. "Belle might not look it but beneath all that butter-wouldn't-melt-in-her-mouth prettiness, she's got one hellacious temper. In fact, she can be meaner than a junkyard dog." Belle stuck her tongue out at him. "You see, Cooper had loaned me his truck," he paused for a sip before continuing, "only Belle didn't know that, so when she saw it parked in front of Lila Coleman's house in the wee hours of the morning she assumed Cooper was messing around with Lila. Talk about jumping to conclusions." Jess let loose a shrill whistle. Belle squirmed uncomfortably beside Cooper. "Belle blew a gasket, got all pissed-off at Cooper and decided to make him pay for cheating on her." He shot Belle a smirk. "Hey, if you ever need a mechanic, Belle's you're go-to-girl." She stuck her tongue out at him again.

As she listened, Raine studied the two men who were a lot alike. Not in looks, though both were tall and ruggedly hand-some, but in temperament and the take-charge attitude. Both were quick to laugh and just as quick to anger and without a doubt should anyone get on their bad side there'd be hell to pay.

"Believing Cooper was cheating, Belle became so enraged she flattened all four tires and ripped out the truck's distributor wires. Only later, when he called to explain he'd be late for their date because some moron had vandalized his truck while it was parked in front of Lila Coleman's house did she realize she'd been wrong. She was even more sheepish, when he explained that I'd borrowed it and left it parked there while I went fishing with Lila's brother. That's when Belle realized she'd screwed up royally."

"Moron?" Glaring at Cooper, Belle smacked his arm. "You called me a moron?" Before Cooper could defend himself she turned on Jess. "In this *moron's* defense, it wasn't until then that I learned you'd even borrowed Cooper's truck. I didn't know yours was in the garage, or that you even knew Lila's brother, or . . . that you went fishing. I wasn't kept in the loop, so how was I to know?" She harrumphed.

Cory nodded vigorously in agreement. "I've always thought it wasn't your fault entirely."

"Thank you!" Belle pouted.

"Cooper had to pull a night shift, so he loaned his truck to Jess. Only thing he forgot, was telling Belle." Cory said.

"Okay, so now it's my fault she wrecked my truck. You women stick together like peanut butter to bread and we're adding another to the fold?" He threw Jess a sorrowful look. "You must be in love, old buddy. Are you sure you want to get tangled up with her?"

"Oh yeah, I most definitely want to get tangled up with her." The double-entendre sent heat waves wafting through her. She wouldn't mind getting tangled up with him again, either, and felt a flush spread from her head to her toes. She seemed to be doing that a lot lately.

From the recliner Cory witnessed the intense attraction between them. In the time she'd known Jess, this was a side of him she hadn't seen regarding a woman. Sure, he was a gentleman and all, but there'd always been an invisible barrier anytime a woman got too close. But with Raine, once overcoming the hurdles, he'd opened his heart and let her in.

"Well," she skewered Cooper with a telling look, "in a way it was your fault. If you'd told Belle what was going on in the first place she wouldn't have gone on the warpath." Cooper grunted but couldn't argue with her. He'd thought the same thing many times. Had he mentioned loaning Jess his truck, things might have gone down differently. But that was something he'd never know.

Crunching a corn chip, Cory swallowed then took up the story. "When Cooper found out it was Belle who'd vandalized his precious truck in a fit of jealous temper, let me tell you he blew his stack. I don't ever remember seeing him so irate."

Belle gave her husband a pained look. No matter how much time passed those terrible memories remained crystal clear.

Cooper, who never raised his voice, had been so rip-roaring furious he'd yelled at the top of his lungs that he hated jealous, clingy women, that she should have trusted him instead of going off half-cocked. How could she even think he'd cheat when he was crazy in love with her? Madder than hell, and hurt, he'd lashed out viciously that as far as he was concerned they were through and he'd broken up with her.

If Cooper was furious with Belle, it was nothing compared to how Belle felt about herself. Non-stop she berated herself for going off the deep end when he'd never given her any reason to doubt him. She *had* been stupid, had deserved his wrath. Her only excuse being she'd fallen hard for Cooper and the thought of him cheating had torn her heart out. Meeting him had been an unexpectedly precious gift, especially after losing her first husband in the line of duty. The pain of that loss had been almost more than Belle could stand. She was sure she'd live the rest of her life a grieving widow. Never in a million years would she dream she could ever love another man. But then she'd met Cooper Michaels at a police fundraiser, and it was an instant attraction. The darkness she'd been living in became a dawning light. It was as though her heart had been waiting for him to bring it back to life.

Sick at heart and feeling seven kinds of a fool, for over a month after the truck debacle she tried every conceivable way to convince him she was sorry but Cooper, still furious, was having none of it. He refused to take her calls, wouldn't answer the door when she came to his house, and if she showed up where he was he either ignored her, or left. The catalyst of their quarrel occurred at his favorite haunt, The Cowboy Club. Learning he was off duty and more than likely there, Belle went there hoping to get him to talk to her. She'd even worn the little black dress he'd given her for her birthday. He was there all right, but to her surprise he wasn't alone. Leaning against the bar, a boozy blond was draped all over him like an octopus with a thousand tentacles. It made her physically ill watching the clinging floozy rubbing herself against him and it was obvious to her, and everyone else in the building, that Cooper was thoroughly enjoying himself.

But Belle was wrong. Cooper had been well aware of her presence from the moment she walked through the door. It had taken every ounce of willpower to ignore her when all he wanted to do was kiss her until neither of them could breathe. But he was still furious and hell-bent on giving her a taste of her own medicine. So, instead he'd drawn the blond onto the dance floor and put on an even more disgusting exhibition. Damn it, if she was going to be jealous then he'd damn well give her something to be jealous for!

As for Belle, she'd had no clue Cooper hadn't ever laid eyes on the blond before that night. Miserable, he'd been drowning his sorrows when the perky blond moved in on him. Not interested, he'd started to give her the heave-ho when the door opened and in Belle had walked. In that moment, he knew what his revenge would be. Very aware of Belle watching from the doorway, he'd drawn the blond onto the dance floor, cozied up real tight, and given free rein to his hands, all the while looking straight at Belle. Unfortunately, despite his anger, the disgust mixed with heartbreak etched on her face made him feel like dirty pond scum.

Cooper's sickening display with the blond was too much. She'd only damaged his truck—he'd just ripped her heart out. His atrocious behavior was intolerable. It was the worst agony she'd experienced since losing her husband. The message was blaringly loud and clear—their relationship really was over—he'd moved on. It was time for her to do the same.

Desperate to get away, she'd escaped out the door without a backward glance. Focused solely on getting the hell out of there before she totally broke down she didn't notice the man lurking in the shadows. One second she was unlocking the drivers' door and the next she was sprawled flat on the hard pavement, a giant of a man astraddle her. Never had she fought so hard for her life, screaming and fighting as he pounded her to pieces. Trying to defend herself, she raked his face with her nails leaving long bloody gouges and tearing her fingernails down to the quick. She even managed to knee him in the groin, but that had only made him angrier, feeding his strength. The proof was in the massive fists that pounded even harder.

Her assailant slammed her head against the blacktop and punched her so many times she lost count. There was hardly any place left untouched by his brutal blows. He wanted to kill her, to feel the life seep out of her battered body. He muttered it repeatedly as he beat her unmercifully. Over-and-over he'd repeated, "I'm glad he's dead. That scum cop deserved to die and now you will, too."

In her pain-fogged mind she didn't grasp what he meant. Later she learned her attacker had been at the house where her husband, who was responding to a domestic violence call, was shot to death. At the trial he'd vowed revenge on anyone related to the cop he'd killed.

Unknowingly, Belle's assailant, released on a paperwork snafu a few weeks earlier, had been stalking her for days, just waiting for the right opportunity to attack. It seemed an eternity that she lay on the pavement beaten to a bloody pulp, her loud screams turning to pain-filled whimpers and still the beating continued. The dark edges of unconsciousness were closing in and she was positive she would die when suddenly he was gone, scared off by a car pulling into the parking lot. Belle would always believe that's what saved her life.

In the glow of the headlights, the couple in the car watched the big man get off the body crumpled on the pavement and run into the woods behind the club. Rushing to help the injured person struggling to get up, their gentle hands eased her back down. It was then they recognized Belle. Calling 911, they made sure the responders knew who they were coming to help. Later, Belle would learn it was Lila Coleman and her fiancé who'd more than likely saved her life — how ironic to be rescued by the very woman she'd thought Cooper had cheated on her with.

Inside the club Cooper's cell phone was blowing up. Though he'd told the blond to get lost, he was still nursing his anger against Belle. Figuring it was her calling to give him hell about the blond, he'd let it go to voicemail but after it went off half-dozen times intuition said check his messages.

Ducking into the men's room where the music was muffled, he listened to them. It wasn't Belle. It was dispatch. Something was happening right outside the club. He needed to check it out.

Stepping outside, he discovered a sea of flashing emergency lights of every kind. Quickly threading his way through to the center of the still-gathering crowd, he saw a familiar couple and paramedics huddled around a body lying on the ground. Onlookers that night swore Cooper's blood curdling howl could be heard clear across the state. Enraged, he'd have gladly killed the person who dared lay a hand on his woman.

Watching Cooper, Raine saw the intense emotion on his face. Even now Cooper's stomach pitched sickeningly remembering that night in all its horrid clarity. It could have been yesterday instead of a year-and-a-half ago that he'd recognized the clothes worn by the person on the ground. Belle had been wearing them not more than ten minutes earlier. He should recognize them — he'd given her the little black cocktail dress and matching heels for her birthday. Kneeling beside her, self-loathing filled him for not going after her. Never would he forget her pain-filled whimpers when he'd gently turned her face toward him, or his shock upon seeing it. He'd wanted to scream in rage and be sick all at the same time. Those beautiful green eyes, normally sparkling mischievously, were dulled with pain, and nearly swollen shut. Her face was a battered mess!

"Belle." His voice was rough with emotion.

Through her painfilled haze she heard him. He was the last person she wanted near her. She couldn't deal with him. Not now. Not ever. She wanted him gone! A spurt of anger surged up from the depths of her soul. Opening her eyes hurt unbearably as tears flowed from them to trail down her battered face. When she attempted to raise up, pain exploded in flashing bursts of bright lights in her head. Added to that, red-hot pokers were searing her lungs. Her tortured body was alive with pain so bad she wasn't sure she was long for this world. Maybe her attacker had succeeded in his mission, and she *was* dying.

Reading her mind, Cooper hunched closer. "No! You're not going to die!" He exclaimed fiercely. "You'll be just fine, sweetheart."

Despite the mess her face was in, there was no mistaking the contempt on it. It cut him deeply, but he deserved it. Why had he been such a damned idiot? Why hadn't he accepted her apology instead of letting his blasted temper get the better of him? If he'd been with her tonight, instead of acting like a jackass with the blond, she wouldn't be laying here beaten to the brink of death.

Belle struggled up only to fall back again. He stayed her movements with a gentle hand. "Don't move, baby. Please don't move."

"Go 'way." The words came out lisped through bloody, swollen lips. Even her jaw hurt and she wondered if it was broken. At that moment she didn't care. She was going to make Cooper Michaels leave her alone, even if it killed her. "Go . . . back . . . to . . . your . . . bimbo . . . I . . . don't . . . want . . . I . . . don't . . . need . . . you. You . . . can . . ." and in one last flash of spirit she told him exactly what he could do with himself. Conspicuous coughs from those near enough announced they'd heard her suggestion.

"You can forget that. I'm staying right here." Tenderly he stroked her rapidly purpling cheek. "I'm sorry, Belle, so sorry, sweetheart. I should have been with you." He didn't care who heard. "I need you baby. I love you. You're not getting rid of me that easy."

Despite the seriousness of the situation another round of snickers sounded when Belle told him where he could stick his love. They quieted, however, at his deadly glare. When they put her on the stretcher her pitiful cries echoed on the night air. Cooper vowed then and there that he'd find the bastard and make him pay. No one hurt his woman and got away with it. He'd kill the monster with his bare hands when he caught him. He wasn't aware he'd spoken aloud until a consoling hand squeezed his shoulder. It was one of the paramedics. "We'll help you, Coop. Don't forget, Belle's our family, too. First thing though, is getting her to the hospital. She's in a bad way, most likely, she has some internal injuries."

After loading her into the ambulance Cooper jumped in. No way was he leaving her side. It was the longest five-minute ride of his life. The whole time he murmured softly in her ear, telling her he had a lot of making up to do, starting right then. He hadn't been there when she'd needed him most, hadn't protected her when she needed him. But from now on he'd be there—forever. Having drifted into unconsciousness Belle didn't hear him

Following the vicious attack, Belle's injuries resulted in nearly a month in the ICU. Miraculously, there were no facial fractures, and even more amazingly, no internal damage. Unfortunately, she developed pneumonia, which was the reason for her extended ICU stay.

Cooper, mired in the depths of guilt-ridden hell, planted himself at her bedside and prayed for all he was worth that she'd pull through. Later, when a recovering Belle was moved to a private room, he planted himself there, too. All the while he endured the barrage of venomous potshots she fired at him. He felt like he was a duck in a carnival shooting gallery.

Already infuriated that he was so caring and solicitous, she became even more irate when upon release from the hospital he refused to let her go home by herself. If she'd been stronger she'd have snuck out of the hospital, but as she was still weaker than a newborn kitten, she didn't have the fight in her. The ride to his house was made in hostile silence. Once there, she'd headed for the guest room while vowing to make his life miserable, slamming the door so hard a picture fell off the wall.

Over the next weeks Belle made good on her threat. Determined to make his life a living hell, her bark, and her bite, were lethal and Cooper felt them every time he got near her. Needless to say, in her meaner than a 'junkyard dog' persona, she quite happily funneled doses of his own bitter tasting medicine down his throat.

Being forced to communicate through the locked bedroom door, Cooper should have saved his breath. Belle refused to speak and turned the stereo volume so loud the house vibrated. One day, as soon as he left for work, for spite, she cut up every pair of his briefs she could find into tiny pieces then scattered them about the yard. His neighbors teased him about the "snow fall" covering his yard in the middle of July. They thought it funny— Cooper not so much. Still, he took each dose of wrath and remained undaunted. He simply bought new briefs and locked them in the gun safe.

Though Belle was furious with Cooper, she was also upset with herself. Never weak and needy, she prided herself on being strong. After surviving the darkest times following her husband's murder, accepting Cooper's tender care was like pouring gasoline on an already blazing fire. This made her more determined than ever to make him as miserable as she could.

In one heated shouting match, again done with a locked door between them, she'd told him the attack wasn't his fault, but making a spectacle of himself, flaunting that floozy just to pay her back was his fault. She needed a man, not some stupid, childish idiot.

The sharp barbs were striking home. Somehow, he had to convince her he was that man. As the days progressed, he remained patient but there are only so many tongue-lashings a man can take, and Cooper finally reached his breaking point. Done biting his tongue, groveling, and apologizing, it happened when he arrived home early to find her packing her bags determined to leave.

Losing his temper, he'd pinned her to the bed, kissed her senseless and demanded she marry him swearing if she didn't say yes he'd lie there on top of her until she turned old and gray. Life was too short and both of them had already paid too high a price. It was time for forgiveness on both their parts, that alone or apart, they would always love each other. Finally, Belle realized he was speaking from his heart. He was right, they had both been stubborn and made mistakes. It *was* time for forgiveness. That's what she'd been trying to get through his thick head for weeks before her attack. To everyone's delight, *and* immense relief, they were married within the week with Jess and Cory as their witnesses.

# CHAPTER TEN

**ALWAYS A SOFTIE** for happy endings, Raine was misty-eyed, especially seeing the leftover guilt shadowing Cooper's face at just how close he'd come to losing Belle. Apparently, she and Jess weren't the only ones to go off half-cocked doing idiotic things. As if sensing her thoughts, he grinned at her.

"As for my attacker," Belle spoke now, "he was apprehended a few weeks later and returned to prison. Not long after that we learned he'd been killed by another inmate." She added fiercely, "and I can't say I'm sorry he's dead. It'd be a bald-faced lie!"

This was the connection she felt with Belle. She'd also suffered at the hands of a violent man and lived to talk about it. It also didn't go amiss that the three of them had beaten their adversaries. Cory had literally run her tormentor off with a shotgun. Belle's had died in prison. And no, she didn't blame her for not being sorry. *She* absolutely wasn't sorry Addison was behind bars. She was only sorry he was getting out. Once released, there'd come a day of reckoning. Of that, she was sure. The thought sent a shiver through her. Not only fear of Addison, but also for Jess. When he found out she was baiting Addison he'd be livid. Hell hath no fury like Jess Harper when he was upset. She ought to know.

Seeing the shiver, and completely misreading the cause, Jess did blame Addison. If he'd known what she was up to, there would have been another knock-down drag-out right then and there. Instead, he rushed to assure her everything would be all right. "I don't want you worrying about Addison getting to you."

*All right Blondie, this is where you confess what you're up to,* shouted her conscious. She ignored it, especially when he continued. "That's why I asked this crew over tonight." One shapely brow shot up. He ignored it. "I just didn't mention it because you'd have flat out refused any help."

"You got that right, buddy boy!" She shot him a miffed glare.

Jess rolled his eyes. "We don't know for certain he'll try to find you." *That was a stupid statement. Of course he will.* "But it won't hurt to have some professional back up." He flicked an all-encompassing glance at the other three. "Cooper and Cory are law enforcement and Belle is licensed to pack heat." He shot Belle a sheepish grin. "I guess I should consider myself lucky you didn't shoot me the other night." They all laughed. "And I can shoot the eyes out of a snake five hundred yards away." Raine made a scoffing sound. "Believe it baby-doll, and I'm legal to carry, too. Surely, you'll agree that's one hell of a team. We'd have your back and Addison would have one hell of a time getting past us. So, what's your answer?"

After pulling a fast one he still expected an answer on the spot? Given her stance on involving anyone else in her problems, she should be tearing strips off him. Needing space, the crackling embers drew her to the fireplace where the flickering flames danced and swayed like glowing marionettes. *How apropos, for she'd been Addison's puppet on a string, dancing and jumping to his every command just like those flames. Well, it was time to burn the damn puppet strings! But she had to do it alone for she wouldn't put anyone else in Addison's line of fire.* As if agreeing, the flames danced faster. Squaring her shoulders, she faced them.

Instantly, Jess wanted to throttle her. Hell and damnation! The stubborn little cuss was going to refuse. "No," she avoided looking at him. "I can't do it. If Addison hurt or, God forbid, killed one of you, I couldn't live with it. My answer is no, absolutely not! If I were smart I'd go back to Phoenix and be waiting when he stepped out of jail for a face-off."

Jess opened his mouth to argue but Belle beat him to it. "First off, you're not going back to Phoenix for any face-off! *If* a face-off happens, it'll be here. Second, you don't honestly believe we'd let you two fight that lunatic alone? No way in hell! That's just plain crazy! We're helping and you'll just have to get used to it!"

Obviously, Belle Michaels was another force to be reckoned with. Put them all together they formed a steel wall no one could penetrate. What bothered her most was Jess. He'd been more worried than he'd let on. And why hadn't she picked up on it. Dammit! This was her fight; she'd ridden the dead horse of her marriage by letting Addison's threats keep her tethered to him. Resolving this mess should rest solely on her shoulders. Pacing in front of the stone hearth, her fingers worried a strand of hair. She was sorely tempted to accept their help, and Belle was right that Addison *was* a lunatic with no filter. He'd do anything, hurt anyone who got in his way. And *that* was what made her thoughts waver in indecision.

Belle watched Raine. At least she's thinking about it, she thought, silently urging her to keep on. *I know you're weighing the possible consequences and I'd do the same thing in your shoes, but come on, you have to let us share your burden. You know it's the right thing to do.*

Tucking a strand of hair behind her ear, Raine mused. "I could have asked for help back in Phoenix, but with Addison's threats hanging over me, I kept my mouth shut." She'd wanted to confide in Molly and Gordon so many times but knew in her heart that it was too dangerous a situation for anyone else to be involved. Molly had been pregnant, and she wasn't about to get her mixed up in this mess. As for Gordon, her attorney and Molly's hot-tempered husband, he'd have killed Addison first, asked questions later, *and* would have buried the body to boot.

"Not having any children, I can't say what I'd have done in your shoes, but I believe if my husband threatened to steal my child, I'd do anything to stop him." Belle said.

"Trust me, you would!" Raine said vehemently. "I thought by putting up with what Addison did to me I could keep him from running off with Katy. Pretty naïve thinking, wasn't it?" She laughed derisively. "And crazy as it sounds Addison never chained me to the house. I could come and go as I pleased, do whatever I wanted so as long as I didn't try to leave. I was on an invisible leash only he and I knew existed. But his temper was getting worse, and it was only going to get even worse. I realized that if he killed me in one of his fits, Katy would have no one to protect her. That's when I finally decided to leave him again. Damn the consequences if he caught me.

I had everything planned right down to the day and time we would leave. Unfortunately, a couple of days before that Addison went off the deep end, and you all know the rest of the story."

But that wasn't the rest of the story. Another chapter waited to be written: The Ending. And how would it end, she wondered? Unquestionably, Addison was cunning and the thought of several pairs of eyes was appealing, but she still opted for no. "I appreciate the risks you're willing to take, but the answer is still no."

Chancing a glance at Jess, his thundercloud expression spoke a thousand words. He was about to turn into Mr. Cranky-Pants. "Right now, my ex-husband is sitting behind bars in some little backwoods jail." At their incredulous expressions she held up a hand. "I know. I know. Ironic isn't it? I agree to a plea bargain so he'll be in prison and instead he's neatly tucked away in some little Podunk jail. And, if I know Addison, he's got everyone eating out of his hand. He may not be free to come and go, but he's not hurting, either. I'd even bet he's found a way to get his feel-good drugs in jail."

"I'd like to find out if that's true." Cooper interjected. "That would shoot that plea deal all to hell. Give me the information where he's at and I'll do a little snooping around."

"Good luck with that." She scoffed but rattled off the memorized information. At this point it really didn't matter what Cooper found out. Addison was getting out and coming after her. "As far as I'm concerned, this is my battle to fight should he show up. My only concern is making sure he never gets his hands on Katy."

Jess had had enough and indeed Mr. Cranky-Pants made his appearance. "Quit being so damned stubborn! Who are you trying to convince you can handle this on your own? Not me, that's for damn sure!" In two strides he loomed large, his hands firm on her shoulders. "I'm not buying what you're peddling, and I'd bet another roll in the snow those nightmares you're having are making you a wreck. You put up a good front but you're not fooling me. By the time Addison's released you'll be sick with fear."

Yes, she *was* worried that Addison would get by her and make off with Katy. That's why she had to get him to meet her away from here. Suddenly, the voice in her head reached her. *Why not use them to protect Katy and Cora? This could work in your favor, you know. Go along with them and in the meantime keep working on Addison. You're no dummy. You know how he gets when he sets his sights on something. Use their help to your advantage and since he claims to know your whereabouts, call his bluff. Pick a place to execute your plan.* The little voice went off on a tangent of uproarious laughter before calming down. *No pun intended but that was funny. Get it . . . execute? Anyway, know your plan like the back of your hand so he doesn't . . .* That little voice rattling non-stop in her head made sense and it finally convinced her to go along with them.

Ignoring a ripple of guilt, Raine gripped Jess's strong hand and gazed into his brooding eyes. "Jess Harper, you have a way of getting into a person's head." She gave a slight smile. "You sure as heck always seem to know what's going through mine." Not really, or he'd have already blown his stack and taken the cabin roof off with it.

"Just keep that in mind whenever you get in another snit about something." He retorted, relieved she'd come to her senses. Still, something didn't sit right.

Raine's chin shot up and those gorgeous blue eyes he could drown in flashed sparks. "I'll have you know I don't get into snits!"

"Uh," He scoffed, jerking his thumb toward the door. "Tell that to poor old Santa Claus. He's the one sporting a hole in him. So, what's it to be? Are we a team?" One dark brow rose, nearly getting lost in his hair.

Another sticky prickle of guilt made her hesitate. She hated tricking him, but she justified it by thinking they could protect Katy and Cora while she took care of Addison. A false sigh of capitulation slid out of her. "All right." And despite her deception, a tremendous weight was lifted from her shoulders. "If you're sure you want to get involved in this mess then I'll accept your help. Between all of us we should be able to keep Addison from getting his hands on Katy or hurting Cora."

Belle and Cory shared a worried look. It didn't go unnoticed by either that Raine didn't include herself in their protection. No matter, *they'd* make sure she was protected should the lunatic show up.

Seeing Belle's green eyes turn flinty, Cooper recognized only too well what she was thinking. His wife was itching to get her hands on Raine's ex-husband and mete out some serious punishment. You go girl! He championed. I'll help you, too.

In the meantime, Cory thought she ought to polish up her daddy's old shotgun. It hadn't been fired in a really long time. And just where the hell was her no-good ex-husband when she needed a little target practice?

"Raine," Cooper said, "we won't let anything happen to any of you. For now, I'll see if my contacts can scope out what's going on with the jailhouse situation. I'd love to stop that early release." *That makes two of us*, she thought as the cell phone in her sweater pocket vibrated. Addison must really be ticked off at being ignored.

Ironically, Cooper mentioned the communication mode at that moment. "Jess told me about the separate phone and email accounts. That was a great idea," he looked at Jess, "you got yourself one sharp lady there. We might try enticing her to join the force." Then he grinned wickedly. "And I've seen first-hand she can hold her own. Just look at how she took you down, old buddy."

As their laughter filled the room, a chagrined Raine blushed red to the roots of her blond hair. She'd never live that embarrassing moment down.

"Ha! Ha! Ten million comedians out of work and I've got a whole cabin full of them." Jess grumbled but joined in the laughter.

Cory moved to Raine's side. "We've all been at the mercy of violent men and came out the other side. It's a situation we never thought to be in, but we should consider ourselves members of the survivor's club."

"Cory's right." Belle agreed. "The three of us survived violence and came out the other side for the better. Cory has her fireman, I've got my cop, you have your marine, and now you have us. You were meant to be here."

Observing the special bond forging between these three special women, Jess's chest swelled with emotion so strong he could hardly breathe.

# CHAPTER ELEVEN

As they gathered around the table Raine noticed the pages of notes Jess had been keeping and her stomach twisted in dismay realizing just how worried he really was. Why hadn't she seen through *his* pretense? Both had been harboring secrets. Had been?—she still was!

Opening the folder in front of her, Raine saw the collection of old newspaper articles along with several pictures of her and Addison. Picking one up, she took a step back in time. The picture had been taken right after Katy was born. It was her first outing and despite the sleepless exhaustion of having a newborn, they were beaming with happiness. It was before the drinking and drug habit Addison had kept so well hidden jumped front and center spiraling their relation down the path to destruction. It was a reminder of everything he'd thrown away and the destruction yet to come.

Looking up, she found Jess watching her with a mixture of anger and jealousy before he glanced away. Without a word she reached for his hand, squeezing it.

He knew it was ridiculous, but he couldn't help the jealousy that filled him when she got lost in the past with Addison. Addison had destroyed their world, now she was his. She belonged with him!

As Raine perused the scant file, she knew they needed a more in-depth look at who they were dealing with. Releasing a pent-up breath, and still holding Jess's hand, she dove into the down and dirt-ugly details about Addison and the things he'd done to her. The only thing she didn't mention was the photos taken at the hospital. At the moment they were hidden in the top of her closet where Katy couldn't get ahold of the horrific images. Actually, she didn't want anyone seeing them. They were reminders of how vicious Addison could be and just how close he'd come to beating her to death.

Throughout the re-counting several colorful descriptions emerged of what they'd do if they ever got their hands on Addison. The majority vote was putting the sadistic monster down. Heaven forbid they see those photos. They'd load up their guns and go after Addison tonight. It'd be just like one of those wild west shootouts where the white-hatted good guys took on the black-hearted bad ones. However, in today's world they'd all end up sharing a cell together.

Though knowing the details, hearing them again enraged Jess just as much as the first time she had recanted them to him. He smacked his fist on the table. "The S.O.B. doesn't belong in jail. He belongs six feet under! You can rest assured that if he shows his face here I'll make damn sure that happens!"

*That was why she had to reach Addison first,* she thought. *She couldn't have Jess making good on his threat and winding up in jail for murder.* Of course, she'd have preferred no one die. She preferred that he would be locked up until he was old and feeble-minded. She really didn't want Katy's father dead but that decision rested solely on his head.

It was approaching ten o'clock when Cory made her exit. "I've got a date with my fireman. I bet when I tell Paul what's happening he'll jump right in with us." When Raine started to protest Cory stopped her. "Paul's licensed to carry and most definitely knows how to use a gun. We're not a vigilante-minded crew but we do believe in protecting our own."

With Cory leaving, Jess hoped the other two would follow suit, but he was totally mistaken. Instead, they settled in for another drink, their shared smirks proof they'd done it just to annoy him knowing he was impatient for some alone time with Raine. When Cooper, shooting a guiltless grin at his scowling friend, finally drained his glass and said, "Come on, sweetheart, let's go home. I'm sure these two want to get to bed," Jess was ready to toss him out in the snow.

"And you," Cooper addressed Raine, "try not to worry too much about what's coming down the pike. We'll make sure we've got your back."

Raine hugged Belle, apologizing once again. "I can't say how sorry I am for saying those horrible things about you."

Merriment danced in her twinkling green eyes. "I've already told you Jess is to blame. If he hadn't been acting like a jackass you'd have never jumped to the wrong conclusion."

"And here we go again." Jess grumbled, tugging the ends of the scarf wrapped around Belle's neck. "Cooper, take your curly-mopped troll home before I strangle her with this fancy scarf."

"Come on you curly-headed troublemaker, you've caused enough trouble for one evening." Grabbing her hand, he dragged his giggling wife out the door.

Closing it firmly behind them, Jess expelled a huge sigh. "I thought they'd never leave!" Then he gave her an appraising look. Talk about knocked for six. Though he'd experience her temper before, her reaction to seeing Belle was beyond spitfire fury. He thought of poor old Santa being kicked to smithereens and their tussle in the snow. Undoubtedly, he'd be the butt of a certain three people's jokes for a long time to come.

She must have read his mind. "I really *am* sorry for making a total idiot of myself in front of them."

"Are you kidding? Anytime they can get a laugh at my expense they're one happy bunch." With a gleam in his eyes, quick as lightening, he hauled her into his arms. "And you're not sorry at all and you owe me a much better apology." Both were breathless when they came up for air. "I've wanted to do that all evening, but there were just too many nosy people here." His hands rested on the curve of her hips.

Still a bit in la-la land, she was thinking the man could give lessons in kissing. On second thought, she was the only one he'd be kissing from here on out! "Yeah, but those nosy people love you, and I'd bet the same goes for you. You can't wait to catch each other in a pickle, but you have each other's backs like the musketeers—one for all and all for one."

Jess gave a contemplative shrug. "I never quite saw us as "musketeers" but I don't know anyone else I'd rather have in my corner then those three, and now you."

"I'll always be in your corner, Jess. Never doubt it." Her simple assurance impressed on him to make sure she never had any more regrets where he was concerned. And, he thought with a bit of wry humor, he guessed he'd better send Inez a big bouquet of red roses in thanks. After all, it was her chicanery that had brought them together.

Tucking a strand of silky hair behind one ear, he asked. "Can you stay or do you need to get back to the girls? One of my favorite Christmas movies is on."

"I love Christmas movies and the girls are down for the count. Cora said not to hurry back. Those two little scamps ran us all over the mall, at least five times." At his chuckle she scowled and smacked his arm. "That's not funny! Just wait. You're turns coming, buddy. And don't think you're getting off that easy getting your friends involved in this mess with Addison. Care to explain how you conveniently forgot to tell me?"

All righty then, at least she'd waited until they were alone before taking him to task. One round of harassment from his friends was all he could stand for one evening. "I didn't forget. I just know you well enough that had I told you my intentions you'd have puffed up like an aggravated bullfrog. Look. I can't explain it, but my gut says Addison knows where you are." He didn't want to compound her fears, but he had to be honest.

Guilt rippled up her spine. Now was her chance to confess about the text messages she and Addison were exchanging. Of course, there'd be a monumental explosion, but at least it would be out in the open. Thinking of Addison, she could only imagine the types of torture he was salivating over after reading her taunts. He was probably pacing his small cell and cursing her

68

with every breath. And if she were to believe him, he *did* know her whereabouts. Despite using Cora's vehicle and information since leaving Phoenix nothing was totally hidden from Addison's grasp.

A flash of ire rippled through her. She wanted her life back to normal. She was tired of living on the edge. She wanted to come and go and not look over her shoulder. She wanted the freedom to see her best friend. She missed Molly something fierce. Although they talked every few days, it wasn't the same as seeing her in the flesh. An idea took seed. Maybe she could talk Molly and Gordon into relocating here. Gordon could get his law license here and there was that place just up the road that, with some TLC, would make a grand place to raise a family. It had caught her eye when she'd first moved here and every time she passed it she heard it calling her name. She needed to snap it up before someone else did!

Her thoughts turned back to Addison. There were strings associated with him back in Phoenix that needed cutting that played no part in her future. But she thought with a bit of trepidation, all of that hinged on the outcome of the looming confrontation. She reflected on Addison's bragging that he knew where she was. If he *had* found her, how had he done it? Then the light bulb flashed on in her head. The snowstorm they'd been caught in a few weeks back! Blizzard conditions had made the roads treacherous and, unfortunately, they'd been caught out in it. They'd been so close to home when a crazy driver hit Jess's new truck sending it spinning out of control and careening off the highway smack dab into a bluff. Fortunately, the only fatality had been the truck and luckily, though severely banged up, they'd walked away from it. As for the snowstorm, one of the worst in years, it had made national headlines, including the accident, and their heated kiss.

Better face it girl, if Addison had access to a television he more than likely saw you kissing Jess in front of the world. Molly certainly had and taken great delight in razzing her about the lip-lock. In that moment they'd given no thought to the television crews filming. They'd just been in a horrible accident and thought the other dead. The sheer relief finding it not true had been so overwhelming they'd been in each other's arms, oblivious to anyone else.

Had Addison seen them, he'd be out for every drop of blood running through her body. Shuddering at the thought, her conscious prodded her to confess right then. After all, wasn't Jess doing everything he could to keep them safe. Nevertheless, she couldn't bring herself to tell him. Not yet. She needed concrete proof Addison knew her whereabouts. In the meantime, playing on that possibility, she would scout out a location to get him to meet her.

"You were right to ask them to help us." She admitted. "I know you're just thinking of my safety."

"I'll take every precaution to keep Addison from slipping past us but no plan is infallible. That's why we need eyes and ears everywhere." Snuggling her against him, the mere thought of Raine being harmed again made him sick. *Never would he forget his first sight of her so painfully beat up. And, by then, she'd had several weeks to heal. How bad had she looked initially,* he wondered.

"When he sets his mind on something, he won't let anything get in his way." *Addison is dangerous, but so am I,* she thought. *He just doesn't know how dangerous he's made me. Should he show up he'll find out just how far she'd go when pushed over the edge.* Though she didn't want him dead it didn't mean she wasn't capable of doing the deed. *If fate demanded it, it would be another fight to the death!* On that thought, she put Addison on the back burner of her mind. After all, he was months from being released from prison, and she'd rather focus on the man holding her.

Her heart swelled with love for the man willing to take on her dangerous ex-husband. After what Addison had put her through, she'd sworn off men, but this one had gotten to her and the cranky-pants man she'd faced off with in his driveway had stolen her heart so suddenly that her heart skipped a beat.

Turning in his embrace, the scent of him, fresh outdoors, and a subtle spiciness, wafted over her. A delicious rush of heated desire rippled through her. Until recently, she hadn't known if she could ever tolerate any kind of intimacy again. She had even wondered if Addison had killed the desire to feel pleasure in another man's arms. Happily, with Jess's tenderness, she could report that was *not* the case!

Nuzzling his neck, the soft flick of her tongue sent an aching longing through him. Memories of their lovemaking were never far from his thoughts. "That's feels so good, honey. I love it when you touch me. You can't imagine how many times over the last few days I've wanted to whisk you away to be alone with you."

Knowing the cruelty she'd endured at the hands of her ex, Jess was amazed she even wanted anything to do with another man. He could barely wrap his head around how a person could inflict so much pain on the woman you vowed to love and cherish. Talk about sleeping with the enemy! She had scars, not just the physical ones but emotional ones also to show for it. Just thinking of the silvery marks marring the creamy-smooth flesh of her back enraged him. All he needed was five minutes with that piece of scum and he'd never lay a hand on anyone again!

Thoroughly reveling in the tender caresses, Raine felt the sudden tensing coil of anger in him. He was thinking of what Addison had done to her. Well, he was just going to have to forget about Addison, and she knew just the way to do it.

The movie ended about the same time they came up for air. Much more and he wouldn't let her go. As if reading his mind, she sighed, "We keep this up and you'll never get rid of me."

"Sounds like a plan to me. There's nothing I'd rather do than keep you here. But it's probably best I take you home." It wasn't what he wanted but he'd meant what he said the other night—the next time they made love she'd be staying permanently in his bed.

A short while later, snuggled under the cocoon of quilts, Raine was wishing Jess was with her when a ridiculously funny thought made her snicker. When they met face-to-face, she'd have to thank Addison, for without the hell he'd put her through she'd never have met Jess.

Her eyes closing, she drifted into the most delicious dream in which she and Jess were making love in his giant, king-size bed. Suddenly, it was Addison touching her and the dream became a rip-roaring nightmare as his evil laughter resonated with relish while he made his intentions quite clear. Terror engulfed her seeing the all-too-familiar belt in his hand. She fought him while frantically searching for a glimpse of Jess. She cried out in horror as she spied him sprawled on the floor bleeding. Once again, everything changed again as smoky shadows swirled round her. This time it was the Addison she'd once known, the loving man he'd once been that was on bended knee begging forgiveness, but in the blink of an eye the evil Addison was back, his crazed laughter echoing as he started whipping her unmercifully. The pain was unbearable! She had to make him stop! Suddenly, a gun appeared in her hand and she squeezed the trigger over and over and over

The loud reports jerked her awake. Quickly switching on the bedside lamp, she peered over the side of the bed. Relief enveloped her as she realized that Jess really wasn't lying dead. Bloody hell, the nightmare seemed so real. "Well, that certainly puts an end to another night's sleep." *Was this a premonition*, she wondered as her heart threatened to explode out of her chest.

Crawling from the tangled covers she needed her soothing balm—a really strong pot of coffee. While it brewed, she showered away the dregs of the nightmare. Wiping the steam off the mirror, a ghostly white face with dark holes for eyes stared back at her. "A trailer load of concealer won't help those beauties," she muttered, dabbing moisturizer under them.

With a steaming mug of coffee securely in hand, she settled into the rocking chair relaxing in its gentle back and forth motion. Using the remote, she lit the Christmas tree. Its lights filled the room with a soft ambiance, one that warred with the roiling turmoil inside of her.

As she sipped her coffee, she pondered the nightmare, correction nightmares. They were happening all too frequently. Were they an omen of the future? "Heed the warnings. Trust your instincts." She lectured softly. "Do *not* forget how brutally vicious Addison is." Memories of that viciousness chilled her as a tremor coursed through her. Taking another sip, it warmed her insides.

Why couldn't Addi . . . No, damn it! He would never control her again. She was through being manipulated—consciously or unconsciously. Come-hell-or-high-water, she would never cowtow to him again. When he showed up, as she knew he would, she'd be ready for him. She pictured him trussed up like the proverbial Christmas goose, and deservedly so. After all, hadn't he trussed her up like one? "Come and get me, Addison," she whispered, "I don't want to, but I just might have to kill you."

While she was enjoying the image of Addison trussed up, Jess was also up. Always an early riser, this morning he'd even beat the neighbor's rooster crowing its morning sonata. His sleep had become restless because of a nagging feeling that something wasn't right. He'd even checked all the security cameras a couple of times. And gun in hand had scouted around the place.

Now on his third cup of strong, black coffee, he was reading through the additional information Raine had supplied on Addison. A frown chiseled his features. For sure, the man was one crazy S.O.B. She'd been damned lucky to escape him. A cold chill swept over him. Raine could have been the one shot. The thought made the coffee set his stomach afire and fueled his rage. He'd be damned if Addison Andrews ever laid a hand on her again!

# CHAPTER TWELVE

**A WHILE LATER,** busy patching the hole Raine had kicked in Santa Clause, Jess heard the kids' traipsing around the snow-covered woods. They were whooping it up so loudly that their voices echoed through the frosty air. Apparently, they were headed to the stables to visit the slick-coated horses they'd become partial to. Given none had ever ridden a horse, with the patience of a saint, he'd taught them. Catching on quickly, it wasn't long before some good-natured competition as to who was the best cowboy started. It made him extremely proud to bring a small amount of joy to their lives.

Finished patching Santa, he headed to Raine's. Knocking and stepping through the door he was greeted by two pajama-clad little girls. "We're watching Christmas cartoons, Mr. Jess. You wanna watch them wif' us?" Katy asked.

"Oh gosh, that sounds like fun, Katy-bug, but I have a whole bunch of things to do and I want to be back for the cookie baking." Looking at Raine, his eyes narrowed at the smudges beneath her eyes. Obviously, another sleepless night; but this wasn't the time for discussion. "I wanted to see if you'd mind picking up the needed supplies. "I'm an eater, not a baker. I've no clue what's needed."

Concerned the kids would get bored, they'd racked their brains for activities. One idea was a cookie baking afternoon in which each child baked their favorite cookie. This was the day! The children and Jess, the biggest kid of all, could hardly wait to sample all the sweet treats.

Raine waved away the wad of bills in his hand while giving him an enticing smile. "No problem; my treat. Want to take a little walk before going our separate ways? Who knows when we'll have a minute alone again?" She was already pulling on her coat. He wasn't about to say no.

The air was crisp as they walked the trail toward the stables. The horses nickered excitedly for the treats Raine carried in her pocket. After feeding them, he led her into the shadowy dimness of the building where he plied her with steamy kisses that she returned just as voraciously. Both wanted more than just a few stolen moments. They wanted hour upon hour, year after year, but for now these private interludes would have to suffice. At least they were alone for a few minutes.

Or so they thought. Robert Ford had been hiding in the thick stand of cedars since first light hoping to get more dirt, so when they'd passed him he'd taken pictures of them holding hands. Of course, he'd thought sure his number was up earlier when those whooping and hollering brats had raced by. Now cold and hungry, he waited until Raine and Jess reached the stables before hot-footing it to his non-descript van. As an extra precaution he'd parked in a different location, so it took a bit longer to reach it. Once there, he cranked the heater full blast then held his icy-cold hands to the hot air blowing from the vents. "Oh, that feels so good." It was a good thing he was getting prime dollar for this job. He was freezing his butt off in this godforsaken place. It was colder than a well digger's . . . well it was cold.

Finally warm, Robert Ford eased down the road only to see a familiar vehicle pass by. Andrews' ex was driving. Obviously, the lovebirds hadn't lingered long at the stable. Sighing in resignation, he guessed eating could wait a while longer. Curious to see where they were headed, he trailed them to town and into a supermarket parking lot. Well heck! They were grocery shopping. Just then his stomach growled loudly and as luck would have it, there was a burger joint across the street. Awesome! He could eat and still keep an eye on them.

A few minutes later he was scarfing down a burger, extra-large fries, and soda while inside the market Cora was scolding a distracted Raine for putting three bags of cornmeal in the grocery cart instead of flour. "You got your head full of that good looking man!" She teased, switching out the bags, "you just push the buggy and let me fill it."

Robert Ford was pleasantly full and half-dozing in the warm sunshine streaming through the van's windshield. Now, *this* was his kind of surveillance. Opening his heavy-lidded eyes he was in time to see Raine and Cora loading groceries into the SUV. Nothing major to report there so he would call it a day. He was past ready to stretch in a warm comfy bed.

It was too bad, Raine thought a while later, watching the chattering group of kids icing the cooled cookies, that Jess was missing all the fun. He'd let her know he was held up because his meetings were taking longer than he'd planned. Learning this, the kids insisted on filling a large cookie tin for "Mr. Jess" and Raine, knowing "Mr. Jess's" sweet tooth, figured the cookies wouldn't last more than one day. Her prediction would prove right.

Twilight had fallen by the time he finally got home. Shutting off the engine, he sat morosely pondering the very rude awakening he'd had concerning the workings of the local foster system. It seemed the powers that be frowned upon a single man being a foster parent. What hog-wash! Their thinking was so archaic they needed to catch up with the 21st century. Still, he'd started the proceedings anyway figuring he had a snowball's chance in hell of being approved. At least he'd received some positive news. All the boys were set to go to foster homes, the transition taking place on New Year's Day.

The not so good news—Kathy would remain in foster care. Jess was still trying to wrap his head around the fact that no one wanted the cute little tyke just because she had deplorable parents. Dad was a drug dealer who'd make a deal with the devil if he could and was serving a long sentence as a guest of the state penitentiary. As for her mother, a strung-out street junkie, it was anybody's guess where she was. His heart ached for the poor mite carrying a double albatross around her neck. The idea of Kathy spending her childhood in the system hit too close to home. He'd been there, done that, thus his decision to try to become her foster parent. The ball was in their court now.

Seeing lights glowing from every window at the cabin Jess was glad the cookie party was still in full swing. He could use some cheering up. Locking the truck, he and his frustration trudged up the pathway. Not too far away Robert Ford sat in the same sheltered cluster of cedars he'd occupied earlier. They provided a good view of the cabin besides being a buffer from the biting wind. He'd rethought taking the rest of the day off, so here he was armed with a thermos of coffee, battery heated socks and insulated coveralls. He even had a lightweight camping chair to sit on. Getting comfortable, he was in time to see the boyfriend approach the cabin.

The second Jess stepped inside he was bombarded by boisterous greetings and the most decadent aroma of fresh baked cookies. "It sure does smell good in here." His stomach growled in agreement. Come to think of it he'd consumed nothing but coffee all day. No wonder it growled.

"When Ms. Raine said you'd be late we fixed you a big tin of cookies." One of the boys said.

"That was a splendid idea." He replied, ruffling the boy's hair.

Leaning against the kitchen counter, Raine observed him, a slight frown furrowing her brow. Though he smiled, it didn't quite reach his eyes. Something was bothering her man. 'Her man'—she liked the sound of it. And he was her man from the top of his jet black hair to the tips of his highly polished, size eleven boots. He's got that *I could use a cup of coffee* look.

Out of the corner of his eye he saw Raine's worried frown and extricated himself from the kids to join her. Accepting the proffered mug, he took a bolstering drink, closing his eyes and sighing appreciatively. "I needed this." Her warm smile eased a little of the angst brewing inside him. When he opened them it was his turn to study her with a worried look of his own. The purple bruising beneath her eyes was more pronounced. His girl wasn't sleeping well and it didn't take a rocket scientist to know why. And oh yes, she was his girl all right, had been since she'd cruised into his driveway. He opened his mouth to quiz her until he saw Kathy and his frustration kicked into high gear.

Seeing the direction of his gaze Raine surmised something was happening involving Kathy and for once was grateful it wasn't Addison upsetting him. Whatever was going on had to wait. The kids, excited he'd finally joined them, deserved his undivided attention. She'd tackle him about what was going on concerning Kathy later. "I could tell . . .," was all she got out before the kids dragged him to the table.

"Oh boy!" He exclaimed enthusiastically eyeing the Christmas tin full of cookies before diving right in selecting an iced Santa Claus. He bit into it. "Umm . . . This is awesome!"

Not wanting to disappoint, Jess ate a cookie from each child's batch, finding something special about it. Their faces beamed, especially when he insisted they had to make more when he ran out. Their joy helped lessen the ache in his heart. Just then, he caught Raine watching him, the love shining from her violet eyes left him breathless. His own gaze took on a possessive gleam as it slid from the mane of corn colored hair in a high ponytail, to the green sweatshirt sporting a trio of dancing penguins, to the clinging jeans. Oh, yeah, she was definitely his woman and he didn't care how sexist it sounded! At that moment, he wished they were alone. Then, he'd show her how much she belonged to him. Grinning, he winked slyly, enjoying her rosy-cheeked blush and her exasperated eye-roll.

By late evening it was an exhausted but happy group, full of Christmas cookies and pizza they'd had for dinner before they trooped off to bed. Katy and Kathy, barely able to keep their eyes open, insisted Jess tuck them in. When he returned Raine was putting the broom away and Cora was pouring chilled Chardonnay into glasses. Passing a glass to each, she settled with a heartfelt sigh into the recliner while Jess drew Raine to the sofa. "We should drink a toast to you," she looked at Jess. "Because of you those kids are having the time of their lives."

"She's right." Raine agreed. "They had a blast today. I bet they haven't baked cookies in ages, if ever."

With his free hand, he reached for hers. "We all deserve a toast. I couldn't have pulled this whole Christmas thing off alone. And heaven knows, they deserve every bit of happiness they can get."

Raine studied his warm, strong calloused hand. It could be gentle yet forceful and she felt safe holding it. "We're all having fun. As for Katy and Kathy, those little stinkers could be sisters. They already adore each other. I know there's not much differ- ence in their ages, yet Kathy seems so much older. I'm betting she's seen her fair share of bad times." Her tone turned wistful. "I hope she gets to go back home soon."

"No. No. No." His dark eyes snapping, Jess shook his head emphatically. "I wouldn't wish that on any kid, not after what I learned today. However, I do have some good news. All the kids, except Kathy, are being placed with foster families come New Year's Day."

"That's awesome! But why isn't anyone taking Kathy?" Cora asked.

"It seems," reiterating what he'd learned from Kevin Forsythe, the director of the children's home, "that every fam- ily that meets Kathy falls in love with her, but her background scares them off. It's unfortunate that no one wants her because they're afraid of what her parents might do. Dad's a drug dealer and mom's a junkie just looking for her next fix. At least he's in prison, but who knows where dear old mom is."

Bingo! That's what's eating at him, Raine deduced.

"And when someone is willing, once they find out her father's one of the biggest, badass dealers in the state, they back off. And the mother's no better, constantly in and out of rehab. I'm not made that way, but I can understand not wanting to take on that kind of trouble." He *was* different and given half a chance, he'd take Kathy. Then, nobody would ever take his little girl from him.

"When was the last time either one had any contact with her?" Raine inquired.

"According to Kevin Forsythe; last year just before Christmas. Her mother called and against his better judgment he let her talk to Kathy. She promised that baby she'd visit her at Christmas and they'd soon be a family again. He said Kathy waited and waited but dear old mom was a no-show. She put on a brave face, he said, but it just broke her heart. So excited, then nothing. Nada. And of course, he wasn't about to let Kathy leave with her had she shown up. He couldn't trust she wouldn't get high and leave Kathy in some dark alley." Taking a sip, he continued, "I'd take her in a heartbeat. Unfortunately, it's still difficult around here for a single man to become a foster parent despite the number of kids that could be placed. However, I'm not letting that archaic thinking deter me. I've taken the steps to become her foster parent. I can only hope for the best."

Picturing Kathy and Katy snuggled together, asleep in the other room, it was clear that they should be sisters. Kathy was starving for a family, and he intended Raine and him to be that family. He just prayed it would all work out in their favor.

"That's just plain ridiculous!" Cora sputtered, appalled. "You're just as capable of providing a good home as any married man. Probably better than a lot of couples, as far as that goes. There sure are a bunch of stupid people in this world and on that ridiculous note," she drained her glass, "I'm going to bed and pray somebody will wise-up and let you have that baby girl."

"I'll be praying right along with you, Cora." He agreed.

The moment Cora closed her door they were in each other's arms, their lips meeting as if drawn by a magnet. Afterward, Jess skimmed a tanned finger down one cheek. "You've got some dandy circles under your eyes, and I know for a fact they're not my fault. Cora said you're having nightmares, honey."

"Cora's got a big mouth, and better hearing than an elephant!" She retorted and swore she heard chuckling from Cora's room. Busted, there was no sense denying it. "Yeah, I've had a few."

"I'd say more than few. I wish there was something I could do." No one has yet figured out a way to stop the mind's working while you slept. He'd suffered plenty of them after the violent skirmishes he'd been in during his years in the service, so he understood the wear and tear that affected not only the body but the mind as well. In fact, very few people knew exactly what Jess had done in some of those god-forsaken places . . . and he never spoke of it.

"I know a way you can take my mind off of them for a while." She suggested huskily, winding her arms around his neck. He had to agree it was splendid distraction!

A long time later a breathless Jess, knowing things could get totally out of hand, reluctantly rolled to his feet and looked down at her. Somehow, they'd ended up lying on the sofa. "After that little session, you probably won't have any nightmares tonight. But my dreams are going to be so hot I won't get any sleep. It's probably a good idea I get out of here before Cora has to get up to chaperone us."

Bemused, she was still under the effect of his kisses when it dawned on her fuzzy brain he'd said he was leaving, and in fact was already at the door. Holly-by-golly! He sure knew how use those lips! But he wasn't getting away that fast! After him in a heartbeat, it was another while before he stepped out into the welcoming crisp air. He was so steaming hot he could have powered a locomotive. "Lock up after me," he bid huskily.

As she did, the sound of the lock sliding into place was over-shadowed by another sound. Instantly alert, Jess scanned the darkness. The other cabins were dark, the only light shining was a full moon in which he caught the shadow of a deer disappear-ing into the woods. He gave a derisive snort. The whole situation involving Raine's ex had him jumpier than a barrel of frogs.

If Jess had glanced upward he'd have found Addison's spy clinging precariously to a tree branch. Earlier, hoping for a bet-ter view he'd taken the chance and snuck up the tree to where he'd been perched ever since. Robert Ford figured he owed the deer big time for saving his hide. Despite the frigid temperatures he was sweating like a hard-run racehorse. Rivulets of sweat ran down his face. Mentally he kicked his backside. He was out of his mind to climb a tree within spitting distance of the boyfriend!

He'd already fallen out of one tree hitting hard with a yelp. He'd lain on the frozen ground for several long minutes, the wind knocked out of him waiting for shots to ring out. This was the first, and last, time he'd ever work for the bloodthirsty Andrews. Nothing satisfied him and the job was getting harrier by the minute. He'd even wanted him to harass her, but Robert Ford wasn't doing that. Andrews could hire thugs for that. If he was smart, he'd climb down from the tree and walk away with the money he'd already been paid. Then he shook his head in self-disgust. Suck it up! You can't do that. You need the rest of it to pay off the bookies. Now calm down before you fall out of this damn tree and someone does shoot you! Only when all the lights were out did he finally shimmy down.

While Robert Ford slinked through the cold night, Jess was intently scrutinizing the tapes. Though it had been only a deer, something still felt off and he'd learned a long time ago to never ignore his instincts. That rule had saved his backside more times than he could count and right now that instinct was in full throttle. For another hour he replayed the tapes until his eyes burned blurry. Alone in the big king-size bed, he wished Raine was curled up next to him. He'd feel a whole lot better. Soon, he smiled into the darkness, very soon she will be.

# CHAPTER THIRTEEN

**A FRESH DUSTING** of snow greeted a crispy-cold Christmas
Eve morning. Frost created shiny diamonds on the café's window panes while inside the air fairly crackled with excitement.
Jess was treating everyone to Christmas Eve breakfast and at the
moment they were gathered at a long table. The kids, giddy that
Santa Claus was coming that night, chattered like a tree full of
magpies.

Raine was seated at one end and Jess at the other. She'd
thought to sit by him but the kids had commandeered him, so
they were separated by a sea of people. Watching him with suspicious eyes, she ignored the continuous vibrating phone in her
pocket. *Addison would not ruin this Christmas. He'd ruined too
many in the past. She'd ignored him the last few days so he must
really be angry,* she ruminated with a touch of humor.

Just then Jess looked down the table, caught her stare and
winked. And it wasn't just any old wink, either. It was the one
he used when he was up to something. She shot him a squinty-
eyed look, he must really be up to something big time given he'd
winked at her at least five times over the past twenty minutes. If
he wasn't careful it'd turn into a permanent tic!

Jess was getting a kick out of her miffed reaction to the
eye-winking business. He had a secret he wasn't divulging until
tomorrow and given her annoyed looks it was probably a good
idea they were sitting at opposite ends of the table.

As soon as everyone was finished eating, he paid the bill
and tried making a quick getaway but she was already outside

waiting to grill him but before she could get more than a "Where . . ." out, he gave her quick kiss, another wink, and drove off.

Shooting Cora an inquisitive look, all she got in return was an evasive shrug. Darn the woman, she did know something! Opening her mouth to grill her, what came out was, "We'd better get going ourselves." Pulling her muffler over her mouth to hide a grin, Cora got in the passenger seat. Subterfuge sure was fun, she decided, as they left the parking lot.

Three hours later they were taking a well-deserved break. Normally a coffee girl, Raine was sipping a rich creamy hot chocolate that immediately sent her into chocolate euphoria. This was her favorite time of year and this Christmas she had so much to be grateful for. She had the sweetest little girl any mother could want. She'd been given another chance at love. And she'd survived Addison. And wouldn't you know it, as if on cue, the cell in her pocket vibrated. Obviously, he was furious at being ignored. Too bad. Until the holidays were over, he could leave all the threatening messages he wanted.

An old adage came to mind about things happening for a reason. It definitely applied to her. She'd had to suffer through Addison's hellishness to get to Jess. As for that other old adage about just desserts, — Addison was certainly getting his. But not for long, she thought dismally, all too soon he'd be free and gunning for her. Well fine! Bring it on!

Her thoughts turned to Jess. Where had the evasive man with the infernal eye-winking dashed off to? If he wanted to get under her skin all he had to do was use that sly-wink thing. It set her off every time. Of course, she was guilty of a few things that set him off too, which proved things wouldn't always be hearts-and-roses between them. Both were stubborn and opinionated to a fault, so there would be plenty of fireworks in their future. But they'd have fun, too, and when they did argue she could speak her mind without fear of any backlash. She'd lost track of the times Addison had slapped her for simply voicing her opinion.

But Jess Harper could be infuriating, too. She remembered the day he'd driven her to the mall to get Katy's dollhouse. On that trip she'd wanted to smack the smirk off his handsome face, especially when he'd decided to do some shopping and bought that sexy black negligee. *Now be honest,* came a taunting voice, *you really wanted to kick his sexy rear-end into the next universe, especially believing he and Belle had a thing going.* And come to think of it, where the heck was that wispy piece of torture? She'd have to tackle the sly dog about it. And, she recalled with a satisfied grin, she had kicked him!

Over the rim of her cup Cora studied Raine. With Addison's hand-i-work finally faded, despite the smudges lurking beneath her eyes, the girl fairly glowed and thank goodness she and that tall-drink-of-water finally worked through their prickly mess. He'd been twisted up worse than a pretzel and Raine had been just a bad. Thankfully, they'd come to their senses, albeit with a mighty shove from her. Much more shenanigans and she'd have boxed their ears! They were a match made in heaven, warts and all. They belonged together like chocolate needed caramel, like peanut butter needed jelly! Hiding a grin, she took a sip of coffee and thought about Jess's surprise. He'd sworn her to secrecy but, for sure, Raine would be over the moon come tomorrow.

By late afternoon the SUV was stuffed to the gills with gifts, including ones from the boys to everyone else. Raine had enjoyed herself especially knowing Addison was not a happy camper spending Christmas behind bars. As far as she was concerned it was the best Christmas present she'd ever received from him. Merry Christmas to me!

It was after eight that night and Raine was wiping down the kitchen counter when she caught the flash of headlights down at Jess's. Good! The sneaky man was finally home. She'd phoned him earlier regarding dinner plans but he'd told her to eat without him, that he was still knee-deep in errands and before she could quiz him, he was gone. She was sorely tempted to march down there and weasel out of him what he'd been up to but a mountain of presents still needed wrapping. Maybe she could find a chunk of coal to put in his stocking! Him and his confounded eye-winking business!

Jess heaved a sigh of relief to be home. He hadn't planned on being gone all day, but his shopping expedition had morphed big-time and he'd found himself thoroughly enjoying it. He hadn't worried about chores as the boys had volunteered to do them. Upon parting company, after breakfast, his first stop had been the jewelry store in the mall to get the ring, the one she'd been captivated by the day he'd driven her to pick up Katy's dollhouse.

Through the bare tree branches Christmas lights twinkled around the cabin. He was tempted to go up, but he wasn't sure he could keep his secret. To further avoid running into her, he'd driven across the river into Illinois to do his shopping. Thank goodness for GPS or he'd still be wandering around in unfamiliar territory. *The things a man did to surprise the woman he loved*!

Once everything was unloaded and the wrapped presents were tucked under the tree, he was ready for a breather. Grabbing a beer, he kicked back in the recliner and found a Christmas movie. Twisting off the cap, he started to take a drink then remembered Katy's dollhouse. A thrill raced through him that he'd see Raine after all and he'd keep the surprise even if he had to glue his lips together. Taking another drink, he thought dourly of the catastrophic evening they'd put the dollhouse together and his horrible actions that had nearly driven her away. A hard lesson learned; he wasn't about to go down that rocky road again.

While Jess watched his movie, Raine heard the two little girls giggling excitedly from their bedroom. They were waiting for her to read them a Christmas story. Her heart twisted a little that Katy was still worried Santa wouldn't find her despite being assured frequently that Santa and Rudolph's red nose would find her any place she was. "All right you two, ready for your story?"

"Yes mommy," they answered in unison. At Kathy's calling her "mommy", a pang hit her heart. If only she could be her mother.

Perching on the bed, she began reading. "T'was the night before Christmas and all through the house not a creature was stirring not even a mouse." Barely two pages in, on simultaneous sighs they'd drifted off into slumber. Turning off the light, she kissed them. Visions of sugar plums may not be dancing in their heads, but she bet there'd be dreams of a jolly fat man in a red suit and a red-nosed reindeer.

Before joining Cora, already busy wrapping gifts, she poured two glasses of Chardonnay. "I thought something fortifying would make this less painful."

"You thought right!" Cora exclaimed, accepting a glass.

"We may need a couple of bottles before we get through this mountain." Grabbing a roll of paper, she got busy. "I barely read two pages before they conked out. But you can be sure they'll be scoping out the presents before the rooster crows in the morning." Cora's mumbling grumble made her chuckle.

With the first round wrapped, Raine was tucking them under the tree when a soft knock sounded at the door. It was Jess with Katy's dollhouse. "Hi."

"Hi yourself." His breath formed a wispy cloud between them. She caught the heady scent of him — clean fresh air and the spice of his cologne. It was enough to . . . umm . . . she really would like to . . . she caught herself mid-fantasy, blushing wildly. "You better put that in Cora's room." She said huskily when he started to set it beside the shimmering tree. "If Katy wakes up and sees it there'll be no sleeping the rest of the night."

"I never even thought of that. Guess you can tell I'm not used to having little ones around. Maybe someday."

"The maybe someday," didn't slide by her and she wanted so badly to tell him she'd have his babies. And she might have had she seen the dreamy-eyed look on his face envisioning her heavy with his child. The picture was so vivid he literally put a hand out to touch her swollen belly only to find thin air. The hand dropped to his side. The idea of conceiving a child with her stirred a yearning he'd never felt before. The image of her with his child would come to him quite often over the next several months.

"Hey, Cora," Jess greeted, sitting the dollhouse down in the one clear spot in the room as he looked around in wide-eyed disbelief. "Did you buy gifts for the whole county?"

"Looks like it, don't it?" Cora chuckled at his stunned expression. "Care to have a glass of cheer? It sure makes wrapping a lot more fun."

"Then by all means, I'll have a glass." He said, shaking his head in amazement.

"I'll get it." Raine headed for the kitchen with him hot on her heels.

Backing her against the counter, he kissed her hungrily for several long moments. "I've been craving your kisses all day, woman." He murmured roughly against her mouth.

"Then by all means we have to feed your craving." And she kissed him back for all she was worth.

Both were breathless when they parted. "Wow! That whetted my appetite a little bit. Much more and I'll have an early Christmas feast—you."

Her cheeks burned rosy red, but not from embarrassment. Visions of their night together wove its silken threads through her mind. If she didn't stop them, she'd be feasting on him, too, right there in the middle of the floor! "I like that idea but there are too many eyes here for that. I think I'd better get your wine."

"Yeah, that's probably a good idea. Let's go wrap all those presents and let Cora chaperone us." Soon Jess was knee-deep in ribbon, tape, and colorful wrapping paper. A little while later he frowned at the pile. "I think this unwrapped pile is multiplying. Just when I think we're done more pop up."

"Better have another glass of cheer," Cora commiserated.

"We may have gotten carried away, but we made our lists and checked them twice, just like Santa and there just weren't any naughty boys and girls. A naughty man, maybe," she teased, receiving an eye-roll and a bop on the head with a roll of wrap.

They stacked the rest of the gifts around the tree, making sure the ones from Santa were front and center. Excited, Raine rubbed her hands in giddy anticipation. "This is going to be the best Christmas ever."

Slipping an arm about her trim waist, Jess gazed into her eyes and couldn't resist kissing her. "Merry Christmas," he murmured as the earlier vision of her with child materialized in his mind.

"Merry Christmas," she whispered against his warm mouth.

Lost in the moment, neither heard Cora's soft goodnight. In her room, she did a fist-pumping victory jig. She'd also asked Santa for something, and he'd delivered on it!

# CHAPTER FOURTEEN

**WHILE THE HAPPY** couple was indulging in heated kisses, over a thousand miles away a raging mad Addison paced the eight-by-eight space he currently called home like a caged animal. He'd done it so many times he'd lost count and with each angry step he called Raine every foul name in the book. It wasn't fair! He shouldn't be here! He was a tax-paying, law-abiding citizen, not some common criminal! Brawny fists grasped the bars of his cell with the urge to strangle something. Raine's slender neck popped into his head.

Dammit! It was Christmas Eve. He should be spending it with his baby girl instead of locked in here. He did another lap around the tiny space. Other people had done worse things and gotten off with a light slap on the hand. All he'd done was remind his wife who was boss in the family and it had landed him here. If that wasn't bad enough, now he'd carry a felony record for the rest of his life. His back teeth gnashed together. The little bitch should be the one in here for shooting him. Those slimy cops made sure her prints weren't on the gun. They probably wiped it clean then put it in his hand while he was unconscious. He'd prove it, too. Then, there'd be even more hell to pay.

"Here man," Sonny, the guard, interrupted his venomous thoughts, handing him a steaming Styrofoam cup of coffee. "I thought you could use this."

"You thought right." Addison said, glum-faced.

Pity filled the guard's eyes seeing the miserable persona Addison wore. "I know this isn't where you want to be right now. Shoot, I'd be mad as a hissing rattler if I couldn't spend Christmas with my kid, that's if I had one. I sure as heck wouldn't let my old lady get away with sticking me behind bars, either. For sure, there'd be hell to pay." Sonny was in a chatty mood and Addison let him rattle on. "You know, I never believed those stories about you. Smearing a good man's repu-tation ought to be against the law. I may work in the justice department, but I know dirty cops exist like the ones that set you up. I bet they wiped that gun clean of her prints and put yours on it. You'd never try to kill that pretty little wife of yours."

Playing the innocent victim to the hilt, Addison gave him a miserable look. "Thanks, man. I'm one hundred percent posi-tive that's what happened while I was unconscious." He feigned a catch in his voice. "I love my wife. I'd never try to kill her. We were just having a little dust-up and the next thing I know I'm shot and bleeding like a stuck pig." That wasn't exactly what happened, but who cared. At least the guard was on his side.

Sonny shook his head. "That ain't right. No woman who loves her man shoots him. She needs to pay for it. Somehow, she has to pay for putting you here. But you got to stay shy of those cops, too. You're in their crosshairs now. Hell, you won't be able to pick your nose without them knowing."

On a roll, Sonny continued, "You need a game plan, and your own phone, a burner one. If mine ever got checked I'd lose my job for letting you use it." Using Sonny's phone, Addison had continued harassing Raine, even after being warned to stop. "Just keep it hidden and be careful when you use it. Then when you're done with it you throw it away."

As Sonny rambled on, Addison's flagging spirits started perking up. He liked where this was going. "You're right. I have been taking chances using yours and I don't want to get you into trouble. I just don't know, Sonny," he sighed dejectedly, "I just feel so damned powerless."

"You're not powerless. I got your back."

*This just gets better and better*, Addison thought. *Now let's see how far he's willing to go.* "Thanks, man. A burner phone sounds great, but how am I supposed to get it? I can't exactly walk to the nearest store to get one."

Eager to gain favor, the guard enthusiastically offered, "I'll get it. Just not around here. It's a small town where everyone knows your business."

Nodding, Addison raised his cup in salute. "You're a good friend, Sonny, and when I'm out of here I'll make sure you're taken care of." An idea started sprouting. Maybe Sonny could do a couple of jobs for him before then. Maybe he'd like an all-expenses paid trip his next days off? He needed to get Raine's attention. The bitch was getting too cocky and Robert Ford was too squeamish to get his lily-white hands dirty. That was another thing. At some point the PI had to disappear.

"I'm looking to improve myself and a job with you would definitely do it. Appreciate it, boss. And I got another idea." Addison looked askance at him. "Somebody's got to know how to get in touch with her. If you knew who it was you could send her a little love note, if you catch my drift."

Muscular arms folded across his chest, Addison studied the man. Sonny wasn't quite the country-bumpkin he came across as. The idea percolating in his head bubbled harder. "Sonny, that's brilliant!" Addison snapped his fingers. "And I have a hunch that someone is her attorney. To prove I'm right let's send my darling little wife that love note. I'll need paper, pen, and an envelope large enough to hold several sheets of paper. It needs to look like a manuscript otherwise he might get suspicious and blow my surprise to smithereens."

"I sure would love to see her face when she opens that envelope." Sonny rubbed his bony hands together. "She needs a really good wake-up call to set her on her ear."

"I like the way you think, my man." *Maybe, his good friend Sonny, plied with enough green stuff, would help him with that wake-up call.* "Sonny, I've been thinking . . ."

# CHAPTER FIFTEEN

**RAINE SWORE SHE'D** just closed her eyes only to be abruptly roused by twin tornadoes making the bed bounce. "Wake up mommy!" Katy tugged one arm impatiently. For such a little thing she was a force to reckon with. "Santa found me, just like you said, and he brought my dollhouse!" Katy tugged harder. "Come see, mommy!"

"And mommy, he brought my baby doll!" Kathy was prying one eyelid up, "and the cookies are gone!" Along with the fingers poking her eye, there was a big pang poking her heart hearing Kathy call her mommy.

"Imagine that!" Raine removed the prying fingers while picturing Jess happily scarfing every last crumb. "Okay. Okay. I'm up." She pulled on a fleecy red robe. "Just give me a minute."

"Merry Christmas," Cora greeted her with a steaming mug of coffee when she finally appeared. She nodded at the girls impatiently scoping out the gifts. "They're as excited as a herd of giggling moose." Peering into the growing dawn she saw lights in the other cabins. "Looks like everyone else is up, too, and here comes Jess." She poured a mug of coffee for him.

He was barely inside and "Merry Christmas" out before the girls tore into the presents. Watching them, a lump of emotion filled his throat. He could hardly wait to be a permanent part of this family. Kathy, her eyes sparkling, was over the moon that Santa had brought the baby doll she'd wanted so badly. Misty-eyed, Raine was positive Kathy hadn't had many happy Christmases.

As for Katy, her deep blue eyes were awe-filled as she thoroughly examined her dollhouse. *Mommy was right*, she thought, *fingering a tiny piece of furniture. Santa would find her wherever she was. Not like daddy...he hadn't even called her so he must not want her anymore!* Her lips compressed into a tight line and her mood became determined. *Well fine! Mr. Jess loved her. And mommy loved her. She didn't need daddy! So there!*

Seeing the sudden hardening of her daughter's jaw, Raine knew it was Addison who'd put that frown on her face. As if on cue, her cell vibrated. Good Lord, did the man never sleep! Ignoring the intrusion, she watched the girls continue opening their presents.

Because Jess's place was bigger, Christmas dinner would be at his cabin. When he'd offered to bake the turkey her mouth had hit the floor with a thud. His cooking a turkey was the last thing she'd expected. "Close your mouth smarty-pants or you'll catch a fly. And yes, I know how to bake a turkey." He'd feigned insult. "I am more than just a handsome hunk!"

Now, the place was rocking and rolling, Christmas carols played in the background and the kids were scoping out the gifts under the beautifully decorated tree. With the fire blazing in the fireplace, it looked like a Currier and Ives Christmas card.

"I just know I'm going to gain ten pounds today." Raine bemoaned, eyeing all the delicious desserts on the counter. Belle had arrived bearing homemade pies — pumpkin, chocolate cream, and her specialty, southern pecan.

"If you ask me you could stand to gain a few pounds." Jess, commented, eyeing her shape critically. "I like my women round in all the right places."

Her eyes flashed impudently as one dainty brow kicked up. "Women?"

"Woman! I meant my woman!" He quickly amended adamantly.

"You better get out of here before you stick that size eleven foot in your mouth again." Cora came to his rescue. "Go see what mischief you can get into."

"Yes ma'am," he exclaimed, making a hasty exit as Raine headed toward him brandishing a wooden spoon.

A while later Raine was checking on Katy and saw Jess and Cooper riding Josie and Becky. With that easy-in-the-saddle-look and cowboy hats pulled low on their heads, she could easily imagine them riding the range. Just then her little scamp raced toward Jess and in one fluid motion he leaned down, scooped her up and settled her in front of him. A knot of panic seized her throat as she started out the door only to have a firm grip on her arm stop her.

"Oh no, you don't! That baby's just fine. Jess won't let anything happen to her. Look at the way he's holding her, making sure she doesn't fall off. He'd cut off his right arm before he let anything happen to her. And see how much fun she's having? It'd break her heart if you made her get down."

Now, she felt silly. "You're right. I'm just being overprotective." Katy was having a blast, and as for Jess, he was beaming; proud as a peacock. Impulsively she wrapped her arms around the older woman. "How'd you get so smart?"

"Just born that way, I guess." Cora quipped, returning the hug and thinking if she'd ever been blessed with a daughter she'd have wanted her to be just like Raine. "Now get busy. We've got a hungry crew to feed."

It was a starving boisterous group that bounded inside just as Raine was pulling a large casserole dish filled with candied sweet potatoes topped with toasted brown marshmallows from the oven. "It sure does smell good in here." Jess called from the mudroom where everyone was removing their outerwear. "I don't know about the rest of them, but all that fresh air's kicked me up a hefty appetite."

"It won't be long now." Cora called above the din of the mixer as she whipped potatoes. "You kids get washed up." As he approached, she shut off the mixer, wrinkled her nose, giving him the once-over. "That includes you grown-up kids too, mister."

"Yes ma'am." He saluted then kissed her rosy cheek. "That's for all you've done for both of us," he whispered, "you made sure Raine was never alone, and you helped me get my head out of my . . . well you know where. I could have lost her otherwise."

"You don't owe me anything, son. You'd have come to your senses eventually," she whispered. "Of course," she added, "you might've had to chase her all over tarnation. Just make her happy and don't hurt her."

"I'd have done exactly that. I'd follow that woman any-where." A steadfast look crossed his chiseled features. "And trust me I've done enough hurting her. From now on I promise to do my utmost not to cause her any grief."

"I believe you. And right here's exactly where she wants to be. Oh look," Cora inclined her head, "she's giving us the stink-eye. Probably thinks we're up to something."

"That's because we are." He grinned conspiratorially. "And thanks for keeping my surprise under wraps."

"It was my pleasure. Now, go wash up or those hungry kids will start without you." Cora shooed him off.

"Barricade the table until I get back!" He exclaimed in mock alarm then passing by Raine, planted a quick, hard kiss on her mouth. "I just couldn't help myself. You look so delicious!"

Flustered, she gaped after him. The man was always catch-ing her by surprise. Suddenly, she was aware the room had gone silent and given their grins, everyone had witnessed the kiss. Cheeks flaming a deep scarlet, she couldn't help but grin.

Seeing Cora's smug look increased her suspicions that the two were definitely up to mischief! Over the last few days they'd become chummier than the Three Stooges, always whisper-ing in each other's ear until she got within earshot then they'd start some inane conversation. Yep! They were definitely up to something and come hell-or-high-water, she was going to find out what!

They gathered round the dinner table and Jess led them in saying Grace. Raine, a lump of emotion lodged in her throat, fully acknowledged that she truly was blessed. By the end of the lively meal she was shaking her head in amazement at how much food a growing boy could put away. Used to Katy's bird-like appetite, it was stunning to see the boys go back for second and third helpings. Afterwards, with so many helping hands, cleanup was a snap, then it was time to open presents.

"This is the best Christmas ever!" One freckled face boy said as they all stared in awe at all the gifts for them. Needless to say, there was a lot of throat clearing coughs and Jess choked back the Texas-size lump in his own throat, especially at their delight when they opened his gifts — each had a remote-control car with their name stenciled on it. No sooner out of the boxes, the good-natured challenges started as to who could win the most races.

And the girls, just as excited, ripped the wrapping paper off two large boxes tagged from Jess. Pulling back the tissue paper, their silent awe was worth a thousand words then came squeals so loud eardrums quivered. Throwing themselves at him, they rained kisses all over his face.

Knowing he'd slammed homeruns out of the park, his chest swelled proud as a peacock. With an idea in mind for the little girls, he'd called several toy stores until he'd found what he wanted and seeing them model their princess dresses, he didn't think there was anything more adorable. They really were his little princesses.

Then it was his turn to open gifts. He did the ones from the boys first. Each watched in wide-eye anticipation. Wisely, he found something special about each one and the prideful looks on their faces filled him with joy. Then, he opened the girls' gifts and it wasn't joy, but shocked dismay that covered his face. Seeing his stunned reaction, Raine barely contained her glee and Cora snapped pictures as he stared at the gaudy red Santa sweater and elf slippers sporting reindeer antlers. Quickly though, he pasted on a delighted smile and pulled the girls in for hugs. "How did you know this was just what I wanted?" Over their heads he shot a smirking Raine a *"I'll get you for this"* look.

But out of all the presents, only one gripped his heart in a tight squeeze — the painting from the art gallery in the mall. He'd felt an instant and unexplainable connection and had even envisioned it hanging above the fireplace. He'd regretted not purchasing it the day he'd driven Raine to the mall, especially later when he'd called the gallery to purchase it only to learn it had been sold. Now, he knew who'd bought it. In front of everyone he pulled her into his arms. "You're just full of surprises, aren't you?" He murmured, hugging her tightly. "I love you."

"I love you, too, and I love my gift." The white-gold, heart-shaped locket with their initials engraved in intertwining hearts meant more to her than anything Addison had ever given her. Thinking of Addison, she couldn't help gloating that he was spending Christmas in jail given his threatening messages. Although she'd sworn to wait until after the holidays to read them, temptation had been too great. Nevertheless, she hadn't responded. He was just going to have to stew in his own juices a while longer.

# Chapter Sixteen

**IT WAS LATE** evening before everyone departed and Cora, a romantic at heart, knew Jess was chomping at the bit to pop the question. "You two haven't had a minute to yourselves all day. You stay and I'll take these two home, they're already tuckered out."

Watching until the lights came on in the cabin, Jess shut the door on a bliss-filled sigh then moved to her side. "She really is something."

"Yes, she is." Thinking he was about to kiss her she lifted her face. Her heart fell when instead he got up and headed for the fridge. The man couldn't possibly be hungry after that large dinner and two pieces of pecan pie he'd eaten. "It was fun, wasn't it and those kids will never forget this Christmas as long as they live, and all because of you." She watched Jess remove a bottle of champagne from the fridge and take two champagne flutes from the cabinet. Ah, they're toasting to the happy day.

"I can't take all the credit. It was a group effort, honey." Pouring the champagne, Jess's hand trembled and a whole herd of rambunctious butterflies started dive-bombing his stomach. Fearing they'd fly right out of his mouth, he clamped his lips together. It was a sudden case of nerves, but he had the perfect remedy and gathered her in his arms, his lips claimed her lips in a deep kiss. "I've wanted to do that all day," he gasped when they finally drew apart.

*Whew! The man sure knew how to kiss!* "Me too, and I want more." Putting words to action, she pulled him in for more of the mind-drugging kisses. And drug her they did, taking her under into the deep, sensuous world of wanting where she floated on the decadent waves of desire.

Finally lifting his lips, Jess definitely wasn't nervous now, just the opposite. "If we keep this up I'm going to get a Christmas present I hadn't planned on tonight." The woman was a fever in his blood. All she had to do was look at him and he wanted to love her into oblivion. But he wanted more. No other woman had ever affected him this way, not even his long-ago first wife. Over forty, he'd definitely not been celibate, choosy—but not celibate. And until Raine came along, no female had made him want to get permanently entangled again.

Suddenly, a ripple of unease slithered through him that he might be moving too fast. Just because she loved him didn't mean Raine was ready for the ultimate commitment. She could have reservations after her horrific first marriage. Well one thing was for damn sure—he was nothing like that low-life, wife-beating dirt-bag! He'd never raise a hand to her. On that thought, the unease disappeared and only a few lingering butterflies remained. As he went down on one knee, the one she'd kicked not so long ago, he grimaced.

Seeing it, Raine almost giggled until he removed a jewelers' box from his pocket then a hitch of excitement caught her breath. It couldn't be what she'd hoped for, even asked Santa for. Giddy elation engulfed her when he opened the box. *Yes! Yes! Yes! It was even the ring she admired the day he'd driven her to the mall.* Huskiness tinged his voice and his hands held a tremor again. For a man not easily flustered, he was jittery than a cat on roller skates. Any second he expected the butterflies to soar out of his mouth. "Raine, will you take this cranky, set in his ways ex-jarhead to be your husband? Will you marry me? Will you love me forever?"

Ecstatic beyond her wildest dreams, she threw her arms around him planting a kiss on him that gave him her answer. "Yes! Yes! Yes! I'll marry you. I'll marry you even if you are a cranky, set in your ways, ex-jarhead. I love you, Jess Harper!"

"I love you with all my heart and I want my ring on your finger." And slipping it on her left hand, he kissed her again . . . and again.

When they finally came up for air, she was as breathless and excited as Katy had been that morning that Santa had found her. Though she'd prayed for it, it was the last thing she'd expected. Admiring the shimmering stones in the lamplight it dawned on her the ring was a perfect fit. "Just how did you know my ring size?"

"Would you believe a little birdie told me?" He asked, drawing her up.

"Un-huh and I'm guessing that little birdie's named Cora?" Her tone was drenched in skepticism.

"I guess we can't fool you on anything." Looking from her eyes to the dark sapphires in her ring, he thought they matched perfectly. "Cora had me figured out a long time ago and set me straight. She didn't mince words, either." He shuddered in remembrance. "Anyway, when I told her I was determined to marry you, even bought the ring, she was more than happy to help me, even took it for sizing."

"So that's what all the whispering's been about. Knowing you wanted to propose tonight no wonder she was eager to take the munchkins home."

"I hoped to, but I wasn't sure how long everyone would stay, or if you'd go home with the girls. I have to say, she's awesome. She's like Inez when it comes to getting things done." He was feeling pretty proud of himself having succeeded in surprising her. He had a feeling that wouldn't happen very often.

"You don't have to convince me. I would have managed these past months, but Cora made things a lot easier. From the moment she learned what happened she, and her sister, Ethel, were by my side. I was such a mess those first days I could barely get around. They not only took care of Katy, they took care of me. And when it was suggested I leave Phoenix, Cora wouldn't hear of us going off alone. She's the mother I never had, and she treats Katy like a granddaughter. Heaven knows, Addison's

parents aren't the get-down-on-the-floor-and-play type."
Bitterness welled remembering her former mother-law's doubting Katy being Addison's. If only Roberta knew how badly she
wished that were true.

Seeing the displeasure on her face, and privy to the crude
accusation, he refused to let a spite-filled woman intrude on
their special moment. "Quit thinking about your witch of an ex-
mother-in-law and kiss your fiancé! That's a lot more fun." And
he was right.

It was several minutes before they came up for air. As he
caught his breath another niggling of doubt passed through
him. Might as well get rid of it, he decided. "Are you sure it's not
too soon to be doing this?"

"Oh no, you're not rushing me. The day I drove away from
Phoenix I started looking ahead. I'm ready to start a new life
with you." One dainty brow shot up. "What about you? You've
been a swinging bachelor for a long time. Are you sure you want
to take on a ready-made family?"

Jess tugged her hair. "I may have been single for a longtime
but the only swinging I've been doing is with that squeaky porch
swing. And I already love Katy like she's my own. Hopefully,
we'll give her a little brother or sister sometime down the road."

A delicious shiver wafted through her thinking of having
his babies. "Maybe several baby brothers and sisters. Perhaps
enough to field a baseball team." She mused dreamily.

One dark brow shot up as he sat down abruptly. "Now just
how many are you planning on having?" He'd thought one or
two, but it sounded like she planned on a houseful. But hey, if
that's what she wanted then he'd be quite happy being a very
willing participant. The baseball team comment coupled with
the errant hand tracing a heated path slowly up his thigh nearly
derailed his idea. Maybe they should start those babies tonight.
It suddenly occurred to him neither had been concerned with
birth control the night she'd returned from Phoenix. Maybe
they'd already made a baby. However, before they took any more
chances he had an idea, one she'd hopefully agree to.

"Oh, I don't know. Nature can decide how many." Her hand was wandering up his thigh.

"Behave yourself!" He growled, grabbing her marauding hand.

"Spoilsport!"

Jess pulled her to him. "So, how do you think Katy will react to you marrying me? She knows I love you and she knows you and Addison are divorced." Raine had explained in the simplest terms about her and Addison not living together anymore. "I overheard her telling Kathy that Addison didn't want her anymore because he never comes to see her. It almost broke my heart and I wanted to break Addison's face." Unknowingly his fist clinched.

"There'll be no face-breaking unless I'm doing it!" She scolded, her small hand covering his large fist. "I've explained to her that we're not married anymore, but I'm not sure she quite gets what I'm talking about."

"I don't know. Katy-bug's pretty smart. I bet she understands a lot more than you give her credit for. I know you tried shielding her from Addison's . . . outbursts, for lack of a better word, but I'll wager she knew something was wrong, probably even heard some things."

"I've a feeling you're right." A frown furrowed her forehead. "It still infuriates me about the powder incident. That he'd use cocaine while she was with him is crazy. What if she'd ingested it? She could have died."

"Obviously, his addiction is stronger than his concern for his daughter!" Jess was getting riled up and if she didn't redirect his thoughts he would be on the next flight out to break Addison's face.

"I think she'll be over the moon having you as her dad and I think we should tell her together. But," she had to caution him, "Addison's still her father, and I know she loves him despite being hurt that he hasn't been in touch with her. That may be why she told Kathy what she did." A sudden chuckle burst out earning her an inquisitive look. "Although, she seemed more concerned about Santa than Addison." She explained.

"I can't say I blame her." Palms up, he weighed the options. "Santa on the one hand, Addison on the other, I'll take Santa hands down every time. And I don't plan on taking his place in her heart. I'm only hoping there's enough room in there for me, too."

"You don't have to worry about room in her heart. She fell hard for you the first time she laid eyes on you. Don't let it go to your head, Mr. Harper, but you were her first crush." He grinned arrogantly. Even four-year-olds found him irresistible. "Yesterday the girls were having a tea-party in their room, so I did a little eavesdropping. Katy asked Kathy what she'd asked Santa to bring her. I thought I'd cry when she said she asked for a mommy and daddy. That's when Katy told her she'd asked for you to be her daddy. Said you were nicer and loved her and spent more time with her than her old daddy." At the sudden sheen in his eyes Raine twined her fingers with his. "You are a good man, Jess Harper, and I can't believe it's me you fell in love with."

"How could I not fall for that feisty but terribly messed up woman who showed up in my driveway? I didn't want to admit it but two seconds in you had me. It was fate that you met up with Inez and now you're to be my future." He smiled at her. "That sounds pretty darn good. I love the sound of it."

"I love the sound of it, too. Mrs. Jess Harper. Raine Harper. It has a nice ring to it."

Happiness surged through him as he fingered the ring on her hand. "I don't want to rush you but what do you think about getting married as soon as possible, say Valentine's Day?"

*He thought that was soon*? "Surely, we can get married sooner? I love you and can't wait to be your wife."

The tempting look in her eyes almost made him forget his plan. "Well . . . we could, but you do realize we've never formally dated. . . . I have an idea."

Raine acknowledged things had moved pretty quickly, and they *had* skipped the getting-to-know-you part. "Okay. What's your idea?"

"This. I want to court you properly. You know—dinner, dancing, walks in the moonlight. Of course, if you'd rather not I'm just as happy getting married sooner." Whatever she decided was fine by him though he believed she deserved to be courted in the old-fashioned way, especially given they'd done everything backwards thus far.

Pondering the idea, a sudden gleam sparkled in her eyes. "Okay, let's do it. But," a mischievous grin joined the gleam, "let's make this courtship even more fun."

It sounded like she was issuing a challenge, especially with that wicked gleam in her eyes. "And just what might that be?"

"How about until we're pronounced husband and wife we don't do anything—if you know what I mean. Just think how hot our wedding night will be."

Immediately the blustering started. "Now wait a minute. I don't know about not being able to make love to you. I'm not sure I can hold out that long. Every time I'm near you I want you so badly I can hardly think straight. Just like now." He placed her hand on the proof of his statement. A second later, he hissed, "stop it!" Though it was the last thing in the world he wanted.

She barely got, "You started it!" out before his hand was under her sweater meting out the most deliciously punishment. As much as she loved him touching her, she would play by the rules and removed his hand, albeit with a reluctant sigh.

"Now who's the spoilsport? I was just getting started." Not making love to her during their courting hadn't been part of the plan, but she had a point. Come their wedding night they'd be so hot they just might set the world on fire. Abstaining until then? It wasn't like he hadn't taken cold showers the last few nights, anyway. "Okay. We'll play by your rules. Until our wedding day we'll be as chaste as a blanket of newly fallen snow. If you can do it, so can I."

"You're on." She stuck her hand out. "Shake on it."

He gave her a wickedly sexy grin. "I'd rather seal our bargain in another way." Abstinence could start afterward.

"Too late!" She shook her head vigorously. "We're now officially engaged and a wedding date's set."

"You're one tough woman, Raine Andrews, but I'm glad as hell you're my woman. Now, you be ready at seven tomorrow night. It'll be our first official date." He said before lowering his head.

All was quiet for a very long time as they plied each other with heated kisses that soon had warning bells ringing loud. With a frustrated groan, he rolled to his feet when he realized they were entwined on the couch. "I think I'd better take you home before I forget our bargain."

Languid from his kisses, her eyes were mistily glazed. Stretching with feline grace, her golden hair caught the glow of the flames from the fireplace. A hot ember popped. Lord, but she was so tempting. "Well . . . we could start our bargain tomorrow."

He shook his head. "You had your chance to have your way with me." He pulled her to her feet. "Come on woman, before you lose control and ravish me."

Sultry laughter followed him to the mudroom. "I'm thinking the ravishing would be mutual and you don't have to walk me to the cabin."

Helping her into her coat, he eased her blond tresses, soft as silk, free of her collar. "Oh, yes I do. I consider myself a gentleman and I always walk my date to her door. Besides, it means I get to kiss you some more, and might I remind you, you're not just my date, you're my fiancé."

With a pert toss of her head she hooked her arm through his. "Then by all means, Mr. Harper, walk me home."

The stars shimmered like tiny diamonds in the velvety heavens. With the ring on her finger sparkling in the moonlight, a strong tide of emotion swept over her stealing her breath away. She could hardly believe that she was marrying the man God had truly meant for her to wed. Her world was good, and nothing, she vowed, or no one — specifically Addison — was going to ruin it.

Jess was doing some musing of his own. Before Raine had swooped into his life he'd enjoyed his freedom and had absolutely no desire to marry again. He'd even boasted quite proudly that there wasn't a female on either side of the muddy Mississippi he'd ever sacrifice his freedom for again. He'd been down that rocky marital road once and swore never again. At the first sign of any clingy female hinting permanency, he bid them adios. Just goes to show you never know what life will throw your way. It still amazed him how the feisty woman had cruised right into his life, stolen his heart, and in just a few weeks she'd be his wife. Life sure was unpredictable!

Upon reaching the cabin he drew her against him. "I get another goodnight kiss, actually, make that several." His mouth closed firmly over hers and, once again, the mystical magic of desire pulled them under its spell. This time it was a reluctant Jess who pulled away first. One of them had to be strong if they were going to stick to their bargain. Tonight, it was him. "If you don't get inside right now, I'll forget about our agreement and make love to you right here in the snow. And I can promise you the impressions will definitely not resemble snow angels."

That vision would stay with her for a long time. "Okay, okay," she grumbled, "but I can hardly wait to sleep in your bed every night, make love with you, and wake beside you every morning."

"That's our bed, our home, our place. What's mine is yours, sweetheart."

The man sure knew how to get to her. "The same goes for me. Whatever I have is yours."

"All I want is for you to love me and let me be a dad to Katy. There's nothing more I could ever want."

"You'll have that and so much more." She promised softly.

Before he succumbed to temptation and carried her back to his place, Jess opened the door. "In you go. I love you and I'll see you tomorrow. Be sure to lock up after me."

He started to pull the door closed but her firm grasp on his jacket stayed him. "I love you, Jess Harper. You've given me the best Christmas I've ever had."

"The same goes for me, sweetheart, and this is the first of many." He kissed her again then gently pushed her back inside. "Lock the door." He ordered before setting off with a jaunty whistle.

Smiling at the happy sound, she just had to have one last peek at him. Standing in the open doorway, she watched until Jess was out of sight before turning around. She let loose a sharp yelp finding herself nose to nose with Cora. "Cripes! You just about gave me a heart attack!"

"Get yourself in here! I want a good look at that ring!" Grasping Raine's hand, she sighed in awe. "My, oh my, I think that's the most beautiful ring I've ever seen. And those sapphires match your eyes perfectly. That man sure did pick out the right ring for you. It suits you to a tee."

Raine gave her a caustic look. "Oh, he knew which one to pick, all right. He saw me fawning over it the day we picked up Katy's dollhouse. He's as sneaky as you are . . . and don't pretend you didn't know. He said you even helped him."

"Guilty as charged." She grinned smugly. "Did you know he actually bought it that day?"

That surprised her. "I told you he's as sneaky as the day is long."

Cora rushed to his defense. "Yeah, but he's crazy about you, so that negates any sneakiness. Now, when's the wedding and don't tell me months away. There's no earthly reason why you two should wait to tie the knot."

Smiling coyly, Raine twined a strand of silky hair around her finger. "Valentine's Day, and until then Jess wants to court me. It sounds kind of old-fashioned, doesn't it, but he pointed out we've done everything backwards. So, until then we're going to just date."

"I think that's sweet . . ." Cora started then trailed off at the wicked grin on Raine's face. "Did you say, 'just date'?"

"I sure did. And close your mouth before you catch a fly! Jess reacted the same way." A schoolgirl giggle burst from her. "I had to sell him on how hot our wedding night would be." Just talking about it made *her* blush.

"You're a devious woman, my girl, and a very shrewd one. That man will be hotter than a chili-pepper by then, and you too for that matter." These next weeks should prove fun. "I might have to chaperone you two, even put you on a curfew," she teased, hugging her. "I'm happy for both of you, honey. After everything you've been through you deserve all the happiness that comes your way.

Oh boy," she rubbed her hands together. "We've got to get on the stick. We've got a wedding to plan and the day will be here before you know it. Tell you what! You two just concentrate on the courting. I'll enlist Inez, Belle, and Cory to help me organize it. Oh gosh," she was giddy with excitement, "this is going to be totally awesome. I always wanted a daughter to plan a wedding for and you're as close as I'm ever going to get."

A huge lump formed in Raine's throat. "You'd have made a wonderful mother, Cora, and since I don't have a clue about mine, I officially make you mine."

"And if I'd had a daughter I'd have wanted her to be just like you." Misty-eyed, she found a tissue and dabbed her eyes. "I'd hope she'd be as strong and courageous as you are. After what you've been through, you deserve all the happiness that man can give you. And he is a good man."

Later, snug beneath the covers, Cora's words played in her head and she whispered a heartfelt prayer. "Thank You for leading me to Jess. Cora's right, he is a good man and I promise to always love him and treat him well. With him beside me, I can face anything."

As she slipped softly into sleep, her nemesis was stretched out on his bunk sipping coffee and plotting his next move. Sonny's idea of a burner phone was excellent. Having his own phone meant he could taunt Raine anytime he wanted, not just when the deputy was on duty. He could toy with her like the big bad cat toys with a trapped mouse, then once released he'd toss it and get another. Plus, having the phone would keep the deputy out of hot water, which was necessary. Believing him the injured party, the man was eager to help. Fluffing the pillow beneath his head, Addison decided Sonny would be perfect for his plan, and he'd be paid handsomely. All he had to do was visit the little backwoods place to play games with her.

"I promise you, you little bitch, as soon as I'm out of here I'll blow your little play-house to smithereens." He made an explosive sound as the Styrofoam cup in his hand crunched sending scalding hot coffee over his fingers. Ignoring the burning, he wished the cup was Raine's throat—he'd squeeze the life out of her. And sometime in the future he might just do it. In the meantime, he had to propose his little plan to the guard. "Hey Sonny, you got a minute?"

While Addison detailed his plan to the enthusiastically nodding deputy, Raine shifted restlessly as menacing shadows intruded on her dreams.

# Chapter Seventeen

**THE NEXT EVENING** it was a spiffy-looking Jess that
escorted Raine to his newly washed truck. Spiffy-looking he
might be, but he was nervous as all get out. You'd have thought
it was his first date ever. And Raine was no better. All fumbling
fingers, Cora thought she'd have to dress the girl. It was pure
relief to shut the door after them. But weren't they just the cut-
est! Pouring herself a well-deserved cup of coffee, she curled up
in the recliner and called Inez to update her on the lovebirds.

As soon as Jess parked in front of the very same restaurant
he'd pulled his hair-brained stunt he should have realized he
was just asking for trouble and sure enough the mischievous
imp in her made its appearance. "You didn't invite any old
flames to join us for dinner, did you?"

Scowling, he opened the door. "You think you're cute, don't
you, and no, you're the only one showing up tonight. And yes,
that wasn't one of my finer moments. But you had my head so
messed up I didn't care what I was doing." The conversation
paused while the hostess seated them, provided menus, and left.

"Don't blame me. I could say the same thing about you. Only
I decided I was running back to Phoenix." Her words darkened his rugged face. "Thank God we finally got our heads on
straight. I thought sure Cora was going to have us committed."

Jess grimaced. "Yeah . . . she wasn't too proud of us."

"That's putting it mildly." She opened the menu in front of
her. "I'm sure she was tempted to take us out behind the wood

111

shed a few times. So," she eyed him innocently, "what are you having? I see they have a special called Crow- ala-Harper."

"I hope it's tasty!" He muttered, rolling his eyes while she chuckled.

And so, the getting-to-know-you-courtship began. Their next date was New Year's Eve. Knowing she loved to dance, Jess made reservations at The Blue Eden Supper Club. Situated on the majestic bluffs overlooking the rolling Mississippi, it was renowned for its superb dining and top-notch entertainment, a perfect place to take his bride-to-be for some slow, cheek-to-cheek dancing.

For their special night Raine went on the hunt for something that went beyond the proverbial 'little black dress'. She wanted a certain man incredibly hot all night long and to hear his awe-struck, "WOW!" in reaction to the short, sequined red dress that twirled about her shapely thighs with every movement.

At midnight, beneath the glittering ball, they ushered the old year out and the new one in. Raine bid a heartfelt goodbye to the past. Later, bathed in the soft glow of the porch light, they wanted the beautiful evening to go on and on, but at last it was a reluctant Jess that pulled away. "Get inside woman, before I forget our agreement."

Raine's deliciously soft laughter followed him to the truck. His head was filled with the little blond she-devil and how many cold showers he'd have to endure until their wedding night and not on anything security related, otherwise he'd have done his customary check and noticed Addison's newest flunky brazenly lurking within a stone's throw of the cabin.

On Addison's instructions, Sonny had flown to St. Louis, picked up a rental car and with directions in hand headed south out of the city. Although the vehicle had GPS, he wanted no digital footprint. Easily enough, he found his destination and had been there long enough to see Andrews' ex and the guy leave. No doubt they were celebrating New Year's Eve while her poor ex was locked away.

Earlier, using a few tricks he'd learned over the years, he'd scouted out the lay of the land without drawing attention to himself from anyone in any of the cabins. As for the security cameras, dressed in black from head to toe, they might pick up his form, but not his face. Night vision goggles helped him to see. Save for the cold, which he'd prepared for, the job was a piece of cake. The money Andrews was paying would be his new nest egg since the paycheck from the jail paid the bills. Working for Addison Andrews was going to make him a very rich man. He didn't care what was asked of him as long as he made the healthy fees.

Finally, all the lights out, it was time for some mischief. Using a new sling-shot with the ability to shoot a hundred yards, he aimed at the nearest wall of the cabin and let his ammunition fly. Raine had just dozed off when the loud thud of something hitting the cabin jerked her awake. When it happened again, she flew out of bed into the living-room faster than a sneeze, flipping lights on.

From his vantage point Sonny watched lights come on and the curtains pulled aside. Soon after, a face appeared in the window. It was her! The no-good bitch who'd put an innocent man in jail! Talk about looks being deceiving. She was pretty as an angel but possessed the heart of a she-devil. No wonder the boss wanted revenge. Well, he'd be happy to help!

"What the heck was that?" Cora asked, scurrying into the room.

"I don't know. Maybe somebody's night hunting and shot in this direction. I should take a look."

When Raine started to unlocked the door Cora grabbed her arm. "Oh no, you don't! Neither one of us is checking anything out until daylight. Under cover of darkness evil things happen." Privately Cora thought something smelled rotten and carried the stink of Addison Andrews. "Maybe the place has a ghost. Anyway, there's nothing to see tonight. Let's go back to bed and check it out in the morning."

Back in bed, Raine's intuition screamed it was neither a night hunter nor Cora's ghost. Addison may be behind bars, but his evil tentacles could reach far and wide. Without a doubt his unscrupulous minions would gladly take his money to track her down. Though she had been careful over the past months, nothing was fail-safe. Raine wasn't backing down from Addison ever again. An image of Addison behind bars made her gloat. "Happy New Years, Addison. I'm making a resolution. Actually, it's a promise. I'm taking your sorry soul down. I'm thoroughly sick of you looming over me, threatening me with more beatings, even death. I refuse to look over my shoulder any longer. If it's a showdown you want, a showdown is what you'll get. Bring it on and may the best *woman* win. Come and get me!."

Sonny waited another ten minutes after the lights went off again before slithering under Cora's SUV. With deft movements he punctured the right front tire and sliced the brake line. The flat tire would be an easy fix but the cut brake line, undetected, could prove fatal. Hopefully the ex-wife would get her comeuppance.

Scouting around the cabin the next morning they didn't see anything out of the ordinary, so by tacit agreement didn't mention their late-night intrusion to Jess. There was no sense getting him up in arms just yet, especially since the kids were leaving today.

Since Kathy wasn't going to a foster family, it had been pre-arranged that the boys depart first. They were as excited as Kathy was deflated. It pulled at Raine's heartstrings to keep her in the dark, but unbeknownst to Kathy, a grand surprise was coming with the arrival of Kevin Forsythe. She'd enjoy a happy ending, too.

With Jess already trying to become her foster parent, Raine had joined him in the quest. The only buzzard that could've impeded the process was Addison and she vowed she'd double-damn make him pay if they were turned down. Worried, she shared her concerns with Jess. "Kevin Forsythe might think Kathy could be in harm's way should Addison find me."

"He might, but I don't think so. I'm sure he'll take it into consideration, but you were forthcoming about everything. That's why I feel confident things will be fine. Plus, he knows we'll be married before Addison gets released. Don't worry, we've got this." *He* might be confident — Raine, not so much.

At their first meeting with the director she'd been nervous as a cat with its tail near a fire. However, his pleasant manner put her at ease, and before long out spilled the good, the bad, and the downright ugly things she'd been through with Addison. Briefly she'd wondered if bringing Kathy into their family was the right thing to do. But on the flipside, the child needed a loving home and she'd be protected just like Katy. Leaving the meeting she'd felt more optimistic than when it had started.

On the flip side, Jess might've *sounded* confident, but he'd sat anxiously waiting until Kevin Forsythe called them to his office. "I've reviewed everything, did backgrounds on both of you plus I've spoken to Ms. Andrews' attorney and the detectives in Phoenix." He chuckled. "They all used some pretty colorful terms describing your ex-husband that I won't repeat. Nor do they trust him any further than they can throw him. They believe he'll try something when he gets out." At that point Raine figured it was all over but the crying. "However, Kathy's lived with enough what-ifs and maybes and I'd much rather see her with you than here. At least you're willing to take her. Furthermore, I know you'll protect her."

"You can bet we'll do whatever it takes to protect her." Ranie replied vehemently.

Kevin Forsythe had no doubts. "I believe that. And Kathy shouldn't miss out on a loving home based on what-ifs. She deserves a nurturing family just like any other child. She's not had it easy. I honestly believe she'll never enjoy a stable home with the parents she's saddled with. Kathy belongs with you two." His handsome face had brightened with a sudden idea. "Tell you what. I'll take care of the formalities and bring Kathy's things out to you. If you can keep it a secret, I'd like to surprise her. I want to see her reaction when she learns she's staying with you permanently."

Raine's gaze had flipped between the two men like they'd sprouted horns and grew eight eyes each. "How on earth am I supposed to keep this a secret? I can't hold out that long!"

"Sure you can. It's only three days! I have the utmost faith in you." Jess said, tongue-in cheek as they exited Kevin Forsythe's office. That's easy for him to say, she groused silently, buckling her seatbelt. Three days was an eternity to keep her lips zipped!

"I can't believe they would torture us this way." She grumbled to Cora on day number two. Jess had taken the girls with him to run errands, so they were alone.

"I think the rascal enjoys tormenting us," Cora retorted, "and I'm a little insulted he thinks we can't keep our mouths shut!"

"Unfortunately, he's not too far off the mark. We've both had our moments nearly spilling the beans."

When the boys bade her goodbye, Kathy put on a happy face, but inwardly she was crying. Nobody wanted her, not even her own mommy and daddy! If only she could stay right here and have Ms. Raine and Mr. Jess for her mommy and daddy. It was the only wish Santa hadn't granted her.

Seeing through her charade, Cora flashed an irritated look at Jess. "Come on, Kathy. Let's go to town for ice cream." She'd baked a cake to celebrate Kathy's surprise and getting ice cream was a good excuse to give Raine and Jess time to talk to Katy about *her* surprise. "We'll be back in a jiffy." She was back sooner than a jiffy and not a happy camper. "I've got a flat tire."

Jess handed her his keys. "Take my truck. I'll change the tire later and have it fixed. It probably picked up a nail." He missed the perplexed look exchanged between the two women. The noise they'd heard during the night and the flat tire were just too coincidental.

"Katy, while Cora and Kathy get ice cream why don't we go visit Becky and Josie." Always up for the horses, she grabbed her coat. They set off on the snowy path through the woods, with Jess trailing behind them. Their boots crunching the snow, Raine looked down at her recalling the last time they'd walked this same path. At that time she'd explained to Katy what divorce was and though it had only been a few weeks, she figured she'd better do it again, just to make sure she understood. "Katy-bug, remember when mommy told you that she and daddy were getting a divorce?"

"Un huh." Katy nodded.

"Remember, it's what people get when they don't want to be married anymore. It means you don't argue and hurt each other's feelings anymore. That's why daddy and I got a divorce and he doesn't live with us anymore."

Katy dropped her eyes. She remembered a lot of things. Like daddy saying mean things to hurt mommy's feelings and making her cry. And he'd hit mommy, too. She'd seen him do it. One time he was hitting mommy and she started to go protect her then she heard daddy say he'd take her away from mommy forever if she didn't keep her mouth shut. Scared, she'd hidden in the closet until all the shouting had stopped. She loved daddy when he was nice, but not when he was mean to mommy. And mommy must have kept her mouth shut too because daddy never ran off with her.

Daddy had been mean to her, too, then made her promise not to tell mommy. She didn't like keeping secrets from mommy and was glad daddy didn't live with them! "I'm glad you and daddy are 'vorced 'cause he made you cry. I don't like it when you cry." She didn't dare mention seeing daddy hit her. That would make her sad. Mommy laughed all the time now, not like when daddy was around. Mommy had a pretty laugh and she wanted to laugh just like her when she grew up.

Close enough to hear, Jess raged inwardly. Just give me five minutes, he swore, and he'd pound Addison into the ground. Picking up on the violent vibe, Raine shot him a 'behave-yourself-look' before turning back to Katy. "Well, we don't have to worry about that anymore, but would you mind if mommy married Mr. Jess and we lived with him forever."

A quiver of excitement raced through Katy. Would she mind? Oh, boy! Mommy didn't know it but every night when she said her prayers she added one more: That Mr. Jess would be her daddy. Her old daddy didn't want her anymore. If he did, he'd come see her, and daddy didn't keep his promises like Mr. Jess did. Best of all, Mr. Jess didn't make mommy cry.

Katy knew Addison hadn't been nice for a long time. He was always yelling. He'd even yelled at her when she'd surprised him playing in mommy's powder. Afterward, he'd said he was sorry but made her cross-her-heart and promise not to tell mommy about him playing in her powder. She'd felt real bad keeping daddy's secrets. When she'd finally told on him, boy oh boy, mommy got really mad that he'd played in her white powder. Mad was too simple a descriptive when Raine realized Addison was using coke around Katy.

At the stables, Becky and Josie ambled their way over in hopes of treats. While Raine obliged, Katy turned to Jess. Apprehensive, Raine kept both ears tuned to their conversation.

"Mr. Jess, if you marry mommy will you be my new daddy?"

Squatting to her level, he stared into eyes the same shade of blue as her mother's. "If that's what you'd like, then I'd love to be your new daddy."

"I do." She nodded emphatically. "My old daddy doesn't want me anymore," then glancing back at Raine, she whispered, "he's mean, too, I saw him hit mommy, so I want you for my new daddy."

Obviously, Katy hadn't told Raine about seeing Addison hitting her. Swallowing back his rage, he clasped her mitten-covered hands and whispered, "Then I'll be your new daddy, Katy-bug, and if your old daddy comes . . . well, we'll just have to see what happens then, sweet pea."

"Yippee! This is the best Christmas present ever, next to my dollhouse." She wound her arms around his neck in a strangle-hold. "I love you, Mr. Jess."

"I love you, too, sweet pea." He said gruffly.

Ecstatic that Mr. Jess was going to be her new daddy, she couldn't wait to tell Cora and Kathy. "Come on!" Bounding off to the cabin, apparently, she'd forgotten all about the horses. At the top of her lungs she was shouting, "He's going to be my new daddy! Mr. Jess is going to be my new daddy!"

Feeling quite smug, Jess draped an arm around Raine's shoulders. "I told you not to worry." Despite being overjoyed, he longed to put an end to Addison Andrews. Later, he'd tell Raine about Katy's witnessing Addison's violence.

Back from the store, Cora and Kathy heard the exuberant shouts well before Katy burst through the door. "Mommy's going to marry Mr. Jess and he's going to be my new daddy and we get to live with him! Kathy, we get to live with Mr. Jess!" No one could say she wasn't thrilled.

"That's awesome, Katy-bug." Cora scooped her up on her hip. When Raine and Jess had shared their concerns, she'd told them they had nothing to worry about. "That little girl will be over the moon." And obviously, she was.

"That's great, Katy," was Kathy's not so enthusiastic response. She wasn't jealous, but she wanted Mr. Jess to be her daddy, too. Once again, she was being left out. Mr. Kevin would take her back to the home and it'd be really lonesome with the others gone. Her heart ached in despair. It wasn't fair! She tried to be good and not get in trouble, but it didn't matter. No one wanted her no matter what. If only she could stay here. She'd never ask Santa for another thing!

As Katy gushed on and on, Raine watched a dejected Kathy quietly steal away only to return wearing her backpack and pushing the prized baby doll in its stroller. She just couldn't keep the secret any longer. Opening her mouth to tell Kathy the surprise Jess stopped her with a firm hand, showing her the text message from Kevin Forsythe. He was two minutes out. "Surely you can last two more minutes?" He whispered.

"Fine." She muttered but in the end the wait was worth it. When Kevin Forsythe walked through the door carrying

Kathy's meager belongings, first she looked puzzled, then fully grasping what was happening, she launched herself at Raine and Jess, hugging them as tight her little arms could. Santa had come through after all!

Seeing firsthand the love the couple had for Kathy, Kevin Forsythe knew the right decision had been made. And, if for some god-awful reason things changed concerning Kathy's parents, they'd cross that bridge when it reared its ugly head. Yes indeed, he whistled happily driving home through the late afternoon sunshine, the New Year was definitely starting out on a very happy note.

# Chapter Eighteen

**NOT EVERYONE WAS** as ecstatic as the two little girls. Several hundred miles away it was a totally different story as a very irate Addison pounded his anger out on an innocent punching bag. Thanks to his father and a sheriff who gladly accepted "donations," a cell had been converted into a gym of sorts boasting a treadmill, exercise bike, and the speed bag Addison was currently beating to death.

In rapid succession he threw one punch after another making the bag bounce crazily on its spring hook. It was a wonder it didn't go flying across the cell. With each punch he pictured Raine's face. He'd shown the bitch mercy the last time he'd punished her. This time there'd be none. This time she'd pay double! No two-bit lawyer or scummy cops could save her then.

Throwing another series of punches, this time it was the two-bit lawyer's face he attacked. He'd never like the arrogant S.O.B. and only tolerated him because of Raine's friendship with Molly Hanson, the S.O.B.'s wife. Briefly, he considered taking Gordon Hanson out. But he knew the finger would automatically point in his direction. Instead, he would stick to the plan to make the bitch pay, then disappear with Katy.

Thinking of Katy reminded Addison of everything he'd missed since this mess started. Things like seeing her in her Halloween costume and taking her trick-or-treating. He'd missed Thanksgiving and the turkey picture she always colored for him. Suddenly, his throat constricted with emotion. He'd missed Christmas, too, and watching her open her presents from Santa Claus. That's when it dawned on him that he had no clue what she'd even wanted for Christmas.

*You're such a role model for fatherhood,* mocked the voice of his conscious. Addison ignored it but guilt made him pound the bag harder. How dare Raine think he could harm a hair on Katy's head! It was preposterous! He'd never do anything to hurt her! He loved Katy more than anything in the world. *Not as much as your little joy powder,* taunted the voice again, *you even used it while you were supposed to be watching her. Well bucko,* that irritating voice continued, *no wonder she doesn't trust you. You're a sorry excuse for a man let alone a father. You go crazy when you're tanked up on the booze and drugs and lose control. So, who can blame her for not trusting you. This mess is your fault so pull up your big boy tidy-whities, quit blaming her, and move on.*

God, how he wanted to punch that irritating voice! None of this was his fault! He'd been a good husband, a good father, provided an excellent living for his family. Raine hadn't needed to work. She'd been a stay-at-home mom while continuing her freelance editing career. She'd lived in the lap of luxury! With all that, the ungrateful bitch had turned on him! Most definitely, she was going to pay!

Viciously attacking the speed bag again, sweat ran off him in rivulets. The muscles in his arms and shoulders burned, but it didn't help lessen the rage that festered like an infected wound. The only medicine that would cure him was *revenge.*

Sheer exhaustion finally forced Addison to stop, but his anger hadn't expended itself. It wouldn't until he'd taken care of the bitch. He had to admit she deserved an Academy Award for her crying-wolf performance, claiming he'd tried to kill her and playing the poor battered victim so convincingly. And those cocky detectives had believed every lying word! It didn't matter that he was the one with the bullet hole in his chest, bleeding all over the place. Hell, he hadn't even stepped outside the hospital when in two shakes he was cuffed and carted off to jail. Thank goodness he'd listened to his attorney and taken that plea deal.

That decision had definitely worked in his favor, and the icing on the cake . . . word had come down he'd be walking free even earlier than agreed. Whatever the reason, he sure as hell wasn't arguing. Wiping his dripping face, he suddenly felt measurably better. "Hey Sonny, I'm going to shower off."

"You know where your things are." Instead of using the coarse jailhouse linen, Addison had his own private stock. Fifteen minutes later, freshly showered, he was reclining on the clean sheets of his bunk, channel-surfing for a football game. It could be a lot worse in here, he guessed. With a little palm-greasing, the lawman in charge bent over backwards to accommodate him.

Sonny was doing the subtle harassing of Raine, and his folks were doing their best to buck him up, visiting often and spending the holidays with him instead of in the comfort of their home. Being 'in here' was definitely not the same as being in his own home, sleeping in his own bed, free to come and go as he pleased. Most definitely the bitch would regret ever crossing him. He'd start by punishing her with his favorite — a good old-fashioned whipping. A vision of her begging for mercy with each lash sent a thrill of anticipation racing through him. The occasion called for a brand new belt. With that thought in mind, he pulled the little brown bottle from his pocket. It was treat time.

Afterwards, his stomach started growling. Between the solid work-out, thinking of punishing Raine, and his little pick-me-up, his appetite was ferocious. "Hey Sonny, anymore of that pumpkin pie my mom brought? If so, how about we have some, and don't spare the whipped cream on mine."

# CHAPTER NINETEEN

**WITH THE HOLIDAYS** a joyful memory, life returned to a semblance of normalcy around the Harper place. Raine went back to editing the stacks of manuscripts from Gordon. Before leaving Phoenix she'd had her mail forwarded to his office then he would send it to the P.O. Box rented under Cora's name. Gordon was also keeping her updated regarding Addison's release. The last time they'd spoken was the weekend before Christmas. "Nothing's changed since you were here," referring to her trip to Phoenix after Thanksgiving. "I do know dear old mom and pops spent Thanksgiving at the jail, even catered dinner for everyone."

"Awe, wasn't that special." Sarcasm coated each word. Leave it to Addison to have all the comforts of home. "I hope your spy-man got plenty to eat."

"Oh, he did." Gordon chuckled. "He's working as a janitor at the jail. Not only did he get plenty to eat, but he also got an earful of bitching about you."

"I can only imagine. Just make sure he knows he'll be well compensated. It's too bad he can't find a way to spike Addison's food with some rat poison." She was surely going to hell for wishing Addison dead, but at least he'd be permanently out of her life.

"You sound just like your sidekick. She said the same thing. I half-way expected her to even buy the poison."

"And that's why she's my bestie. Great minds think alike. By the way I found a place just up the road that you and my bestie can relocate to."

"And have you two getting knee-deep in trouble again!" He joked. In better days his wife and Raine had been partners in mischief, but that was before Addison had taken the slithery slide to hell ruining everyone's good time. "There's a package on its way. You should be getting it pretty soon."

"Good. I can't remember when I've had so much fun during Christmas. It'll be nice getting back to work—and some normalcy." Well, as normal as life could be given the circumstances.

"Things would get back to normal quicker if Addison went missing the day he walked free. Under less watchful circumstances my guy could make that happen, and I'm not talking rat poison."

"Good luck with that. At least we'll be notified when he's due to be released. He wants his pound of flesh. So, you can bet he won't waste any time hunting me down. And you know what—I want him to. I'm tired of looking over my shoulder. I want this over, one way or another."

An edginess in her tone set alarm bells ringing in Gordon's head. Was she thinking of doing something reckless? Thus far, she'd been cautious, but a person could only be pushed so far. Surely she wouldn't—"entice," for lack of a better word—Addison to her door. Of course she wouldn't, but she'd given him pause for concern. "Don't do anything stupid!" He cautioned sternly.

"Don't you think that warning comes a little too late? Stupid started when I kept my mouth shut about the things he was doing." Recrimination hung on every word.

"That's not what I'm talking about, and you know it!" Frustrated, he wanted to reach through the phone and shake her. "I'm talking about you doing something rash. And you weren't being stupid. It's called survival. Addison threatened to disappear with Katy. You were in a life-or-death situation when all hell finally broke loose. It could easily have been you shot that night."

"You call it what you want, I still call it stupid. However," she crossed her fingers, "I promise I won't do anything rash." *Yep, she was definitely going to hell. She'd better head straight for the nearest church and confess her intended sin.*

Hanging up, her promise rang hollow in his ear. Gordon wasn't convinced she wouldn't do something reckless—like lure Addison to her. He'd shared his concerns with Molly. "You know how her mind works better than I do. You don't think you're partner in crime would really do anything crazy, do you? In her shoes, I know you would."

"And you'd be right, but no, I don't think so. It'd be a foolish move on her part putting everyone in danger. Besides, Jess would stop her." She might have sounded sure, but Molly was filled with doubts, too. "Oh Raine," she prayed silently, "don't do something you'll regret."

"I sure hope you're right." But his gut instinct was telling him to call Jess. Still, he gave Raine the benefit of the doubt.

As for Jess, he was also glad to get back to normal. The New Year was starting off on a very positive note. Not only were he and Raine engaged, but a tech company had approached him about manufacturing his security designs. However, before making a commitment he wanted firsthand knowledge of the operations. Luckily the company was located in Kansas City, only a few hours' drive from home.

The opportunity, if it panned out, couldn't be passed up. The income, though not necessarily needed, would go a long way in providing his soon-to-be family with the kind of life he wanted them to have. After what Raine had endured living with Addison she deserved to be treated like a princess, sparkly crown and all. Of course, if he ticked her off, she'd tear the darn thing off and smack him with it!

Not the bragging kind, Jess however, took pride that this manufacturer considered his designs worth producing. Who knows, he thought, stowing his gear in the truck, maybe this was the beginning of a legacy he could leave to his children. Giving Raine a lingering kiss, he said. "Anything happens call Coop first, then me. I still wish you'd come with me." In the back of his mind was the cut tire and brake line incident.

He'd wanted her to go along but she'd told him she'd use the time shopping for clothes for Kathy. When putting the child's belongings away, she'd been dismayed at how sparse they were. "I'll go on the next trip. You just be careful . . . and call me." She watched until the truck disappeared from sight before going back inside.

"You do know we'd have been just fine if you'd gone with Jess." Cora, sitting at the kitchen table, remarked.

"I know, but he needs to do this alone. There'll be plenty of other trips when I can go with him. Besides, I have some things I need to take care of. I can work on some articles later this evening. I plan on contributing to the family coffers, too."

"You don't have to." Cora took a freshly baked cookie from the plate on the table and bit into it. Her eyes closed, savoring the sweet crunchiness of walnuts and chocolate chips.

"I know," Raine reached for one and bit into it, "but I like being self-supportive as well as adding to the family income. We're going to be a couple who works together. Whatever I have will be Jess's and vice versa. He knows how I feel."

Chewing slowly, Cora nodded. Those two reminded her so much of her and her deceased husband, Ben. They'd even made the same pact and it had stayed in place until the day the Good Lord called him home. A lump of emotion welled up. She still missed him something fierce, always would. As for Raine and Jess, she'd had some serious doubts they'd ever get on the same page, but thankfully they'd come to their senses. That didn't mean they'd always see eye-to-eye. Shoot, she and Ben had been pie-eyed crazy about each other, but they'd also *thrown* a few pies during some heated arguments.

A smile tilted her lips remembering their first Christmas together. They'd been at her mama's and Ben had said some-thing snarky about her cooking—that she could take a few lessons from her mom. The next thing she knew she was hoisting one of mama's homemade chocolate cream pies at him. It was a good thing she'd made four or there'd have been no dessert. As for mama, she sure was madder than a wet hen at both of them. And they didn't get any pie. Still, even when they were spatting, they'd had each other's back. It would be the same with Raine and Jess. Those two had a mighty big challenge headed their way in the not-too-distant future. *If only,* she thought with resignation, *there was some way to head it off.*

"While he's gone, we're going shopping. Kathy could use some new clothes." Raine interrupted Cora's trip down memory lane with a nudge as she walked by to refill their mugs. "And you thought with Christmas over you were done shopping." Cora's grumble made her chuckle.

Reaching the interstate, Jess set the truck on cruise. As the miles sped by, he contemplated the potential dangers Addison posed. Acid burned a swath through his stomach knowing the atrocious things he was capable of. Like a rabid dog, the man should be put down. It was purely wishful thinking he'd step in front of a fast-moving train (or truck). Images of the scars on Raine's body flooded his head. How could the man profess to love her, then inflict such cruelty? He was pure cokehead evil and shouldn't be allowed to walk the face of the earth. It was an atrocity that he wasn't locked up forever! Since that wasn't happening, he'd protect her any way he saw fit—especially after learning from the garage mechanic that the tire and the brake line had both been cut on purpose. It was sheer luck he'd noticed the brake fluid on the ground and had the vehicle towed in. The burning in his gut intensified—a warning something more was going to happen.

Activating the truck's computerized call command, he gave it a number. Cooper answered on the second ring. "Hey bro, what's happening? You and the bride-to-be still getting along or has she face-planted you again? The guys are chomping at the bit to know when she takes you down again." Cooper loved jerking Jess's chain.

"Kiss my backside, Cooper Michaels! Next time Belle wrecks your truck, don't come crying to me," he tossed back.

Cooper laughed good-naturedly. "I guess we're even. So, what do I owe the honor of this call? And where are you?"

"Headed to Kansas City for a meeting, but I need a favor."

"Name it." It was a given the favor had to do with Raine.

"Can you keep an eye on the place until I get back? I'm only gone over night, but given what happened to Cora's SUV I'd feel a hell of a lot better knowing my girls were checked on while I'm gone."

"No problem, you know I will." Cooper frowned. Somebody was messing with Jess and they'd play hell when he caught them. This should be a happy time for his friend. After finally finding the woman he loved beyond distraction all should be shiny bright, not tarnished by a ruthless ex-husband. Something really ought to be done about the scum-crawler. "Any ideas on who did it?"

"I can imagine who's behind it, but nothing shows on the security videos. And keep this on the Q.T. I don't want Belle blabbing to Raine. She'd just raise holy hell." Cooper snickered. "She thinks she's quite capable of taking care herself." Of course, Miss Independent had set him straight on that score, too. *I'm a big girl, not some helpless female that gets upset over a hangnail. We'll be just fine.* He hadn't argued, knowing when push came to shove, she'd use her head. "Anyway, she knows to call you if she needs anything."

"You got it, pal. Anything looks suspicious, I'll be on it. How about we meet for a beer when you get back?"

"Will do, Coop, and thanks." Disconnecting, he felt some-what better.

At that very moment the stubborn object of their conversation was passing the old logging road adjacent to the property. She gave the mud-splattered van parked there a cursory glance then forgot about it. It wasn't the first dirty vehicle she'd seen there. Hunters used the road all the time.

Robert Ford watched the SUV drive past. Now he had a choice to make—follow them or do some snooping. He opted for snooping but decided to wait a bit longer just in case they came right back. Earlier, he'd watched the boyfriend stow a bag in the truck and leave, obviously he was taking a trip. Now, with the others gone he had the whole place to himself. First though, since getting caught wasn't part of the plan, he pulled a camouflage ski mask over his face.

Unbeknownst, all the ski mask did was keep his face warm for Jess had recently placed swiveling video cameras along his property line, which ran parallel to the logging road. It was an added precaution, especially after the sabotaging of the tire and brake line. Someone had done it on purpose, and it scared the hell out of him that they'd gotten that close, and he'd not known.

With a furtive glance around, Robert Ford picked the lock and cautiously opened the door. He fully expected an alarm to start screaming but instead, he was engulfed in silence. He'd have sworn the place would have been wired for sound. "Thank you, Ms. Andrews, for making breaking and entering so much easier."

Looking around the large room, he took in the coziness of the combination living and dining area. It had a certain charm, that is, if you liked backwoods rustic. It was warm inside, so he shed his coat and stuffed the mask in a pocket. Not wanting his prints on anything, he kept the gloves on.

Starting in the kitchen, he searched through cabinets and drawers but found nothing of interest. Next, came the girls' room, then Cora's, but still he came up empty handed. It was in the last room, the one Raine was using, that he found handwritten drafts for wedding invitations.

"Raine Andrews and Jess Harper *request* . . ."

So, they were getting hitched. Andrews would blow a gasket. Instead of disturbing the pieces of paper, he snapped several pictures with his phone. Staring at the feminine handwriting, another zing of consciousness rolled through him. The woman didn't deserve what was coming at her. If he didn't owe those gambling debts, he'd chucked the dirty job. Instead, he carefully sifted through dresser drawers and the closet, but found nothing else. A glance at his watch said he'd been there nearly an hour. It was time to go. Staying any longer was just asking for trouble. As if fate agreed, sirens suddenly echoed in the distance. Oh hell, he must have triggered a silent alarm after all! Not wasting another second, he grabbed his coat, locked the door, and hastened back through the woods to the van as fast as his feet could take him. If the cops were after him, he'd just claim to be a hunter. In his haste, he forgotten to don the ski mask.

The driver's door was barely closed when two patrol cars flew by, their sirens wailing, lights flashing. Tossing out a dozen Hail Mary's, Robert Ford didn't waste another second. Hitting the blacktop, he stomped the accelerator to the floor. It was time to get out of Dodge.

While he was speeding away, Raine was just stepping into the mall when her cell phone rang. Caller ID showed Jess. "Hey."

"Hey beautiful, I'm just checking on my girls." Hopefully, he didn't sound worried nor was he going to mention Cooper checking on them. It'd just tick her off and he was looking forward to a romantic reunion. Well . . . , he thought dour faced, *as romantic as you can get considering their bet.*

"Your girls are just fine. We're at the mall shopping for clothes for Kathy and a wedding dress for me."

"You could wear a feed sack and still look beautiful. You did set the alarm when you left the house?" He asked.

"Flattery will get you everywhere, and of course the alarm's set. Do you think we're that scatter-brained?" She shot a quizzing look at Cora who mouthed, "I didn't." She couldn't remember setting it, either, and if she mentioned her doubts, he'd raise holy hell and call out enforcements to stand guard.

Laughing, he said. "I'm not about to answer that. On that note, I'll let you ladies get on with your shopping. I'll call you later tonight. Love you." Then he was gone. Well, that was short-and-sweet, and no, he hadn't been able to disguise his worry. *Damn Addison.*

Once Kathy was outfitted with jeans, tops, and a few dresses for church, they were off to the bridal shop. The wedding day was fast approaching, and a feed sack was not an option, no matter what Jess Harper said. An attendant showed her a selection of long bridal gowns that were all beautiful, but she had a distinct vision of what she wanted. She'd already had the big wedding dress with yards and yards of satin at Addison's insistence. This time she'd dress herself and have the small wedding she'd wanted instead of the grandstanding party the Andrews clan had insisted on. Spotting the tea-length lace dress in a soft ivory, it was love at first sight and when she tried it on she thought, *it could have been made especially for me.*

"Mommy, you look bu'ful." Katy sighed in wide-eyed awe.

"You do, mommy," Kathy echoed.

Cora nodded in approval. "They're right. You look beautiful. That dress is perfect."

A bit giddy, Raine twirled in front of the mirror. It was perfect! "This is definitely the one!"

Changing back into her clothes, Raine made another decision. "Come on ladies. Let's get you the prettiest flower-girls dresses we can find." And twenty minutes later, they were pirouetting in front of the mirror modeling lace dresses that closely matched her own dress.

Watching them, Raine was again amazed how alike they looked. In fact, if she didn't know better she'd swear they were true sisters. And they just might get to be. An idea had been swirling in her mind for several days. She just hoped Jess would be for it. But she wasn't getting her hopes up yet. There were a lot of obstacles to overcome, especially given Kathy's circumstances of still having parents with rights. It could be they wouldn't relinquish them. And then there was Addison to consider.

After a dinner of burgers, fries, and chocolate shakes so thick you could turn them upside down and they wouldn't dump out, they headed home. Just as Raine parked beside the cabin her neck prickled painfully. So as not to alarm Cora, she did a cursory glance around but saw nothing strange. It was when she unlocked the door and silence greeted her that she figured out the cause of them. It also confirmed no alarm had been set. Sharing a look with Cora, unspoken they agreed not to mention it to a certain man. He'd just pitch a hissy fit. Later, sitting at her desk reviewing the wedding invitation draft, an eerie sensation of something being off came over her but couldn't put her finger on it. She chalked it up to not setting the alarm. However, the uneasiness followed her into a fitful sleep.

# CHAPTER TWENTY

**EARLY THE NEXT** afternoon Jess was making fast-tracks for home. The meeting had gone well, and he was excited to share the details with Raine. As soon as he pulled onto the interstate, he called her. "It's a done deal, sweetheart. I was really impressed with the whole operation and Jensen Wainwright, the CEO, wants to take a look at some of my other designs." There was no mistaking the pride in his voice.

"That's wonderful. I know you wouldn't contract with them if it didn't feel right." Jess was a smart man, good at reading people, so they must have thoroughly impressed him.

"That's right. Now, if nothing delays me, I'll be back in time to take you on a dinner date."

"Sounds like a plan to me. Just drive safely. I don't want you crashing." He heard the catch in her voice. Obviously, the accident they'd been in a few weeks back was still in the back of her mind.

"I'll be careful. I love you, babe." He disconnected, feeling a bit disconcerted. She might say everything was okay, but something in her tone said otherwise. He was glad she apparently hadn't noticed the extra sheriff's patrols and he wasn't about to confess asking Cooper to check on them. That'd be like stirring a hornet's nest. She might say everything was fine, but he'd check in with Cooper.

Cooper was cruising right by Jess's place when his cell rang. Using the hands-free button, he said. "Cooper Michaels."

Jess got straight to the point. "Hey Coop, tell me all's well at the homestead?"

"Driving by it right now and everything looks hunky-dory."

"Good, I feel better. Raine said everything was fine, but she sounded strange. At least she didn't notice the extra patrols or she'd definitely knock me on my rear."

Cooper heard the relief in his voice. "If you're bride-to-be figures out we're keeping tabs on her she'll do more than knock you on your rear-end. Though I have to say, I thoroughly enjoyed that show you two put on." Cooper laughed. "And the guys in the department still want to hire her."

"You just had to mention that humiliating scene! And yes, I do consider myself lucky I came away with only a sore knee and bruised shin. The girl can kick like a Missouri mule. Anyway, the meeting went well. I believe I made the right decision. Of course, I investigated them thoroughly before agreeing to meet with them. Jensen Wainwright runs a tight ship."

"Glad you have confidence in them. Besides, keeping it American-made will go a long way for marketing them." They were of like minds in supporting American-made products. Cooper started to say something else, but his police radio came to life. A patrol was needed to check out a B and E. "Jess, I've got to go. I'll catch up with you later. Call me and we'll catch up over burgers and beer." Then he was gone.

Relieved by Cooper's assurances, Jess relaxed. As the truck ate up the miles, he pondered what this venture would mean financially. When it had just been himself, he hadn't worried about financial security. He had his service retirement, plus investments, and lived quite comfortably. But now he wanted his family properly provided for, especially should something happen to him. Raine made good money with her editing career, but he considered that money hers to do with as she pleased. Of course, his feisty fiancé hadn't seen it quite in the same light. "We share fifty-fifty, or we share nothing at all." That brought a smile to his lips. There was one thing she had he looked forward to sharing and their wedding day couldn't get here soon enough to suit him. *Damn that bet*!

It was turning twilight when he parked beside his home. Anxious to see Raine, he hadn't stopped along the way. Quickly stowing his things, he freshened up and made tracks for the cabin. He had one booted foot on the porch when the door flew open and Raine launched herself at him, kissing him as if he'd been gone months instead of just overnight.

"God, I missed you," she whispered against his lips. "It seemed like you were gone forever."

"I know what you mean. I couldn't wait to get back." Tucking a strand of silky hair behind her ear, he kissed her again only to be interrupted by two little munchkins tugging on each pant leg.

"I think you've got competition." Hoisting each on a hip, he kissed their silky-soft heads then sat them on their feet.

"Hey Jess. I see you've got a welcoming committee." Cora greeted him while handing him a mug of freshly brewed coffee.

"Thanks, Cora." Taking a sip, he sighed with pleasure. "Just what I needed, there's nothing like your coffee, Cora."

Her round face beamed with pleasure. "Well, you just sit yourself down and enjoy it while Raine finishes getting ready."

"I'd like to, but I've got to see about Becky and Josie." He set the mug on the table.

Cora shook her head. "Raine and the girls already took care of them." She chuckled at his surprised look. Pointing at Raine she continued, "You're turning her into a real country girl. Better watch it or she'll be tooling around on that new tractor pretty soon."

"God forbid!" Mock horror covered his face.

"I heard that! And I can't do any worse than you, big boy. At least I haven't tried rearranging a cliff face."

"She's got the ears of an elephant. And you can't blame me for that little fiasco!" He retorted. A crazy driver's disregard for treacherous road conditions had hit Jess's truck sending it spinning willy-nilly before it careened through a guardrail and smack-dab into a rock bluff. Though both had suffered injuries, it could have been a lot worse.

"Yeah. Yeah." She teased, re-joining them. He stared appreciatively at the black jeans that fit her like a second skin. "I'm ready when you are. So, where are you taking me?" She asked, blushing at the desire darkening his eyes. She almost caved, then remembered their bet. Nope! Not happening.

"I've a hankering for spaghetti and that melt-in-your mouth cheesy garlic bread from Collette's, but since you're trash-talking my driving, I don't think you deserve to go." He gave her a put-out look.

Collette's. Just the name made her mouth water. It was truly authentic Italian cuisine using family recipes handed down generation to generation from the old country. Raine swore it was the best Italian food she'd ever eaten. "If I promise to be very good will you'll take me there?" She batted her big violet-blue eyes at him.

"You? Good? That'll be the day!" He scoffed and received a smack on the arm for it. "And you're mean, too!" He complained as they went out the door.

The spicy aroma of garlic and yeasty dough permeated the air even before Jess opened the door of the small pizza parlor. "Mmm. This smells wonderful. Too bad they can't bottle this scent. They'd make a fortune selling it."

"Honey, if you wore this as perfume, I'd be nibbling on you all the time." He grinned wolfishly.

Seated in a corner booth, the mischievous imp inside her came to life. Looking around as if searching for someone, she asked. "So, got any old girlfriends joining us tonight?"

With an exasperated sigh, he groused. "I'll never live that down, will I? And no, Miss Smarty-Pants, you're the only girlfriend on this date. And yes, that wasn't one of my finer moments. But you got your evens by messing with my head so much I didn't know if I was coming or going."

"I might point out you did the same to me. I was ready to pack up and head on down the road. Thank God we finally got our heads on straight. I thought Cora was going to have us committed." Poor Cora. They'd nearly driven her crazy.

Jess grimaced. "Yeah . . . she wasn't real proud of us."

The conversation paused while the waiter took their orders for spaghetti and the scrumptious garlic cheesy bread. They skipped the salads. "The spaghetti's too good to fill up on salad." Jess also ordered a bottle of Merlot. Good food, good wine, a beautiful woman sitting across from him, life was good. Looking at her askance, he noticed, with a furrowed brow, that the beautiful woman sitting across from him had suddenly become noticeably lost in thought.

Raine was pondering how to broach the subject of adopting Kathy and the butterflies dive-bombing her stomach weren't helping. Unconsciously she fell back on a forbidden habit. Fidgeting. Thankfully it was Jess sitting across from her instead of Addison. Addison would have probably snapped her wrist. Suddenly, she winced as a phantom pain shot through her right wrist as if reminding her he'd done just that.

Noting her fidgeting, it was a sure sign something serious was on her mind. For anyone else it was a natural reaction when they were nervous, but not Raine. She never did it and recalled why—Addison, in his viciously controlling manner had broken her wrist to make her stop.

Just as he started to ask what was wrong, the waiter returned with their wine. Picking up his glass, he immediately set it back down before he snapped the delicate stem. Jess wished the stem was Addison's neck—he'd squeeze the life out of him. Shaking the murderous thoughts from his head, he had to find out what was wrong before he sprouted any more gray hairs. A horrible thought suddenly sent his stomach plunging, like riding a runaway rollercoaster with no way off and the crash eminent. Had she changed her mind about marrying him? He couldn't stand the suspense any longer. Reaching across the table he gently stilled her restless fingers. "Okay, sweetheart, what's wrong . . .

and don't say nothing. You're not getting cold feet on me, are you?" Though just teasing, his stomach knotted painfully.

Raine's head rocketed up. "What!?" She caught his hand in a fierce grip. "Oh no! Absolutely not! No cold feet for me, Mr. Harper. You proposed and I've got the ring to prove it. I'm not giving it back! I can't wait to meet you at the church and become Mrs. Jess Harper."

A huge breath swooshed from him. "Thank God! For a minute there you had me worried. Now that I know you're not breaking my heart, what's got you fidgeting all over the place making me think you're chickening out on me." Still, she didn't speak. "Raine," he coaxed, "you never have to be afraid to say what's on your mind."

Releasing a pent-up breath, she said. "Okay, there is something I'd really like to do, but I'm not sure how you're going to feel about it."

"And I won't know until you tell me what it is." He encouraged her.

"All right, I think we should adopt Kathy. Fostering's great, but that little girl needs a forever family. If God's willing, we need to make her ours forever."

No wonder he was crazy in love with her. "I was thinking the very same thing, but I wasn't sure you'd want to add to the fold right away."

In the flickering candlelight her pretty face glowed. "I most definitely want her in our fold. The sooner she's permanently ours the better. We already love that little girl, and she needs us to be her mom and dad. What still worries me is Addison. It's bad enough Katy and the rest of you are in harm's way without adding Kathy."

"She'd be in no more danger adopted as she is fostered." He assured her. "We need to hire an attorney who handles this type of thing, though. I'd imagine getting her biological mom and dad to relinquish their parental rights would be the first step."

"If they care one iota they will do the right thing. Surely, they want what's best for her? How could they not?"

"You'd think." He concurred, ignoring the kernel of doubt. So far, they hadn't cared one wit about her.

As they ate they discussed Kathy's pathetic background and the two albatrosses hanging round her neck—a big-time drug dealing father doing time in the state prison and a strung-out junkie for a mother. "Kevin Forsythe said there's been no word from the mother since just before Christmas a year ago. Either Kathy hasn't noticed her total absence, or she's just not saying anything."

It was the latter. Kathy, at that very moment, was burrowed beneath the covers quietly crying and trying not to wake Katy. She was thinking about her mother and the broken prom-ises she had made. Mommy had not been with her both last Christmas and again this year. Didn't she know it hurt when she made promises then broke them? Last year she'd promised to come but she'd never showed up. Then this year, despite all the wishing and praying, she hadn't even heard from her. Hot tears trickled down her cheeks. Didn't mommy care that it hurt real bad when she promised they'd be a family then it never happened? Mommy didn't want her anymore, and as for daddy, he was in some place called 'the big house'. That's what she'd overheard the bigger kids calling it. She was no dummy. It meant prison. And daddy didn't want her either or he'd quit doing bad things that put him in prison. Well fine! I don't need them, either! She'd pretend Ms. Raine and Mr. Jess were her mommy and daddy. *If only*, she gave a wishful sigh as her teary eyes drifted shut, *there was some way I could stay here forever.*

# Chapter Twenty-One

**KNOWING IT'D TAKE** a while to work through the process of attempting to make Kathy a permanent part of their family, they immediately hired the attorney Kevin Forsythe recommended. At that first meeting Raine again held nothing back concerning her life with Addison and what he was capable of. She wanted nothing on her part—the good, the bad, and definitely the ugly—preventing them from having a chance at adopting her.

Besides contending with Addison, there were other hurdles to jump. Getting Kathy's mother and father to sign away their parental rights were gigantic ones. Given her father's thirty-year term of incarceration, one would think he'd realize how much better off she'd be in a stable home filled with love. As for the disappearing mother, she had to be located. To that end, an investigator was searching, but so far it seemed she'd disappeared off the face of the earth. Still, they weren't giving up looking until every last stone was overturned.

While the search continued, the wedding preparations were being made. Just as Cora had dictated, she and the girls, Inez, Cory, and Belle, were knee-deep in the details. "Don't you worry about a thing," Belle said, picking a black olive off her pizza and popping it into her mouth. Her green eyes flashed mischievously. "We've got everything under control. You just keep on letting Jess court you."

They were having lunch at Collette's. Jess had taken the little ones with him for the day. He wanted to show them off and thought it'd be fun for the old-timers at the feed store to meet his girls. No doubt the old fellas would be wrapped around their too-cute little pinkies in minutes.

"I have to say," Belle continued dreamily, "that's just plain old-fashioned romantic. Sort of makes me wish Cooper and I were getting married all over again."

Cory, in the process of taking a drink of soda choked, spewing it everywhere. It took several back-wallops from her mother before she caught her breath. "Mom, I swear you enjoy beating the tar out of me!" She wheezed.

"Should have done more of it when you were a kid," Inez quipped.

"Are you kidding me!" Cory rasped. "I was the angel out of the bunch of heathens you birthed. They're the ones needing thumping." She shook a stern finger at Belle. "And dear lord, Belle, no way in hell are you and Cooper getting married all over again! Not one of us could survive another range war like you two waged last time!"

"Well Miss Smarty-Pants, I *said* it *sort of* makes me want to get married again. I didn't say we were. Besides, we're planning on another kind of celebration." Curious eyes shot up, but she shook her head. "It's still in the planning stages. Right now, we have to concentrate on getting those two hitched." Her not-ready-to-spill-the-beans expression warded off any further questions.

Eyes downcast, Raine nibbled the point of her pizza and wondered what they'd do if she divulged that she had something else in the planning stages, too — a come-to-meeting-moment with Addison. That would certainly set them on their ears *and* on the phone to Jess quicker than she could make her escape. As for him, he'd explode into a blazing inferno. Under the right — or wrong circumstances the man could be just as scary as Addison. *Nope, better keep my mouth shut. My mess, I'll clean it up.* As if on cue, the old cell in her pocket vibrated. She ignored it.

"Cora, before we head home I need to pick up the mail. I'm expecting a package that should be here by now." Though having everything in Cora's name was a precaution, she'd be glad when it was no longer necessary. She'd considered having Gordon pay Addison a visit to put the fear of God in him, but who was she kidding? Addison feared nothing save losing his pipeline of feel-good powder and at that very moment probably planning his attack.

*That's right,* the little voice in her head piped up, *he's planning something all right, and whoever has the better scheme will emerge the victor. He's sly and will strike like a thief in the night, so you'd `better be on your toes, little Missy. It's all right to be afraid, just don't let it control you. If he even gets a whiff he'll go for the jugular.* That scary vision jerked her back to the present. Now the pizza tasted like sawdust.

Entering the post office an hour later, Robert Ford followed her inside. Sporting sunglasses and a ball cap pulled low on his forehead, he stationed himself at a table near the wall of boxes while she opened one and extracted a bundle of mail. Heading back out, she looked in his direction and smiled. The innocent gesture sent a wave of guilt rolling through him.

Later, sorting through the thick package she made a pile for herself and another for Cora. When her fingers touched one particular piece it instantly raised the hair on her neck. It had her name and old address but no return one. Who would send a . . . then it smacked her right between the eyes. Addison! Going boneless, she dropped the envelope on the desk as if she'd grasped a snake. Any second now she expected it to open and Addison come slithering out yelling, "Gotcha!"

"Oh Addison, you think you're so clever, but it took you long enough to figure out Gordon would know how to contact me. That little white powder must be eating brain cells or you'd have thought of it sooner."

Using a letter opener, she slit it open. Inside was a thick pad of paper and a plain envelope containing a note in Addison's bold scrawl. Goose-bumps peppered flesh as she read:

"No matter how far you run I will always find you. Just like now. I know where you are, and I will come and get you."

That was it—short, sweet, and threatening.

Unconsciously she tapped it on the desk. Obviously, Addison hadn't pulled this off on his own. He had to have an accomplice. She should tell Gordon but decided to wait a little while. Instead, she was going to taunt Addison—have some fun at his expense. Besides, what difference did it make how far she pushed him? He would show her no mercy either way. However, this new twist needed a dandy taunt. She needed time to think about it. Not wanting anyone to see the note she stuffed it back in the envelope and hid it beneath her mattress.

# Chapter Twenty-Two

**AT LONG LAST,** and to the couple's everlasting joy (or was it fevered relief?), the happy day arrived. The heavens graced them with one of those rare, balmy February days that teased at spring when only the day before it'd been a blustery thirty degrees. The sunshine streaming through the stained-glass windows of the church cast it in a heavenly glow.

The girls, precious in their matching dresses, waited impatiently at the back of the church. Jess, watching from the altar, expected them to race like excited puppies down the aisle. Kathy was the flower-girl and it just seemed befitting Katy the ring bearer carrying the symbols of their love. Seated in the aged pews were most of the people who meant the world to them. Raine just wished Molly and Gordon could have been there. And just as Jess had known, his friends had taken his new family under their wing and dared anyone try hurting them.

As the strains of the bridal march began, Jess saw his radiant bride appear in the entryway. An overwhelming rush of love gripped him. Beside him, Cooper whispered, "She's beautiful." Choked up, all Jess could do was nod.

As for the bride, her heart was hammering so hard she expected it to burst right out of her chest and ping pong around the church. That was bad enough, but suddenly a roaring filled her ears. Oh no! If she fainted she'd never live it down. She could already hear Jess bragging to their grandkids: "Your grandma was so excited to marry me she fainted right at my feet the day we got married." Inhaling deeply, the ping-ponging eased as did the roaring and she was able to focus on how devastatingly handsome her groom looked decked out in his new silver-gray Western-cut suit. The man was gorgeous and in a few more minutes that gorgeous man would be her husband. A funny thought nearly made her giggle aloud. *Thank you, Addison. You did me a big favor.*

As soon as the minister pronounced them husband and wife, Jess kissed his bride immediately and thoroughly. Cupping her face, he stared into eyes so intensely blue he thought he'd drown in their depths. "I love you, Mrs. Harper," he whispered, kissing her again.

Totally lost in the moment, it took several coughs and snickers to finally bring them back to earth. Passion flowed like warm mulled wine between them and if not for the afternoon reception he'd have whisked his bride off to the nearest private spot and make love to her slowly and sweetly. Instead, they joined their friends in the church hall for a luncheon to celebrate their union.

When the newlyweds were ready to depart for their honeymoon, a very serious looking Katy pulled Raine aside. "Mommy, you make sure you bring Mr. Jess back. He's my new daddy."

Hugging her tightly, Rained whispered. "Don't you worry, sweet-pea, Mr. Jess will be your daddy forever, and if you want to call him daddy, you can."

Later, sharing what Katy had said, Jess was delighted. "Yes indeed, I'll be her daddy forever."

Caught up in the excitement, neither felt the aura of threat hovering in the form of Addison's spy. From his vantage point, the pretty little park across the street from the church, Robert Ford snapped dozens of pictures of the happy couple and thought of his client, of how hell bent he was with punishing his ex-wife. Her remarrying would further escalate that fury. There was no telling how far off the deep end he would dive. Just the picture of the invitation had sent him on a rage-filled tirade.

While the ladies had seen to the wedding details, Jess, with the perfect place in mind to honeymoon, had made reservations at a lakeside resort requesting a secluded honeymoon cottage. As they drove through the countryside the man beside her claimed her total attention. From the moment they'd pulled out of the church parking lot her hand had claimed his muscled thigh and the heated caresses were driving him to distraction. If he wasn't extremely careful they'd be plunging into another bluff. And he'd be damned if he was spending his wedding night in a hospital bed!

Shifting to ease the ache, her knowing giggle filled the truck. "Now, aren't you glad we waited until our wedding night to make love?" Her voice was husky with desire.

"You're really enjoying driving me crazy, aren't you?" He growled.

By the time they reached their destination both were in need of very cold showers. Hopefully no one could tell what they'd been doing for the last few hours. When her gaze dropped below his belt, she giggled. He glowered then his laughter filled the truck.

Within minutes they were parked in front of their cottage. Out of the truck in a flash, he opened the door and swung her up in his arms to carry her over the threshold. "I've always wanted to do that." He really was a romantic at heart. "I've been waiting weeks to make love to you, my beautiful wife." Hungrily, his mouth hovered above hers. "I can't wait a second longer."

"Then don't." Just as eager, he wasn't the only one who'd lived for cold showers. She'd even considered rolling naked in the snow a few times just to cool down!

Raine stepped out of her shoes. He pulled his boots off. His jacket came next along with the rest of his clothes while she struggled with the zipper of her dress. "Come here." Turning her about, he unzipped the delicate lace. When it slipped to the floor his eyes nearly fell out of his head in surprise for beneath the dress she was totally bare, save for silk stockings held up with lace garters. Fire blazed even stronger in his dark eyes. "Woman, you've had nothing on underneath that dress the whole day?" He demanded.

"I believe," she leaned against him, "it's called going commando, darling. Do you know how many times I started to show you I had this little surprise waiting for you?" The hot huskiness of need threaded through her.

"If I'd known you had nothing on under that dress I'd have driven you as crazy as you did me!" Nuzzling her neck, their eyes connected in the mirror as he caressed her tenderly. Raine swore it was one the most sensual things she'd ever experienced.

"Love me." She whispered as her eyes drifted shut.

"I'm going to, sweetheart." And not just her body, but her heart, her soul, for years and years. "For always."

Laying her back on the silken sheets, he eased down beside her then took her mouth in a slow, drugging kiss, sending them into the darkest waters of sensual pleasure. The throaty moans coming out of her were swallowed up by his mouth.

One thing was for certain, he conceded, just before losing himself in the mind-blowing passion flowing between them, waiting until their wedding night made him ache with a fiery, all-consuming need for his woman — his wife. This night was going to be well worth the wait.

Reading his mind, Raine purred in agreement. She'd yearned to make love with him for weeks. She promised herself that she wouldn't make the first move because of that crazy challenge. Then, this morning her last-minute idea of going commando had definitely stoked the fires of desire burning within her. Her lips twitched with humor. The minister would have had a cow had he known the bride was going commando!

A long time later, breathless and bathing in the warm afterglow of their loving, they returned to earth. "I'd love to stay like this, all wrapped around you. I wish I could keep you naked all the time."

Pressing light kisses to his neck, delicious shivers rippled through him. "That's quite an appealing idea, but we seem to have too many people around for that. Where are you going?" He protested when she stopped the kisses and slid from their wedding bed.

She caught his hand "Not me. We," and tugged him from the bed. "are going to take a shower."

Jess couldn't remember the last time a shower had been this much fun. In fact, he believed it was the best one he'd ever taken. Only after the water turned cool did they leave their watery playground.

"Are you hungry?" The bedside clock read eleven-thirty. He couldn't believe they'd spent the last three hours making love. *If this was any indication of the future, he'd be hiring someone to help tend the property. He'd be too busy making love to his beautiful wife.*

In harmony with his thoughts, she said. "I can't believe we've been making love for this long." Soft fingertips trailed over his broad chest.

Catching her wandering hand, he brought it to his lip. "You keep that up you'll never get any food. I happen to know you haven't eaten anything except the bite of wedding cake I fed you. You'll need your strength for what I have planned for the rest of the night."

"M . . . m . . . m, I like the sound of that. But if eating's what you want, eating's what we'll do. I still like my idea better."

"Me too, but its food you need now." He said sternly, giving her backside a swat. "I plan on a very long wedding night, Mrs. Harper, and you'll need to keep up your strength. I'm a starving bridegroom who intends to feast on you all night. The concierge said there's a restaurant that stays open until two in the morning."

It was a good idea until she opened her suitcase and got quite a shock, unable to believe what she was seeing— or not seeing. Obviously, checking her suitcase would have been a good idea given Cora and Inez packed it for her. Those rascals, she thought, bursting into gales of laughter.

"What's so funny?" He glanced her way.

"This." And held up a miniscule nighty. "Apparently some wily women decided what wardrobe I needed for our honeymoon." His whistle of appreciation filled the room as she looked in the suitcase again. One particular item snagged her full attention — the little black number he'd purchased the day he'd driven her to the mall to get Katy's dollhouse. Not knowing who he'd bought it for had driven her crazy for weeks. And here it was in her suitcase. "What on earth? Where did they get it?"

"Me." He grinned unabashedly. "I bought it the same day I bought the ring hoping sometime down the line you'd be wearing both. You've no idea the number of cold showers I've taken picturing you in that thing."

"I know when you bought it. I was there." Her tone was just a tad snarky. The man was just full of surprises. "You are really sneaky, Mr. Harper, and you have no idea how many times I wanted to kick that sexy derriere of yours into the next universe worrying who you bought it for. I promise to model it for you."

"I can hardly wait! I have to agree with the girls' wardrobe choice." He teased, tongue in check. "Don't worry," he slipped an arm around her, "we'll get you some clothes tomorrow."

Suddenly, her eyes twinkled recalling Belle's comment about Cooper having a surprise for Jess. "Um . . . you might check your own luggage. Cooper . . ." she didn't get to finish.

"Not to worry. I did my own packing . . ." Opening his own suitcase, he stopped short seeing the contents — or lack of. "Well I'll be damned!"

It was empty save for two packages of his favorite chocolate bars and a note taped to them. In big bold marker Cooper had written: "**CLOTHING NOT NEEDED — CHOCOLATE TO KEEP UP YOUR STRENGTH.**" Half-groaning, half-laughing, he should have known Cooper would get in on the pranking, too. "He must have pulled the switcheroo while I was in the shower."

"It's a good thing they're our friends." She bemoaned wryly. "I'd hate to see what they'd do otherwise. So, what do you propose we do? I hate getting dressed again." She twirled a scrap of wispy red lace around her finger enticingly.

"Well, we've got the chocolate bars and strawberries, and the champagne." He grabbed the scrap of lace mid-twirl. "You keep twirling that bit of fluff and I'll show you what I propose to do."

"Promises, promises," she touted, tugging the belt of his robe loose. He shrugged it off, a hot gleam shining in his eyes. This was a much better idea than eating, she decided as her own robe hit the floor.

Laying quietly beside his new wife, a shaft of moonlight angling through the curtain fell on Raine's bare shoulder. She breathed softly in sleep. Whisper-light, he traced the silvery scars marking her creamy flesh. As far as he was concerned, they were badges of courage for what she'd endured. His stomach knotted painfully for even in the darkest reaches of his mind he couldn't fathom the terror she'd suffered living at the hands of the vicious madman who was her ex. What kind of man did that to the woman he professed to love? The kind that needed putting down, that's who and by God, he wanted so badly to be the one to do it. Curving his body protectively around her, he vowed that if the monster came near her, he'd personally kill him, dump his body someplace no one would find it, and live happily ever after without an ounce of guilt. With a contemplative smile on his lips, he drifted off to asleep.

The days that followed were idyllic. They spent their nights locked in each other's arms and played tourist during the day. One day they rented a boat and leisurely explored the coves of the beautiful lake. Another, they parked at the end of the dam and strolled hand-in-hand up and down the old tourist strip. Her love for the old-time shops had her dragging a mildly protesting Jess into every one of them where they bought souvenirs and cedar jewelry boxes for the girls that when the lids were lifted the tangy scent of cedar wafted out. Knowing Cora's sweet tooth, they bought salt-water taffy that was pulled right in front of them. But they hit the mother of all jackpots at the fudge shop. A bell tinkled announcing their entry and immediately their senses went on sugar overload, enticing them to sample every flavor. It was only by sheer willpower they didn't buy out the whole shop. Instead, they settled for thick slabs of peanut butter fudge, maple fudge, and chocolate fudge chock full of walnuts pieces. Leaving the shop, they continued their stroll while munching on the decadent sweets figuring they'd have to buy more before heading home.

They also explored the winding back roads. It was then they stumbled across a junk store, aptly name Treasured Junk, so far off the beaten path the GPS couldn't get a signal. Of course, Raine insisted on stopping. "You never know what treasure you'll find. You know the old saying—one person's junk is another person's treasure."

He gave her a skeptical look but sure enough, rummaging through the cluttered store his bride unearthed a ratty, battle-scarred rocking chair that, in his opinion, should have been tossed on a bonfire. Raine, however, declared that with a little TLC it'd be perfect to rock their babies. At her words the most indescribable feeling stole over him envisioning her rocking them. Suddenly, it occurred to him that he hadn't used protection and knew Raine wasn't on any form of birth control. Maybe they *had* already started that baby. Surprisingly, she hadn't become pregnant on their first time together. Once again elation coursed through him picturing her carrying his child.

Catching Jess's dreamy-eyed expression, Raine gave him an inquiring look, but his answer was one of his infernal winks as he carried the ratty chair to the truck. The man, she decided, following behind him, definitely had something on his mind. Just then the cell phone vibrated in her pocket reminding her of another man with something on *his* mind.

Their last morning found them alongside the lake, its glassy surface glistening like crystalline ice in the morning sunlight. Clasping his hand, Raine said wistfully, "How about we make it a tradition to come back here every year for our anniversary?"

"I'd like that, and I like the idea of having traditions." Raising her hand to his lips, he kissed it. "Come on Ms. Harper, let's go home. Our girls are waiting for us."

Still in a state of honeymoon euphoria, again neither felt the aura of evil that followed them. In fact, Robert Ford had dogged their every move and despite his qualms had taken numerous shots that would help increase the growing wrath of a vengeance-seeking Addison.

Three hours later, with a heads-up to Cora, they rolled into the driveway. There was a welcoming committee of culprits proud as pirates who had made off with their bounty, royally pranking the newlyweds. "Just remember, old buddy," Jess's squint-eyed gaze landed on Cooper, "paybacks are hell. Believe me we will get back at you." Then glancing around and seeing no little ears listening, he added, "Course you all were right—we didn't need the clothes." While everyone laughed uproariously, Raine blushed scarlet from the tips of her pink painted toes to the top of her shining blond head.

# Chapter Twenty-Three

**TWO DAYS LATER,** Jess came through the back door of his home toting another box of toys from Cora's. Katy and Kathy followed at his heels supervising the move. Raine hid a grin as the girls instructed Jess where to put the box. *The man had the patience of a saint!*

Cora had been invited to move with them but had declined. "You need to bond as a family. But if you don't need the cabin I'd just as soon keep living there." The munchkins thought having Cora right up the hill would be as neat as cherry flavored jelly beans.

Excited to be living with Jess and still sharing a room, the girls insisted on having bunk beds and Jess wasn't about to say no. "If bunk beds are what you want then bunk beds it is! Come on. Grab your coats. We're going shopping."

The local furniture store had a good selection, and it was a set of glossy white beds engraved with princess crowns that stole their hearts. "We want these!" And immediately jumped on the bottom bunk and refused to budge until he said okay. And of course, he wasn't about to deny his little princesses their hearts' desire.

With the bed selection completed, Raine had taken the girls looking for decor for their room while Jess moseyed around the store ending up in the little boys' section. At the sight of the western bedroom display befitting a little cowboy, his heart turned to mush. Maybe one day he'd have a little cowboy of his own.

At bedtime that night the two little munchkins eagerly crawled in between the crisp new sheets of their bunks. It had taken a game of rock, scissors, paper to decide who got the top bunk. It was a secretly relieved Raine who'd breathed a huge sigh when Kathy won. Later on when she checked on them, both were sound asleep in the bottom bunk.

As for Jess, he quickly found himself in a dilemma and wished it could be resolved with a game of rock, scissors, paper. Used to living alone, he'd received a very rude awakening. Having three females in the house meant a race to the bathroom of which he was never the winner. Even the two they had weren't enough. Leaving him always last in line. He guessed he should be grateful the little stinkers knocked instead of just bursting in — now. Thank goodness he'd had his bathrobe on that time they didn't knock! Since then, he made darn sure the door was locked. No doubt about it, the bathroom situation needed remedying ASAP. He refused to be relegated to an outhouse!

Cringing at that thought, he grabbed pen and paper and began sketching. As he drew, several ideas emerged. Raine needed her own work space. It was amazing how she could be pages deep in edits yet handle any interruption without missing a beat. It must be a 'mom-thing' and, he thought with a kernel of pride, he was getting the hang of the 'dad-thing'. When he was finished, not only was there another bathroom and an office for Raine, but there were an additional three bedrooms. Studying the sketch, another idea popped into his head. He was just full of great ideas!

While Jess was in his office sketching his surprise, Raine was doing a load of whites and having guilty thoughts about her own surprises. If Jess found out she was plotting to meet Addison head-on, he'd definitely put on his cranky-pants and she'd be paying holy hell for years to come. He'd rant and stomp around, eyes blazing black fury. She could just hear him yelling, *what the hell were you thinking*?

*And what could she say . . . I thought he might want to join us for dinner? Wouldn't that put a kink in Jess Harper's boxers — except, he didn't wear boxers!*

Since receiving the "sweet" little letter, for which she'd yet to respond, Raine was thoroughly convinced someone on the outside was helping Addison. What she needed, she decided, adding bleach to the washer, was concrete proof. To get it she would taunt him, calling him a blow-hard liar. Addison would jump at the taunt like a long-whiskered catfish going for the fat worm. As full of boast and arrogance as a strutting bull, he thought he could get away with anything. In his warped mind, there wasn't a line he wouldn't cross to get his pound of flesh. He considered himself ten-feet-tall-and-bulletproof, well . . . not so bulletproof, she snickered.

But underestimating him would be her folly. Sly and brazen to the bone, she wouldn't put it past him to pull right up to the front door and stroll in like he owned the place. If only it were that simple. She'd take a page out of Cory's book and greet him at the door with one of Jess's 12-gauge shotguns. Maybe that would make a believer out of him, and he would leave her alone. If not, then she just might have to pull the trigger. *One way or another, the madness had to stop!*

Pondering her plan to trap Addison, she realized that there were a couple of obstacles, or rather watchdogs, named Jess and Cora to get around. It wasn't even near time for Addison's release, but they stuck to her like glue. Somehow, she had to get off by herself. Just then the sound of the back door closing interrupted her musing. Glancing out the window she watched Jess heading to the barn with that sexy gait of his. *My oh my, but that man cut a fine figure!* And that same fine-looking man would blow his stack if he caught wind of her plan.

Twenty minutes later with the load of whites in the dryer, she pulled on a coat and went in search of him. The sound of hammering led her to the barn where he was framing a . . . frowning,

156

she wasn't sure what it was — a chicken coop, maybe? Whatever, he was hammering to beat the band. "What are you building?"

"Aren't you the nosy one?" He teased, removing the nail tucked between his lips.

"You didn't accuse me of being nosy this morning. In fact, you were quite willing to help me on my little expedition." She reminded him.

"I'm always willing to help you." Standing back, he admired his handy-work. "I'm building the girls a playhouse."

It still looked more like a chicken coup to her, but she kept her opinion to herself. What did she know about building things, anyway? She looked around for them. "I'm surprised they're not helping you."

His eye-rolling grimace spoke volumes. "They were, but I sent them up to Cora's."

"Okay, what'd they do?" *Obviously, something he wasn't too happy about.*

His humor returning, laughingly he said, "Well . . . where do I start? Let's see. Katy wanted to hold the boards while I hammered the nails. That worked for about two seconds, then she thought it would be funny to let the board drop just as I hammered. After about the fifth time I'd had enough. As for Kathy, she thought my tools needed a bath."

"So, that's why she wanted her plastic bucket filled with water." She surmised with a chuckle.

"That's not funny!" He retorted. "Now, I have the cleanest tools this side of the Mississippi. But the last straw was when they wanted to wash the new tractor. That's when I sicced them on Cora."

"They're just showing you how much they love their new daddy." She teased.

"Un-huh," he grunted, casting a wary eye toward Cora's place, "and no doubt they're showing Cora how much they love her, too. Any second I expect something to come sailing my way in retaliation." He looked back at her. "So, how about holding this board. Just don't pull a Katy on me."

With a mischievous look she held the board while he hammered. It wasn't the first time she'd helped him. Wanting to pull her weight fifty-fifty, she dogged his heels pestering him to show her how to do things. Sure, she could feed and water the horses but there were other things like mowing and grading. What she *really* wanted to learn was how to drive his shiny new green John Deere tractor. When he'd mentioned digging a lake to stock fish in, she'd dashed out the door racing for the tractor. "Come on, Jess, teach me how to drive it!"

That sent him into a conniption fit hot on her heels. "Hands off, Blondie! You stay away from that tractor!"

When she wasn't helping him, she was busy working on manuscripts and being a full-time mom with two very energetic little girls. At night she was in the loving arms of her husband. On more than one occasion she snuggled in his arms listening to his even breathing as he slept and marveled at how happy she was. It was also in the dark of night she quit pretending she wasn't scared to death of meeting Addison head-on.

While Raine was scared, Jess was flat-out enraged. Meeting for a burger and beer at a local pub, Cooper filled him in on what his contact in Arizona had unearthed. It wasn't good. "This Andrews' character is bad news ten-times over. Besides his hellacious temper and expensive snorting problem," Cooper sniffed for effect, "there are skeletons in his closet rattling their bones to get out. He said it's a miracle Raine survived given the number of trips to the ER over the last couple of years she had endured." Hearing that, Jess vowed Addison wouldn't need an ER when he got through with him. A grave six-feet deep would do the trick nicely.

"Visitors have been his folks and his hairdresser," Cooper snorted in disgust, "guess a jailhouse haircut isn't good enough for our 'boy'. Anyway, there's a guy who shows up periodically named Robert Ford." The unknown visitor bothered both men.

Lifting his beer to his lips, Jess said. "We need to find out who this guy is. I've got a feeling Addison's got himself a couple of flunkies on the payroll." One of the flunkies had sabotaged Cora's SUV and the other one was sitting right outside the pub.

It took a few days before Raine finally got her chance to get away from her guard dogs. On the pretext of going to the Post Office and grocery store, she refused the offers of company. "I'll be gone long enough to take care of mailing this . . ." She held up a large envelope, "back to Gordon and going to the store. You have that business call and Cora and the girls are baking cookies. I'll be fine on my own."

Though Jess didn't like her going off alone, this time it couldn't be helped. Kissing him goodbye, the pestering voice of conscious started heckling her. *"When he finds out what you're up to you're going to be in big trouble, Missy. You ought to confess what you're plotting, or just not do it at all."*

Ignoring the pesky voice, Raine set out on her mission and luck was on her side—neither of Addison's minions was around. She quickly mailed the package, but instead of going directly to the grocery store she headed out of town toward the state park she and Jess had taken the girls hiking at a couple weeks earlier. It was then she'd decided this secluded place would be the perfect spot for her rendezvous with Addison.

Driving the narrow two-lane blacktop, she spotted the location she'd been seeking. It was the same place they'd parked and hiked the trails. Zipping her coat up snuggly, she headed down the snowy trail into the woods looking for a particular campsite number. She found it. Tacked to the scaly bark of a bare tree was the campsite number 13. The number sent a shiver racing through her. Was it an omen of bad luck–hers or Addison's? Only time would tell.

Back in the SUV, she turned up the heater, found a pad of paper, and drew a rough map for Addison. Now, she was ready to give him a hard time over the note he'd sent. Pulling the old cell from her pocket, she took a picture of the map, attached it to the message she had typed then hit send. That should really fire him up, she thought gleefully, heading back to town and the grocery store all the while ignoring the pesky voice that niggled her conscience.

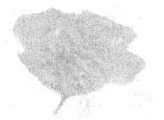

# CHAPTER TWENTY-FOUR

**MARCH ROARED IN** like a lion, dumping several more inches of snow making it hard to believe Easter was fast-approaching. Fortunately, spring-like weather came the week before Easter when Inez called to see if the girls could go with her to Branson with her family. "We promise to have them back in time for Easter Sunday."

"I know they'd love it, Inez, but Jess and I can't get away right now," Raine explained regretfully while Cora, having a cup of coffee with her, waved her arm frantically to get her attention. "Inez, hold on a minute." Covering the phone mouth piece she asked. "What's up?"

"I'll take them. Inez mentioned the trip yesterday." Cora had joined the little coffee group and had quickly made friends with the coffee-drinking gang. "I'd already told her I'd go if you two couldn't. They plan on leaving right after church on Sunday."

It was fine with her but before committing she wanted to okay it with their dad. "Inez, if Jess doesn't mind then its fine with me. I'll call you back in a bit." Disconnecting, she grabbed a jacket from the mudroom. "Will you keep an eye on the chicks?"

"Sure." Cora grinned knowingly. "Go consult with dad."

Dad was mucking out the stalls of his four-legged babies when their excited nickering alerted him Raine was near. She spent a lot of time with the two mares and they'd become quite attached to her. Of course, it had nothing to do with the sweet-treats she carried and she didn't disappoint them this time, either.

Resting the pitchfork against a wall, Jess joined her at the rail. "You have something sweet for me, too?" His sinfully sexy smile practically turned her knees to water.

Going up on tip-toe, she kissed him, murmuring against his mouth. "I thought I gave you your treat this morning."

"Ah . . . indeed you did," his dark eyes took on a dreamy remembrance, "but you know how crazy I am about sweet things. In fact, you're so sweet I just can't seem to get enough of you. I could nibble on you all the time." To confirm it he pulled her into his arms and nibbled her earlobe.

When it ended, she was breathless and fanning herself. "Whew! I almost forget what I came up here for."

"You mean you didn't just come up here to tumble with me in the hay!" He clutched his heart in mock hurt. "I'm wounded."

A tumble in the hay? Hmm . . . now that sounded like fun. "Sorry to burst your bubble, babe, but Inez called. Her crews' taking a trip and wanted to know if the girls can go along. They'll be back the day before Easter. I told her we couldn't get away but Cora's offered to go along. What do you think? Could you stand having your wife to yourself for a few days?" Fluttering her big violet-blue eyes at him she added a bonus incentive. "We could run around naked and no one would see us. It could be like another honeymoon."

"Another honeymoon! Absolutely they can go! Are they gone yet? I'll race you back to the house to see who can get naked first." Laughing, his teeth flashed white in his tanned face. "Sure, they can go."

"Great. I'll call Inez back." Pressing her mouth to his, she savored the taste of him: coffee and peppermint, then she gently pulled away. "Lunch will be ready soon. I'll see you back at the house." She'd taken a couple of steps when his husky voice stopped her.

"Raine," She turned back. "Thanks for asking me about the girls' going. You didn't have to, you know."

"Yes, I did. You're their dad. Anything to do with our children involves you." A rush of emotion so strong nearly brought him to his knees. And to think he'd nearly driven her away. Thank God he'd come to his senses and now he had to do everything in his power to keep his scared-to-death bride from her evil ex-husband.

Despite her bone-deep worry, happiness and the crisp air put a rosy glow on Raine's cheeks. Add in the alone time they'd have . . . she did a little dance right there in the middle of the woods.

Robert Ford, ensconced in a hunter's deer stand, watched her little jig and knew she wouldn't be 'happy dancing' much longer. Once again, his conscious poked him to ditch the whole sordid mess.

Cora had offered up the use of her SUV for the trip, so as soon as Sunday church services were over they headed for the McCullins. While Raine kissed the girls goodbye, Cora pulled Jess aside. "You call me if anything crops up."

There was no need to ask what she meant. With Addison's release looming they were all on tenterhooks. "Don't worry. He's still locked up. Gordon told me so last night."

Her brow furrowed. "Raine didn't mention him calling."

"He didn't. I've had an uneasy feeling, so I called him while she was giving the girls a bath. Nothing's changed. Rest assured, if it does he'll call right away, so don't worry. You have fun and I'll keep her safe."

"I know you will, son." Cora hugged him tightly. "You just be careful, too. Addison won't care who he runs through to get to her."

"I'll be careful. After all, I've got a whole passel of women to look out for."

They stood in the McCullins' driveway until the SUV disappeared out of sight then made a dash for the truck. By the time they reached home their clothes were undone. Once inside they were out of them. Cuddling amongst the overstuffed cushions on the floor they made love the rest of the day, taking breaks to nibble on chocolate and strawberries. It was a fond reminder of their honeymoon.

The next day Jess was working at the stables. Raine was quickly realizing her husband was quite a talented man. He could design, build, and fix just about anything he set his mind to, an example being his security designs. Her morning had been spent editing three magazine articles. Now, it was break-time. Time to surprise her husband. Dressing for the cool weather, she struck off for the stables in glee-filled anticipation of his reaction to her surprise. After all, hadn't he come up with the idea?

Sitting on a bale of hay mending a harness, the horses nickering had him looking up. "Hey you, this is a nice surprise." Setting the harness aside he patted the space beside him.

Thankfully he'd turned the heat on, so it was toasty warm; perfect for her surprise. "I missed my man," she kissed him, "so I came to see if you wanted to take a little break."

Against her lips he murmured, "I'll take a break for you anytime." Given the chilly weather, he didn't think much about the long leather coat or the thigh high boots the color of warm honey until she untied the belt of the coat. Then his eyes did a double take in surprised appreciation as the coat fell away. Save for those sexy boots, she wore absolutely nothing.

"You're just chock-full of surprises, aren't you!" Fiery desire filled him as he slipped out of his own clothes then drew her against his hot body. He wasn't sure if it was her heart, or his, thundering out of control as storms of longing consumed him.

A while later she picked bits of straw out of his hair. "So, did you like my surprise? Actually, it was your idea for a tumble in the hay." There was smug satisfaction in her husky voice.

"Oh yes ma'am, I love your surprises! You can tumble me in the hay anytime!" He replied enthusiastically as he helped her back into her coat before pulling his own clothes back on. With a sigh of regret, she guessed it was time for them to both get back to work. "You can surprise me like that anytime. As a matter of fact, I've a few surprises of my own planned."

Raine's face lit up. "Is it making naked angels in the snow? No one would see us way back here." Had she known they were being observed at that very moment she'd have been screaming bloody murder.

"Oh no, I'm not telling. It's called payback for keeping me in the dark about your little commando escapade." His eyes glittered in remembered amazement. "I have to admit that was a splendid surprise, and so is this one." Kissing her, he gave her a gentle push toward the door. "Now, let me see if I can concentrate and finish what I was doing. Go keep the home fires burning and I'll be down in a little while. We'll pick up where we left off."

Happily bemused, they were totally unaware of the motion-activated camera hidden in the stable. Feeling brazen, Robert Ford had snuck into the stables as soon as Jess and Cooper had left for the wedding and set up his own hidden mini-system before high-tailing it to spy on the wedding festivities. He'd bugged the stable because Andrew's ex-wife spent a lot of time there. Now, as he watched her return to the house, his conscious screamed to stop the bad things that were about to happen to her. If he was any kind of man at all, he'd spill his guts and get the hell out of Dodge. Unfortunately, there was no turning back. Those bridges had been burned with flame throwers. He needed the rest of his fee or he wouldn't live to see spring—that was the final warning two days ago from the Vegas bad boys.

But there was an even scarier bad boy arriving later that night. An involuntary shiver shook his frame envisioning Addison Andrews foaming at the mouth in anticipation of getting his hands on his ex-wife. Once again, his conscious bit him to do the right thing. Scraping a cold hand through his buzz-cut hair in guilt-ridden frustration, he shoved the notion away. It was too late to stop. The wheels were already in motion. All that was left now was to show Andrews her location, get the rest of his money, and he was history.

If he'd had a crystal ball showing that Addison *was* truly planning to make him history, he'd have hot-footed it to Raine's door, ratted Addison out, and gone to ground — to hell with the money.

As for Addison, at that moment he was ensconced in a plush hotel room enjoying his first meal as a free man. With each bite of the thick-cut, medium-rare steak, he happily gloated. There was nothing like a good steak, a glass of fine wine, and a good cigar. Fate and good fortune were still riding his shoulders.

Taking a sip, he pondered Robert Ford's guilty conscious. Wondering if he'd already spilled his guts to the authorities. Would the cops be waiting for him the second he stepped off the plane? The answers had to be 'no'. Money was a driving force. So, he'd wait until he had it in his grubby little hands. The guy had gambling debts out the wazoo. He'd get his money, all right, and then he'd get dead. What was one more body to dispose of anyway? With a satisfied smile, Addison wiped his mouth, bit off the tip the cigar, and lit it.

# Chapter Twenty-Five

**EXHILARATED AFTER HER** visit to the stable, Raine hummed a happy little tune as she settled back to editing when, without warning, the familiar prickling rippled across her neck. Her first thought was Addison! Then she relaxed. Addison was still in jail. It couldn't be him. "Don't be silly," she chided herself aloud. "You're just paranoid. You know Addison's still behind bars. Gordon said so yesterday."

"There's nothing to worry about, yet." He'd assured her then snickered. "As of thirty minutes ago I left the scumbag looking like a caged monkey locked tight behind bars. Come to think of it, that's insulting a monkey. Anyway, I promise to be on the horn the second he steps on free dirt. Now quit worrying. You're still a newlywed. Go have fun with your husband. Molly and I are looking forward to meeting him, too. We just wish we could've come to the wedding. From the pictures you sent he must be crazy about you given his sappy-eyed look."

At first, they'd been full of misgivings regarding the quickly developing relationship but the more they'd faced-timed with Jess, those qualms disappeared and they happily accepted him with open arms. Gordon especially felt a kindred spirit in Jess realizing the man wouldn't back off from a fight with Addison. In fact, Gordon sensed Jess's aching need for Addison to bring it on.

As for Jess, he liked the no-holds-barred, kick-ass attitude Gordon Hanson possessed. His opinion,—no one got by the man unless he wanted them to. And they were in total agreement that eliminating Addison once and for all would make the world a much safer place. "I wish I could find a way to make him disappear." Gordon ground out in a private conversation he'd had with Jess.

"You come up with something I'll hop the next plane out to help you."

If Jess had seen Addison's reaction to their marriage, he'd have already jumped the first plane to Phoenix and done the deed. Addison's vicious temper had blazed front and center alarming Robert Ford enough he'd moved out of striking distance. Addison had literally shook with rage and made no bones about pounding his ex-wife so far into the ground nobody would ever find her.

Despite being taken to task after harassing her at Thanksgiving, he'd continued. Once started, he couldn't stop, especially when her taunting replies egged him on. It was like poking a stick at a riled-up rattler just to watch him strike. It did puzzle him that the bitch hadn't turned him in again. They'd been taunting back and forth for weeks. But her last one set his back teeth to grinding. She'd actually had the gall to call him a wife-beating coward. Said he wasn't a real man, that he was afraid to fight a man. By damn, he'd show her what a real man could do when he got his hands on her. And if she thought he was going to meet her some place she picked she was as crazy as a loon! He wasn't about to walk into a backwoods trap, nor was he gullible believing she'd bring Katy to any meeting between them. He had to catch her on her heels. "I'll catch you by surprise and you'll be sorry you were ever born." Once the score was settled, he'd disappear into the wild blue yonder with his sweet baby girl. Revenge was so close he could almost taste it.

At nine o'clock that night, Robert Ford watched Addison enter the airport arrivals area carrying a duffle bag and camouflage jacket. They played at pleasantries but once in the jeep Addison was ready to get the show on the road. "You have anything new for me?"

Ignoring his screaming conscious, Robert Ford handed Addison the envelope containing the shots from the stable, then waited silently for the fireworks.

Opening the flap, Addison removed the glossy eight-by-tens. His fury was instantaneous. The throbbing vein that jumped out on his forehead was proof of that rage. Taking a deep breath, he remained uncharacteristically calm while thinking the little bitch was definitely going to wish he'd killed her months ago. Yes indeed! He was about to make her life a living hell starting with a well-deserved beating.

He touched the belt at his waist, the one purchased just for the occasion. Thanks to his attentive secretary, everything—new clothes, money, plane ticket, had been ready upon his release. And it had all been on the q.t. Few knew he'd even been released earlier than planned, especially not Raine's arrogant ass-hole attorney. As for his folks,—he'd given them some lame story about needing a little space to clear his head before getting back to work and they hadn't questioned his actions. Now, he was a man on a mission to mete out some well-deserved punishment. And with the element of surprise on his side he was going to use it. In anticipation, the thrill of the hunt coursed through his heart, thundering with the thrill of the score he meant to settle.

Silent but exhilarated, Robert Ford drove the ribbon of interstate. This conscious-killing case was almost finished. *All I have to do is show the sicko her location, collect his fee then color me gone.*

Robert Ford would be gone all right, for he knew too damn much. Running scared Addison knew he'd spill his guts to save his own hide. But Addison had an elimination plan for him, too.

Sliding the photos back into the envelope Addison tucked them inside the duffle bag at his feet then began paying attention to the tangle of interstates flashing by. St. Louis was a veritable treasure trove of escape routes and he'd need one once the deed was finished.

It wasn't long before they left the interstate for rural back roads. That surprised him. Who'd have thought the prissy little bitch would like living in the sticks? "That's the place." Robert Ford interrupted Addison's musing to point to the sprawling log home set back off the road.

Muted lights glowing in the windows provided a serene ambiance, but Addison was anything but serene. He was over-whelmed with the urge to strike right then, but he fought it off. Noting the dusk to dawn lamps, he'd have no trouble finding his way around and, luck of all luck, there was the added bonus of the surrounding woods to hide in. Again, the urge to act was strong but he lectured himself. *Stay focused. Don't be rash. You'll get your reward in the end.*

His self-control firmly in place, Addison pulled an envelope from his pocket. "Here's the rest of your fee. You did great. I bet you're ready to head home to warmer weather."

Robert Ford accepted the envelope. "You have no idea."

# CHAPTER TWENTY-SIX

**THE NEXT DAY** Jess had errands to run in town including meeting with the banker. "You're going with me." Snagging a burning hot cookie she'd just taken from the oven, he bit into it.

"I just took…" Too late. His eyes watered and he made huffing sounds trying to cool his burning tongue. Grabbing the glass of water she held out, he gulped it. "No, I'm not going. I'll be just fine right here until you get back. Besides, I've got more cookies to bake." She dipped a finger into the batter and licked it slowly from her finger.

His burning tongue was forgotten as a wildly erotic blush of heat tinted his whole body. "I've got something you can lick that dough off of." Waggling his brows, he laughed at the shocked expression on her face.

Raine punched him lightly on the shoulder. "I'll never be able to bake cookies again without thinking of that wicked suggestion. You're a mess, Jess Harper, but I love you, anyway. Now, go get your business done and leave me to my cookie baking."

Jess was barely out of sight when the prickliness crept up her neck. Although positive the house was locked tight, Raine quickly went from room to room making sure. Afterward she calmed down with a cup of coffee. *You're just spooked because you're not used to being alone. Besides that, per Gordon, Addison's still locked up.*

Unfortunately, Gordon would learn much too late he'd been given the wrong information. By then Addison was stalking his prey.

171

Ensconced in a hunter's tree-stand he'd found by sheer luck, Addison had a clear view of the cabin. Now that she was alone, he was tempted to confront the bitch right then but decided to bide his time. Thanks to a handy-dandy map app, he'd already scoped out the appointed meeting place. With its acres of meandering trails, he had to agree it was the perfect place to get rid of a body. Or two. He pictured Robert Ford's in the cargo trunk in the adjoining motel room.

Feigning hunger, Addison had asked him to get fast food for both and when the PI had stepped away for a minute, he'd drugged his soda. Once the man was down for the count, he smothered him with a pillow. Hopefully, the do-not-disturb sign would deter any nosy maid, and by the time they did find the body he'd be long gone. Smug, Addison sipped coffee from the thermal cup before pulling the new burner phone from his pocket. It had been a while since they'd chatted.

As Raine lifted the cup to her lips the old cell vibrated. A sense of foreboding slithered through her. Addison. After his rage-filled response to her latest taunt he'd gone silent. Until now. And ironically, Jess was gone.

Opening the message, she read. "Just think. Another couple of weeks and I'll be paying you a visit. I can hardly wait to meet you and Katy at the park. Do you remember how much fun we had hiking through the mountains?" He made it sound like a family picnic, not some volatile meeting that could, and probably would, end in disaster.

Pinching the bridge of her nose, she pondered her decision to not tell Jess what she was up to. When he did find out, Mr. Cranky-Pants Harper would rant at her for days on end. So, it was better to wait until the day of the assigned meeting to confess. He'd still rant and rave, but he'd gather the gang and they'd all converge on Addison. In the meantime, she might as well keep Addison riled up.

"I remember, all right, and it's too damn bad you didn't fall off one of those mountains! Come to think of it, I should have pushed you off when I had the chance!" *That ought to get him worked up*, she thought, hitting send. Sticking the phone back in her pocket, she went back to baking cookies and happily humming.

The phone's vibrating alerted him she'd responded. Reading it, his temper rose. Once again, he was tempted to attack right then. So, she wished she'd pushed him to his death. The high-and-mighty bitch! He'd give her an extra dose of medicine for that!

While Addison was having a meltdown, Jess had a nagging feeling his bride was keeping something from him, but he'd be dogged if he could figure it out. Fleetingly, he wondered if she'd somehow contacted Addison thinking of luring him into a trap. No, she wouldn't do that. Or would she? Would she brazenly invite the devil to a come-to-Jesus-meeting? Knowing his spitfire wife, she most certainly would! As he'd heard directly from her lips, "I'm tired of Addison hanging over me."

Gripping the steering wheel until his knuckles shown white, Jess understood her feelings. Part of him wanted Addison to show up, too. Then he'd make damn sure the scumbag never saw the light of day again. And he was quite capable of making it happen without a trace of evidence and no one the wiser. Men had underestimated his killer-instincts and paid the ultimate price.

The stop at the bank consisted of signing loan papers for the new addition then he was on his way to the feed store. Normally, he'd pull up a chair and join the old fellows but today he gave them a sly wink. "Can't stay long, boys. I'm a newlywed and the little woman's waiting for me." Inwardly he cringed. If Raine heard him referring to her as "the little woman" he'd be sleeping alone for a long time. And that would be after she'd beamed him with her favorite iron skillet!

The old-timers glee-filled hoots followed him to the truck. About a half-mile out of town he remembered his sinfully wicked idea. It was his turn to surprise his very imaginative wife. And knew just the thing, having read it in one of the manuscripts she'd been working on. The dialogue had so turned him on that they'd made love on the living-room floor right then and there.

Practically turning the truck around on a dime, he back-tracked to the nearest supermarket. A few minutes later he emerged carrying his surprise while visions of the fun he was going to have that night filled his head all the way home.

The object of his visions was standing at the stove when he walked through the door. Greeted by the combined aromas of fresh-baked cookies and spicy chili simmering on the stove, his mouth watered. "It sure smells good in here." He planted a kiss on her lips as he passed by headed to the refrigerator. Yes indeed, he was a lucky man. Not only was his wife a passionate, loving woman but she was a great cook, too. What was the old saying about the way to a man's heart was through his stomach.

Raine eyed the bag. "What's in there?"

"A little something for later. I've got to unload the truck. Lock up after me."

"Yes boss." She saluted and received an eye-roll as he went out the door.

A rush of love so intense threatened to suffocate her. God forbid Addison harm him in any way. As if tuned in on her thoughts, the old cell vibrated again. Will the man ever give up!? This time he'd sent a picture: of a belt.

Beyond fed up, she typed: "You don't scare me. Bring it on! Come and get me!" Hitting send, she tucked the phone away before Jess came back. She still wasn't prepared to tell him her secret, because when she did, he'd strangle her.

After unloading the truck Jess filled the horses' feed trough and was rewarded with happy neighs as they munched. He loved spending time up here almost as much as he loved spending time with his new bride. Funny, he reflected, sticking a hose in the watering trough, just how happy he was. In fact, it seemed they'd been married forever instead of only weeks. Just thinking of his beautiful wife sent him meandering into cotton-candy land. So, it took several moments before the sudden agitation of the horses penetrated. Dropping the hose, he pulled the pistol hidden in his boot and started scanning the woods, then circled the building, but nothing seemed amiss and the horses had calmed back down, which eased some of his tension. More than likely an animal had spooked them.

"You ladies need to quit scaring the hell out of me. You're as jumpy as the rest of us. I just wish you could tell me what the scumbag has up his sleeve." Ready to head back he had one leg inside the truck when the eerie feeling of being watched came over him. Scanning the woods again, he didn't see anything but when he got back to the house he'd check the perimeter cameras.

Behind a stand of thick cedars, Addison watched Jess's movements through binoculars. It was another perfect place to watch the comings and goings of the bitch and her lover. He — couldn't bring himself to call him her husband. Actually, he kind of felt sorry for the guy. The poor sap hadn't a clue how devious Raine was and now he was saddled with her.

An image of the latest photos turned his face a raging red. That she found an intimacy with this man as she never had with him scraped a festering wound raw. It was just one more thing to punish her for. Touching his chest through his shirt, Addison felt the scar from the gunshot. Yes indeed, her sins were stacking up higher and higher and soon, very soon, he'd exact payment.

With bated breath Addison watched Jess walk to the cabin then pause at the door. So, they're keeping the doors locked. *Silly people! Raine should know a locked door won't stop him. It never had before.* Then it opened and there she was. Even from this distance there was no mistaking the love shining on her face. For the merest moments sunlight glinted off her shining gold hair. Struck by her beauty, it transported him back to a time before the drugs and alcohol had taken control of him. Sweet memories flooded through him of the times she'd looked at him that way, making him feel he was the luckiest man in the world. Then reality returned as he watched her kissing another man.

The pressure cooker inside his head was ready to blow sky high. He needed to start punishing her. He vowed to nail her coffin shut!

Thinking a batch of cornbread would be good with the chili, Raine whipped one up and set it to baking while Jess checked the security monitors. Returning to the kitchen, he checked the oven timer. Fifteen minutes to go. "Since the cornbread's not quite ready, do I have time for a quick shower? By the way, it smells great." After taking a small taste from the pot, he continued, "I don't know what all you put in it, but it's the best I've ever eaten."

"It's an old family secret," her eyes twinkled sassily when she added, "from the orphanage," then giggled when he gave her a playful swat the backside. "Yes, you have time. If you're not back when it's ready I'll come get you."

A while later with heads bowed, Jess said grace. Raine appreciated that. She'd tried teaching Katy that blessing their food and asking God's grace was something very special, but the monster Addison had become hadn't appreciated any of the finer points she tried instilling in their child.

The mouth-watering chili and the golden-brown cornbread would tempt any hardened dieter. It was after his second helping of both that Jess finally sank back with a satisfied sigh. "I think that's the best chili I've ever eaten." He was glad he'd stayed in the bathrobe with nothing constricting around his waist. With no kids around he'd been freer with his dress. However, he drew the line at dining in his birthday suit. Something hot, or cold, might get spilled on some very sensitive places.

The compliment sent a rush of guilt through Raine. Keeping secrets did not make for a happy marriage, but she had to keep this one for a while longer. Otherwise, he'd head for Phoenix and pop Addison the second he stepped outside the jail.

Sensing her sudden mood swing, he mistook the guilt for worry and wished for about the millionth time Addison Andrews would disappear off the face of the earth. Suddenly, the earlier inexplicable eeriness overtook him. It must be her unease affecting him, but to be on the safe side he'd check in with Gordon for an update.

While Jess was experiencing his weird feelings, the neck prickling she associated with Addison was so strong it hurt. "You're just being silly," she chided herself silently while casually touching her neck. "Get over it and enjoy your alone time with your husband." Dipping a tiny bit of chili onto her spoon, she put it to her lips. Her appetite was non-existent. But she knew that if she didn't attempt to eat something Jess would force-feed her himself.

As if reading her mind, he pointed his spoon at the chili. "Eat all of it and you can have a treat. Otherwise, I feed you and you get nothing."

"Fine!" She stuck her tongue out at him, but spooned the bit of chili into her mouth.

"And you call me cranky-pants!" He teased. "Don't forget we have a meeting Saturday morning with the architect Cooper and Belle recommended." The talented man had converted an old barn into a beautiful home for them and the first time Raine and Jess had seen it they'd fallen in love with it. "You're still going with me, aren't you?"

"Darn it! I did forget. I promised Cora I'd spruce up her place in preparation for Ethel's arrival. With her taking the girls it was the least I could do."

"No problem. We can always reschedule the meeting." He couldn't resist another piece of cornbread. Slathering it with sweet cream butter he thought, *If he kept eating like this he'd need a wench to get off the chair.*

Raine shook her head. "The sooner we get started on the new additions the better. You meet with the architect, and I'll help at the cabin. By the time you get back I'll be finished and then it'll be time for Cora and the girls to be home." When she started clearing the dishes, he offered to help. "Go catch up on the world news."

Jess liked to keep abreast of the goings on around the world, especially security situations. He was often called in for consultations. Several schools had requested his advice due to the rising incidents of school shootings. Now that he had children, it was of uppermost importance they be in a safe learning environment. He loved his girls to the moon and back and no one had better harm one golden hair on their heads.

From the corner of his eye he watched Raine store the chili in the refrigerator and wondered how she could miss the cans of whipped cream and cherries. Biting his lip, he asked. "What's for dessert?"

"The chocolate chip cookies I baked today. I didn't fix anything else." She shut the door and headed his way.

"Chocolate chip cookies it is, but I'll have some later." There was another kind of dessert he had a hankering for. Looping her arms around him from behind she nuzzled his neck. He turned his head and met her lips.

When they finally parted, she was left breathless. "While you're checking on what's going on in the world, I'll take a shower."

"If I'm not here when you're finished, I'll be in the office. There's some paperwork I need to look over." As she turned to step away he patted her cute little backside. That was one of the perks of being married. He could pat his wife's delectable derriere any time and any place he wanted. Well, almost any time and place, he amended, certainly not the grocery store.

The old roll-around chair creaked in protest when he settled into it and began studying the bank of screens. Everything looked okay so why couldn't he shake the feeling of being watched? Frustrated, he scrubbed his face. It must be Raine's anxiety rubbing off on him. The woman was jumpier than a barrel of frogs. Her appetite was practically non-existent and she'd lost weight since their wedding. He'd give his right arm to assure her Addison had no clue where she was, but his gut instincts screamed otherwise, and he *always* listened to them. They'd saved his backside more times than he could count.

Opening the top drawer he removed a folder containing updates from Cooper's contact in Arizona. Digging deeper, he'd unearthed more information. Figuring if a man with this dangerous a reputation had one dirty little secret, there were more hiding in the closet. And boy-howdy were there. Cooper's guy had unearthed investigations into alleged drug dealings, and with a word here and there, it came to light he had a gambling problem owing some pretty hefty debts to some not so savory characters. Jess surmised Daddy Andrews had paid them off since Addison still had both kneecaps.

A newspaper article dating back three years associated Addison's name with a couple of businessmen who'd gone missing after meeting with him. Though he claimed they'd been fine when they parted, Jess figured Addison knew where the bodies were buried. Literally. The date of the article coincided with the timeline Raine had given as to when he'd become so violent. He'd also bet a hundred bucks she knew nothing about the missing men or Addison would have made sure she kept her mouth shut.

# CHAPTER TWENTY-SEVEN

**WHILE JESS PERUSED** another article, Raine sighed bliss-fully. The stinging hot spray eased some of the tension holding her in a firm grip. This mess with Addison, plus keeping secrets from Jess, had her wound tighter than a banjo string. One little pluck would send her spiraling into space. Come to think of it, she'd love to strap Addison to a rocket and launch him into outer space. Let him float around in no-man's land until he drew his last breath. But Addison wasn't going into space. He was coming here, at least according to his last text. *"I'm so looking forward to seeing you and our sweet baby girl very soon."*

To anyone else the response would seem innocent, but Raine knew better. The man was a pro at hiding his true colors. It was also proof-positive that he had help on the outside. Poor suckers. Once their usefulness was over he'd make sure they disappeared. He couldn't leave witnesses. And surely, he wasn't stupid enough to believe she'd bring Katy to their meeting? That had just been bait to get him there. No way would she put Katy within grabbing distance. This was a dangerous game of cat and mouse in which she didn't plan on getting caught in her own trap. Nor was she showing up unarmed. She had the gun he'd tried to shoot her with and, if worse came to worst, she could and would use it. Unbeknownst to anyone else, she'd brought it with her from Phoenix. If she fessed-up about her plan and the gun, Jess would take it away and have Cooper cart her off to jail for safe keeping. And that was after he'd ripped into her with an angry diatribe loud enough to shake the state. It wouldn't be a pretty sight! On that grim thought she turned off the water.

*H*earing the shower shut off, Jess quickly stashed the file away. He had plans for a romantic evening involving a delicious dessert and Addison wasn't ruining it.

She padded in barefoot a few minutes later wearing the sexy black negligee. He was reading through some requests that had recently come in. Word was spreading about the place and requests were rolling in like wildfire. Setting them aside he pulled her onto his lap, the scent of something sweet and powdery tickled his senses. "Mm . . . you smell good enough to eat."

"Sound's good to me." She nodded at the letter he'd been reading. "Anything I can help you with?"

"They're requests for summer camps. You can help me with the paperwork." Suddenly, it crossed his mind she might not want to do them. "That is, if we do them."

"Of course, we'll do them. Those kids need something special to look forward to. Just tell me what you need."

Setting her on her feet, he stood up. "Later, right now I've got a hankering for dessert." Boy oh boy, just thinking about it steamed him up.

With his back to the monitors, Jess didn't see Addison's sinister figure inching closer to the house. Moving stealthily, the thrill of the hunt raced through Addison's veins. With each spying stint he'd become brasher in his thirst for revenge.

In the living room Jess added a log to the fire, the embers popping and crackling while yellow flames danced and swayed to soundless music. Next, he arranged several plush throws in front of it. With the girls away this had become a nightly ritual — cuddling in front of the fire and driving each other totally out of their minds. Unable to resist, he dropped a lingering kiss on her mouth. "Why don't you get comfortable while I get dessert?" His voice was husky with desire.

She gave him an odd look. The man wanted cookies right now? Okay . . . then sighed appreciatively as delicious heat wafted through her at the sight of his muscular shoulders and broad chest that tapered to a trim waist kept that way with by all the physical work he did. Even now, at the end of March, he sported a winter tan. Somewhere in his family Indian blood had flowed, for even without the sun he gleamed golden.

Lost in admiration it finally dawned on her that he was deliberately shaking a can of whipped cream. Her eyes widened incredulously. "What on earth are you going to do with that?" It was an asinine question as comprehension dawned in a roll of molten desire.

"Having dessert." His meaningful look sent a deep bolt of heat through her as he covered her mouth. The connection sent velvety currents of need flowing between them. Lifting his head, a sensual curve tilted his lips. It was time to feast! And he didn't hesitate to move in for dessert.

After the initial shock, she thought his idea of dessert divine—and most definitely better than chocolate chip cookies. One thing was certain, between the two of them, the element of surprise and pleasure in their marriage would never die out. By the time he'd had his third helping of *dessert* she was vowing payback. Before the night was over Jess Harper was going to be her dessert buffet.

"That was unbelievably the best dessert I've ever had." He said much later. "You bring something primitive out in me. If we keep this up, I won't live to see forty-two." He teased, resting his damp forehead against hers.

"Then I guess we'd better stop making love so much." That was not an option, either. Jess brought out a sensuous side of her that had long lain dormant. Addison had destroyed all her desire for any kind of intimacy, but Jess had brought it back to blazing life. She'd always chalked those romance novels up to fictional imagination. But now she understood why women read them. She'd even picked up a few ideas to use on him, like the trench coat surprise.

"Put that idea right out of your head, woman!" He said sternly. "I'll be making love to you for at least the next fifty years."

"And I look forward to it." She practically purred stroking the smooth flesh of his back.

"Come on," he eased away. Getting to his feet, he pulled her up. "Let's wash off." Afterward they returned to their cocoon. "I'm sleepy." He murmured, snuggling against her.

Nestled together, they were still unaware of Addison spying on them with blatant hatred carved deeply in every line of his face. "You bitch! You'll pay for cheating on me. I promise you," he hissed. "You'll rue the day you were born."

With the fires of hell burning strong, Addison stayed put while planning the ultimate attack. It would happen right here on her doorstep. No way in hell was he falling into a trap. Did she think he was stupid? She'd have that kick-ass big husband, and who knew who else, for backup.

Awakening from her short respite, Raine watched Jess sleeping. A lump of emotion tightened painfully in her chest as a wealth of love rushed over her. Every day she gave thanks her journey had led her to his doorstep. He was everything she needed—her best friend and protector, her port in a storm, her lover and soul mate, someone she'd had no hope of ever finding. All at once, an impish grin lit up her face. Turnabout *was* fair play. It was her turn to treat him to a round of whipped cream heaven.

Retrieving the can he'd put back in the refrigerator, she stood silhouetted in the lamp's glow, totally unaware of the alluring picture she made with her hair flowing golden around her curves. But Addison was aware, and despite his fury, she reminded him of a golden goddess. It had been so long since he'd enjoyed his wife's delectable body. Lush in all the right places, yet slender. In fact, she seemed thinner than the last time he'd seen her, and right now he ached to storm the house and slake his lust. Then, he'd punish her. But he got his rage—both in temper and the one in his body, under control and watched the next scene play out while keeping a firm grip on his raging emotions. He kept telling himself the final goal was too close to mess it up now.

Oblivious to her audience, a wicked grin tilting her lips, Raine eased the blanket off her sleeping husband. It was his turn to be driven out of his mind and most definitely this was much better than his outrageous cookie dough idea.

The second the cool creaminess touched his flesh Jess shot awake. The heady combination of it and her lips were enough to drive even the steeliest of men out of their mind. He murmured his approval just before she took him on the wildly delicious journey of pleasure. When he was capable of stringing two words together, he pulled her against him. "That was a much better idea than cookie dough. I sure do love you, Raine Harper."

Nuzzling his neck, a delicious chuckle slipped out. "What?" He asked.

"Just wondering what you'll come up with next." She answered then gasped when he suddenly flipped her on her back. "Oh yes, this is most definitely another splendid idea."

Peering through the darkness, Addison was livid that his wife could touch another man so intimately when she'd always refused him. *What did this man have that he didn't?* "You little bitch. You most certainly deserve what's coming to you. You can't put me in jail for something that's not my fault. You can't cheat on me, rip my family apart, and not pay. By God, by the time I'm finished, you'll be beyond begging for mercy." The ragged threats were whisked away on brisk waves of cold air. Numb to the cold that seeped into his bones, he remained hidden in the shadows long after the cabin went dark. The fires of fury consuming him kept him warm as he plotted the tortures he'd inflict on her. It took the loud growling of his empty stomach to finally make him leave.

Another all-night burger joint provided dinner. Addison hated fast food, but beggars can't be choosers. Plus, the fewer people seeing his face the better. Back in the motel room he scarfed down the greasy cuisine then developed the pictures he'd taken. Those photography classes back in college were proving useful, plus the PI had graciously left his equipment. Staring at the images, his wrath burned anew. "You've no idea the hurt about to be heaped on you, bitch!" No man will want her after he was through, even her new husband. And that's *if* she lives through it.

A malevolent smile covered his face. She was definitely going to be surprised at his sudden appearance. Being released early was definitely working in his favor. For the time-being he'd watch. Then, catching her off-guard, he'd make his move.

Downright proud of himself, Addison splashed two fingers of scotch into a water glass. Before downing it, he did a final salute to the PI stuffed in the trunk in the room next door.

# Chapter Twenty-Eight

**IT WAS SATURDAY** morning and Jess was ready to leave for the appointment with the architect. But he was having second thoughts about leaving Raine alone. However, before leaving he'd check on his skittish wife at Cora's place.

The day was a bit warmer, yet still held a tinge of winter's sharpness. It was hard to believe tomorrow was Easter. The calendar might say spring had sprung but it was riding the crisp cusp of winter. Welcome to Missouri. If you didn't like the weather just wait. It could change in a heartbeat. Nearing the cabin he heard music blasting. Why on earth she wasn't deaf was a mystery to him. He figured folks two counties over could hear it. At least it was country.

"Raine? Honey?" He called out. "I'm headed to meet the architect."

"In here." She called from the bedroom she'd once shared with Katy. Suddenly, the all too familiar prickling attacked her neck. She started to rub it then dropped her hand. Jess didn't need to know how spooked she really was. In fact, it was so bad her stomach was uneasy. Guilt was also eating at her for not confessing her plans concerning Addison, but she had her game-face on and was dance-stepping to a George Strait song when he appeared.

Pausing in the doorway, Jess watched her move, appreciating the way her jeans molded like a second skin over her delectable bottom. "Hi." She tossed the cloth on the dresser. As she wrapped her arms tight about him, another wave of unease washed over her.

Sensing it, worry lines creased his face. "You okay? I don't have to go, you know."

So much for fooling him! Leaning back in the circle of his arms she noted the worry. "I'm fine." She assured him. "I just have this creepy feeling I'm being watched." She waved a hand dismissively. "I'm being paranoid because I don't know what Addison's going to do." Liar! Liar! Pants on fire! "It's just my imagination. You go meet the architect."

"You can rest easy. I just checked all the cameras and didn't see anything anywhere." Trying to reassure her, he wasn't about to mention having the same feeling. It would just freak her out even more. At the moment he wasn't sure who he wanted to punch more — Addison, or the judge allowing this travesty. Both, if given half the chance.

"You're right. Addison's still locked up otherwise Gordon would have called. Maybe Addison won't even try to find me." *That's a laugh! You dared him to come after you.* "All I want is for him leave us alone." She looked up at him with earnest eyes. "And just let me make it clear for about the millionth time I really do love you. You were not a rebound. I couldn't love another man the way I love you."

"I know, and I love you, too, sweetheart. It's the age differ-ence that still bothers me. I just hope years down the line you don't start thinking you made a mistake, thinking I really *am* too old for you. Fifteen years is a mighty big span." This wasn't the first time he'd voiced his concerns and each time she'd rushed to reassure him that would never happen.

Her tone was firm, just as were the arms holding him. "Jess Harper, you will be the love of my life until the day I die, be it today, tomorrow, or fifty years from now. I want to have your babies. I want to grow old with you. I want to share the good times and the bad times. Always remember that." A dainty brow arched at him. "Besides, who's to say you won't get tired of me. Maybe you'll decide I'm *too* young for *you.*"

"That'll never happen, babe. You'll never be too young for me. Besides," he waggled his dark eyebrows at her, "I need a young wife to give me enough sons to field that baseball team."

Violet-blue eyes widened. "Baseball team, huh? In that case big boy, I think we should continue practicing so we can get our first home run."

"Hold that thought you little devil." Kissing her soundly, both were breathless when he let her go. "Maybe I should postpone this meeting after all."

Swatting his backside, she walked him to the door. "Go to your meeting so you can get back here to me. We'll have another practice session for that ball team when you come home. And just think," joy filled her voice, "our girls will be home before long. I've missed them."

"Me too, but I've also loved having you all to myself. Maybe we can get Cora to take them on vacation at least once a month." It was a great idea and from the gleam in her eyes she thought so, too. "I'll be back as soon as I can. Lock the door."

Across the road Addison was well-hidden in a thick stand of cedars. He'd been there since early morning knowing this had to be the day to act. Staying much longer could mean getting caught. When Raine had arrived at the cabin earlier it'd taken every ounce of willpower not to grab her. However, he really didn't want to tangle with that big guy. Over the last days he'd learned that wherever Raine was, he wasn't far away. And low and behold, he'd shown up, although he hadn't stayed long. With Jess gone Addison knew he either grab her now or get the hell out of Dodge. He opted for grabbing.

Stealthily reaching the cabin, and knowing success was imminent, he was tempted to do a victory dance. Instead, he crept quiet as a church mouse during Sunday service. He needn't have worried. The blaring music covered any noise he made. She always could immerse herself in music, often tuning him out on purpose. This time he'd use that to his advantage. Easing onto the porch, Addison kept close to the wall. He heard the loud whirring of a vacuum, another noise to mask his movements.

188

From his angle against the wall he noted the screen door wasn't locked, nor did it squeak when he stealthily slipped inside.

Caught up in daydreams of Jess, it took several moments to realize the prickling in her neck felt like tiny knives stabbing her. Instinctively, she glanced in the oval mirror hanging on the wall. In it she saw her reflection and another that gloated with smug satisfaction. Addison! Instantly, the blood drained from her body. She wasn't sure how she remained standing. Her instincts had been right all along that someone was watching her.

Addison reveled in her white-faced shock. "Hello, Raine." His greeting sounded casual, as though she were an old acquaintance rather than the one person he hated most in the world. Turning to face him her shocked eyes met his. They glittered with fanatical excitement, betraying his casual demeanor. "You look surprised to see me, but you shouldn't be. You didn't really think I'd let you lead me into a trap, did you? Give me some credit for being smarter than that."

The evil radiating off him literally touched her, feeding her with fear, making her heart thunder so loudly she could hardly hear. Heaven help her, the devil himself stood inches away and though he appeared calm, the tic working overtime in his jaw said otherwise. It was an all-too-familiar sign of his rage. The handwriting was scrawled on the wall. This wasn't the showdown she'd planned, and it would not end well, especially without the protection of the gun hidden in the back of her closet at the house.

Addison swore he smelled her fear and the most perverse thrill shot through him. A malicious smile curled his lips. "I bet you're wondering how I found you. "Silly girl," he chided, "you knew no matter how far you ran I'd hunt you down. And I wasn't stupid enough to fall for your trickery, either. Did you really think I'd let you pick a place to set me up? Now I'm the one running the show and you'll do exactly as I say. As you can see, I'm out earlier than planned. It's amazing what money can buy. Plus, there was a big drug bust and so they needed the space. Releasing me was the logical thing to do since I was being sprung next month anyway." His gloating was pure evil. "I have to say, that plea deal worked more in my favor than I'd ever hoped for."

"Wha . . . what are you going to do?" It took two attempts before the words came out. She hated showing any weakness. That's when the anger started replacing her fear. Any prior plans walked out the door the second Addison walked in. The look in her eyes hardened along with the straightening of her spine. Bring it on big boy, they challenged.

Addison saw the moment her demeanor changed from frightened to a fighter. She'd always been a scrappy little thing and he liked it when she fought. It stirred his juices, the pleasure he always got delving out her punishment was supreme bliss. "That's for me to know and you to find out."

Glancing around, he said. "Quite a cozy little place you've got here. A bit too countrified for me but whatever floats your boat." Raine darted a glance past him to the door. He saw it. She thought to make a run for it. It was her only means of escape, but he was between her and it. Please do it, he begged silently. Never a shrinking violet, she wouldn't go without a fight and that's what he wanted. Even that last night before she'd shot him, she'd gotten in some good licks.

"You really shouldn't have been out in that snowstorm." The silken censure in his voice made her shiver. "You see, in case you didn't know it, that accident was broadcast nationwide and so were you and lover-boy." Addison growled harshly. "I just happened to see the news and lo and behold, there's my wife in a lip-lock with some other guy. After that, finding you was as easy as taking candy from a baby. In no time my man tracked you down and you had no clue you were being tailed. He even followed you to Phoenix and back, he was even on the same plane. Bet you didn't know that either, and the crème-de-le-crème. He— followed you on your honeymoon." So, her instincts had been right all along, that someone had been watching her,—watching all of them. His tone became surlier. "Hell, you never even knew you and lover-boy were being photo-graphed, either. Talk about some pictures! You could sell them to some smut magazine!" His slimy minion had taken intimate pictures of her and Jess? Her stomach lurched sickeningly. "I certainly hope Katy never saw you."

The vileness enshrouding Addison was palpable. This wasn't the man she'd once loved, had a child with. That man no lon-ger existed. He'd been taken over by this fiendish monster and though her fate might be sealed, she damned sure wasn't going down without a fight. She threw caution to the wind.

"You're a sick son-of-a-bitch, Addison! What did seeing those pictures of me and my husband making love do to you? Did they excite you? Did you get turned on looking at them?" Taunting him, the tic in his jaw hammered faster as his rage grew. "You're twisted even worse than I thought to get off on looking at your ex-wife and her new husband making love. You should be in a lunatic asylum! You're so eaten up from all the drugs and booze they've made you insane! Why else would you do the things you've done? You're not a man! You're nothing but a coke-snorting alcoholic monster! My husband's a thousand times more a man than you ever were!" Goading him, maybe she'd force him into a stroke, or heart attack.

"And . . . he's so much better in bed than you ever thought of being!" She was screeching at the top of her lungs now and given the purplish red of his face, her every word pierced him like a dagger.

How dare she flaunt her cheating ways in his face! Addison took a step then stopped short. No! He was the one in control! He had a plan and she wasn't derailing it. "You really should be scared." This time the silken censure feathered fear up her spine and his sudden calm didn't fool her either for beneath it fury waited to be unleashed.

When he spoke again his voice was low and menacing, nearly drowned out by the vacuum. "You betrayed me on every level, you slut. You shot me. You put me in jail. You cheated on me." Reaching inside the camouflage coat he pulled out a manila envelope and dumped the contents on the floor. "Look at them!" He yelled, shoving them toward her with the toe of his lug-soled boot. "What do you see, dear wife? You know what I see? I see my wife in the arms of another man, doing things she never did with me. I see my wife cheating on me."

Raine recoiled in stunned disbelief. His spy had taken pictures of her and Jess in some of their most intimate and precious moments. And from the hands of her sadistic ex-husband, they'd been delivered. Her fate was absolutely sealed, but still she wasn't backing down.

"Get it through your damned head I'm not your wife anymore. Just the sight of you makes me sick. You're a sadistic coke-snorting snake that should stay locked away. My husband could wipe the floor with you." She flung the taunt like a spear. "He's not a sick creep like you who can only get it up by beating up a woman. You're scum, Addison, the kind he wipes off his boots." Again, she hoped he'd stroke out but so far that hope hadn't materialized. "I must have been crazy to think I ever loved you. And you never loved me. Or maybe you did in the beginning, I don't know, nor do I care. You let the alcohol and drugs turn you into a monster incapable of loving anything but the rush and buzz the drugs give you.

"God, Addison, you're more evil than the devil! You even used your own child to keep me under your thumb. And it worked for a while, but I finally reached my limit. If you hadn't gone off the deep end the night of that party I'd have been long gone come Monday morning. Instead, you went crazy and tried to kill me! You couldn't beat me to death, so you tried to shoot me! I never, not even when you were beating the daylights of me, ever try to kill you. I didn't wish you dead. I just wanted free of you. Besides," she sneered, "you aren't worth going to jail for."

At last his fury exploded and quicker than lightening he backhanded her so hard she stumbled backward over the vacuum, landing on the floor. "Shut up! Shut up!" He roared. "You're lying! You're nothing but a no-good lying bitch! You did try to kill me! You shot me! Then you had the audacity to cry innocent-victim and those damned cops believed you. I'm bleeding to death and it's you they believe! You! I should have finished you off when I had the chance."

"Then do it!" She screamed. The salty taste of blood filled her mouth from the cuts inside it as flashbacks of other times at his mercy filled her head. Any moment the volatile situation would get worse. And she was right.

Punishing her consumed Addison's whole being. She'd caused him a lifetime of trouble and he wasn't about to let the cheating bitch get away a second time. She had sins to anti-up for and by God he'd show her no mercy. "Do it! Do it!" The evil voices in his head egged him on. And he did. Charging, he attacked with feet and fists over and over. One hard blow caught the side of her head causing showers of bright lights to fill her eyes while vicious kicks connected with her ribs and kidneys.

"Stop, Addison. Please don't do this." She finally pleaded. It was difficult getting the words out as pain stole every ounce of breath from her. "Hurting me won't do you any good. I'm not your wife anymore! Just go. Go! I won't do anything." Another vicious kick connected with her side while another caught her low in the back.

"That's where you're wrong. No matter what, you'll always be my wife." With superhuman strength he jerked her off the floor then shaking her like a ragdoll, snarled. "And there is nothing you can do to me!"

Her hair hung in a tangled mess blinding her to the fist coming at her. It caught her squarely on the jaw sending blinding pain shooting through her head. The blow should have rendered her senseless, but Raine fought against the fresh batch of stars dancing before her eyes and swung at him with doubled-up fists. The first blow caught Addison squarely in the nose. The second one landed on his mouth, her weddings rings splitting both lips.

Stunned, Addison wiped his bloody mouth on his sleeve then lunged at her again, wrapping her tight in his arms he grabbed her left hand, intent on tearing off the offending rings. He'd break her fingers if he had to.

Though she balled her hand into a tight fist, he was stronger, bending her wrist painfully backwards and prying her fingers open. Ignoring her pain-filled cries, Addison ripped the offending rings off with a triumphant shout and flung them across the room. Amidst the violence, the diamonds and sapphires sparkled innocently in the streaming rays of sunlight.

In all their years together Raine had never seen the look that now covered Addison's face. It was of a madman gone completely over the edge without an ounce of conscious. Knowing her fate was sealed, she eyed the door. It was so close and her last chance to escape. Emitting a shrill scream, she dodged around him, but he caught her in his vice like grip. Still, she wasn't giving up. She was determined to inflict as much damage as possible. At one point her knee connected solidly with a very vulnerable spot causing him to scream in pain. It would have brought any normal man to his knees, but not Addison. It only inflamed him more and she had a split second to see the angry fist coming at her. The last sound she heard was someone screaming. Her last conscious thought was of Jess then she went down like a stone dropped into a deep, dark well.

For several moments Addison stood over her, gasping for air and willing the pain in his groin to go away. Damn, but she'd put up a good fight. Nudging her with the toe of his boot, she didn't move. Good. He couldn't afford to waste any more time fighting her. It was time to book it. Not wanting anyone to know what he carried, Addison took the throw off the sofa and covered her with it. This was just too easy! Hefting her dead weight over one shoulder, he eased open the door, checking first to see if anyone was around. The coast clear, he headed for the van.

Having blacked out the side windows it was dim inside except for the light streaming through the windshield. He dumped her inside like she was nothing more than a gunny sack of potatoes. Then, not wanting her trying to escape or scream her head off, he made short work of tying her up and plastering tape over her mouth.

"Yes indeed, bitch," he promised, "you're going to pay for every sin you've committed." Grabbing a breast, he squeezed as hard as he could, as if putting his brand on her then not satisfied he hit her some more. When he finally stopped fresh blood smeared her face and his hands. Wiping them on a black tarp, he tossed it over her. Now it was time to get out of Dodge.

High on adrenalin, Addison drove the winding blacktop toward the interstate. He'd done it! He'd slipped in and caught her without her guard dog. Now, he just had to get to the abandoned farmhouse and he could finish what he'd started. The way he figured it, it'd be a very long time before anyone found her, if they ever did, and by then he'd be long gone. Too bad his sweet baby girl hadn't been around, he'd have taken her away with him.

In his haste to get to the van, Addison didn't notice the cell phone fall from Raine's pocket and land near the porch.

# Chapter Twenty-Nine

**JESS, STILL WORRIED** that Raine was alone, was glad the meeting hadn't taken long. With a professional eye, the architect had reviewed the sketches, made some tweaks that would retain the ambiance of the century-plus log home while incorporating the modern additions. Singing along with the radio, his thoughts were on enjoying the rest of the day with his bride before their rambunctious girls returned home. They'd certainly enjoyed the mini-honeymoon and his heart did a happy rat-tat-tat of anticipation thinking of the remaining can of whip-cream in the refrigerator.

Lost in heated fantasies, he meandered along the rural blacktop. With the spring-like temperatures, yellow and pink wildflowers reached for the sun. Tomorrow was Easter and a big celebration was planned. Jess wasn't sure who'd had more fun decorating the yard and house before they'd left on their trip — him or the girls. Their Easter baskets, laden with all kinds of goodies, were hidden away until tomorrow. His whole being overflowed with contentment. Lost in happy thoughts, he gave the dirty van a cursory glance as it passed before a tingling warning said there was something vaguely familiar about the guy the ball cap couldn't hide. It was probably someone he'd seen around town. He memorized the tag number, then forgot about it as his driveway came in sight.

Gloating at his success, Addison's heart nearly gave out seeing the familiar black pickup coming toward him. Talk about going down to the wire! Reacting quickly, he slapped on a baseball cap and averted his face as much as possible. After the truck was past, Addison watched in the rear-view mirror until it was out of sight then floored the van.

When Jess walked through the door he was greeted with silence. Calling her name, all he got was more silence. A slight unease rippled through him. But figuring she was still at Cora's, he headed there. Drawing near and hearing the music still blaring, relief flooded through him only to die a quick death the second he stepped through the door. Then it was gut-wrenching terror that consumed him.

"No! No . . . !" A howl of pure panic erupted at the scene before him. The place looked like an E-5 tornado had torn through it. Furniture was knocked over, shattered glass littered the floor, and somewhere in his head it registered the vacuum cleaner was running. Automatically he switched it, and the blasting stereo, off. The ensuing silence was almost as deafening. His mind spinning, Jess took in the chaos, zeroing in on three things: a manila envelope, photos scattered on the floor, and something glittering near the fireplace. Pain clawed at his insides as he picked up the glittering objects — Raine's weddings rings. There was only one explanation why the place was a mess, why she was missing, and why she wasn't wearing her rings. Addison! The son-of-a-bitch had slipped through their guard and now he had her!

Snatching up the pictures, the images set his head to reeling. Someone had taken these intimate pictures on purpose and given them to Addison. This time it was a cry of pure rage that erupted from the very depths of his soul as he tore back down the hill. Cooper! He had to call Cooper!

Cooper was just hitting the save button on his computer when his phone rang. Seeing the number, he managed a, "Hey . . ." then his mouth clamped in a grim line as he listened to a frantic Jess telling him what he'd found. Cooper's own stomach twisted painfully for there was something he'd never heard from Jess in the all the time he'd known him. Fear — an undisguised, soul-aching black fear.

Jumping to his feet, Cooper went into battle mode motioning for everyone to gather around him. Every second counted in getting Raine back and knowing Jess, he would take matters into his own hands at any minute. "Jess! Don't go anywhere until I get there. Stay put!" He ordered.

"I can't! I have to find her!" Jess yelled through the phone.

"You wait for me!" Cooper ordered firmly.

"Go to hell! That's my wife he's got!" Jess yelled again. Disconnecting, he headed to his office where he did two things: locked the damning photos in the safe. Raine must have died a thousand deaths realizing Addison had them. But how had he come by them? The answer was simple. Addison had a spy. Well, he'd kill the spy, too, when he got his hands on him.

The second thing he did was get a gun from the gun safe. A line had been crossed. His woman, his wife, the love of his life, had been stolen and the man who'd taken her was going to pay. Just then his cell rang. It was Cooper. "I'm waiting! Get your ass out here!" He snapped.

Heaving an audible sigh of relief, Cooper empathized with his friend. Waiting wasn't one of his strong suits, either. "I'm on my way."

Guilt gnawed at Jess. The what-ifs slammed round in his head. If he hadn't gone to that damn meeting, if he hadn't left her alone, she'd still be here safe. Running a hand through his hair in rage-filled frustration he just couldn't stand around twiddling his thumbs. He headed back to the cabin. Once there, standing amidst the mess, he could only imagine Raine's terror coming face-to-face with Addison. The mere thought of what he could do to her left Jess deadly cold. Closing his eyes, he tried thinking of anything he might have missed, even the minutest detail that had slipped past him. Then it hit him like a sledgehammer between the eyes. The dirty van he'd passed only minutes ago! Immediately, he punched in Cooper's number. As soon as Cooper answered Jess explained about the van then rattled off the tag number.

"That had to be them, Jess. They can't have gotten far. We'll alert all law enforcement agencies." Scribbling as he talked, Cooper snapped his fingers at the officers gathered round him again. "Put this out to all agencies. Now!" To Jess he said. "I'll be there in a few minutes. In the meantime, try to think of anything else suspicious that may have occurred during the last few days." Lastly, he said, "just hold on Jess. We'll find her."

Knowing their friend needed them, Cooper called Belle, explained what had happened and to be ready to go, he'd swing by to get her. God forbid, but should Raine not come out of this alive, Jess would go off the deep end.

Less than five minutes after talking to Cooper, police cars, sirens wailing, swarmed the drive. Apparently, Cooper hadn't wasted any time getting the word out. Jess answered every question fired at him while wanting to yell they were wasting precious time. But he kept his cool. It wouldn't do any good to piss off the people who were there to help him.

At the cabin he was ordered to stay outside. His nerves on edge, he paced the length of the porch and frantically prayed. "Hang on, baby. Just hang on." Maybe she could pick up his thoughts. "Please stay with me, sweetheart. I'm coming after you. I promise. And I promise you he'll pay dearly." Jess didn't know if he was trying to assure her, or himself. Whatever, it sure as hell wasn't working for him.

The twenty minutes it took for Cooper to get there were the longest minutes of Jess's life. Several times he started to jump in his truck to go on the hunt. Because of his close friendship with Jess, Cooper was put in charge of the search. There'd been a brief meeting before picking up Belle. Now, they were ready to search for Raine, and support their friend.

Seeing Cooper's vehicle pull into the drive, Jess raced back down the hill. They had barely stopped before Belle was running toward him with Cooper right behind. Reaching him, she wrapped him in a fierce hug. "We'll find her, Jess. I know we will."

"We've got every law enforcement agency alerted to be on the lookout for them." Cooper hugged him, too. "They've got a description of what she looks like and if you remember what she was wearing I can add it."

"Yeah," Jess scrubbed his haggard face wearily, "she had on jeans with sparkly things on the pockets and one of my sweat-shirts. It's gray, has the Marine emblem on the front and is way too big for her. And tennis shoes."

Cooper relayed the information to the station over the mike clipped to his uniform shirt. "Come on." he urged Jess, a com-forting hand on his back. "I want a look at the cabin."

Following behind the two men, all kinds of horrible thoughts raced through Belle's mind. She knew what Raine's ex-husband could do to her. She'd confided some of the things he'd done and imagined there was far worse Raine hadn't imparted. Just imagining it made her stomach pitched alarmingly. Of one thing she was certain — Raine Harper, helpless in this madman's clutches, needed every prayer in the world if she was going to survive.

"This place is a mess, Coop. She must have put up one hell of a fight..." Jess choked up as he fought for composure. "We've got to find her. She's full of grit and will fight him, but she doesn't stand a chance. He's hell-bent on revenge and he'll make her pay with every last drop of blood in her body. Every minute that passes is a minute closer to him killing her."

Grim-faced, Cooper was thinking the same thing. "At least we have a good lead. You actually saw the van, so we can't be that far behind him. With the description and the tag number, a BOLO's being broadcast statewide on all the emergency alert signs as we speak. There's a good chance someone will spot the van and connect it to the alert. Now, start at the beginning and tell me everything. Starting with the van."

Biting back his frustration, Jess repeated word-for-word the same details he'd given the other officers — about passing the van while returning home from the meeting with the architect to finding Raine missing and the cabin in shambles. The guilty voice in his head blamed him for not following the van.

Cooper's cell rang just as he and Jess stepped onto the porch. It was the dispatcher. He had good news — and bad news. The van had already been sighted; then lost. Studying Jess's anguished face, Cooper conceded he wasn't going to be happy. At least now they had a general vicinity of where she could be.

"What?" Jess barked seeing the grim look on Cooper's face. He was barely hanging on by a thread. "Cooper . . . I'm sor . . ."

Cooper cut him off with a wave of his hand. "I'd be the same way if I was in your shoes and Belle was missing. A white van matching the one you saw has been sighted."

Hope flared in Jess's heart. "Where the hell at?"

"A trucker going down I-67 saw the alert. Right about that time a white van flew by him like a bat-out-of-hell. He managed to get the tag number and exit number when it slowed to take the turn west out of town."

Cooper might have sounded positive, but both had lived in the area long enough to know that if a body wanted to get lost and stay lost, there were plenty of places do so off the rural back roads. No matter, they'd search every nook and cranny until they found her.

It also didn't go unnoticed by either that Addison had had time to scout out the area. A renewed sense of dread filled Jess. "That's not good. If he holes up in the country it'll be like trying to find a needle in haystack."

"At least we've got a starting point." Cooper left Jess on the porch. With a professional eye he took in everything including the drops of blood on the floor. Whose was it? He wondered, while praying it wasn't Raine's. Obviously, Jess hadn't noticed the blood or he'd have already been in hot pursuit.

# CHAPTER THIRTY

**THOUGH HE'D TAKEN** a chance speeding, Addison reached his destination without complications. He breathed a sigh of relief when he pulled into the rutted lane so rough the van bounced and rattled along with his teeth. It was beyond him why anyone would live way out here in the sticks. He wasn't complaining though, since it served his purpose. It had been the rusted "No Trespassing" sign nailed to a tree that had caught his attention when scouting the area. Seeing the ramshackle house and outbuildings, he'd known it would be the perfect place to carry out his mission. The crème-de-la-crème was the root cellar. He could lock her away and no one would find her for a long, long time. Maybe years from now someone would stumble across her dried-out bones.

Parking in a shed, Addison quickly strode across the hard-scrabble yard to the root cellar and unlocked the double doors fastened with the shiny new lock he'd installed. He descended the rickety steps into the dank-smelling space. An old iron bedstead rusted with age stood center-stage in the middle of the room. Gloating, he thought the accommodations perfect for the cheating bitch.

Returning to the van, Addison found her still unconscious. Dismay filled him. Surely, he hadn't killed her yet?! Not when he had so much fun planned for her. Pressing fingertips to her throat and finding a pulse, he wanted to shout for joy. He'd have his fun after all!

Hoisting her dead weight over his shoulder Addison returned to the cellar. Dumping her on the grimy mattress, he was quite smug, mentally patting himself on the back for having outwitted everyone. Now let the fun begin!

Untying and stripping her, Addison tossed her clothes aside. Ripping the tape from her mouth, he didn't care that it took skin with it. Next, he flipped her on her stomach and secured her wrists and ankles to the four corner posts with lengths of coarse rope. Show-time! Time to start paying the piper. Crouching down, he briskly tapped the blood-smeared cheek turned toward him. "Rainey. Rainey. Wakey. Wakey."

Fighting through layers of darkness, Raine vowed whoever was hitting her better quit or she'd punched them. Each strike was like a gong reverberating in her head. Hazily she wondered if she'd fallen and hit her head. Maybe that's' why she felt so muddled-headed. It would definitely account for the gong triple-pounding in her skull. Gradually she realized she was lying down and that really confused her. The last thing she remembered was vacuuming the rug. *Why was she in bed?*

Addison, though thoroughly enjoying her state of confusion, guessed he'd just have to help her remember. Leaning closer, he peered into her face. Feeling hot breath on her face, Raine forced her eyes open. Instantly the face in her line of vision brought everything rushing back in horrifying clarity. "No! No! No!" She shrank away only to realize she was tied down *and* stripped bare. Horrific memories of the last time he'd done this bombarded her and dear god in heaven here she was again at the mercy of the sadistic monster. This time would be even worse. He would kill her. His desire to do so bore into her from hate-filled eyes.

A heart-wrenching moan ripped from her as she came to grasp with the fact that her fate was sealed. Jess would never find her in time. Then, truly despaired, she realized Jess didn't even know she was missing, or where to look. Even still, she refused to give up. Reaching deep into the depths of her soul, she forced herself into survival mode. Struggling against the tight bindings, she let loose a scream of frustration when they wouldn't budge.

"You might as well stop. No one can hear you and you're not going anywhere until I say so. And that could be a very long time, if ever." Gloating, he trailed a finger down her bare flesh.

"Don't touch me!" Her shudder of distaste sent his rage soaring. Whipping off the belt bought especially for the occasion, it made a swooshing sound clearing the loops. The familiar sound sent a fresh wave of terror through her. Even as the first lash bit painfully into her exposed back Raine vowed not to make a sound. Clamping her jaws together, she buried her face in the dirty pillow and used every ounce of willpower not to scream.

That's what pushed Addison completely over the edge. He wanted to hear her beg for mercy. It wasn't enough that she jerked with each vicious blow delivered. He didn't care that inside she was screaming mindlessly. He was incensed, all control gone as he whipped her over-and-over again.

The torture went on forever until Raine finally reached the breaking point. "Stop! Stop!" She was crying so hard he could barely understand her. Perverse satisfaction filled him knowing he'd finally broken her. There wasn't a place on the back of her that wasn't covered in livid red welts and oozing blood.

Despite the chill of the room, sweat poured off Addison. He wanted to continue punishing her, but he was worn out. After days and nights of waiting and watching to grab her, then meting out her punishment, the adrenalin was seeping away. What he needed now was sleep and a healthy meal that didn't consist of greasy fast-food fare. He'd leave now, but he'd be back. Besides, half out of it, she wasn't any fun. Securing the doors, he got in the van and drove a different route back to town.

Hearing the doors slam shut, Raine lay in an agonized stupor, grateful the whipping had stopped. Her body a mass of fiery burning flesh, felt as though it had been doused with gasoline and set afire. Lifting her head she moaned as shafts of pain speared through then blackness claimed her.

While Raine lay in blessed oblivion Jess watched Cooper and the other officers gathering evidence. His mind flashed to the first time he'd seen Raine and the horrible damage Addison had inflicted. Now, he had her in his clutches again doing God knows what at that very moment. "God, please, please watch over her until I can get to her."

Belle's comforting hand on his arm got his attention. "Jess, Cora needs to know what's going on." Her eyes strayed to the cabin. Cooper hadn't allowed her inside either, but she'd glimpsed the mess. Raine must have put up one hell of a fight before her ex-husband had overpowered her. Good for you, girlfriend! She cheered silently.

Jess nodded. "Then I'm heading out to where that van was last seen. I just can't stand around any longer. I'm going crazy. It's my fault he has her. I promised to protect her and I failed!" He railed with pent-up guilt.

Grabbing him, Belle gave him a brisk shake. "You listen to me, Jess Harper! No one failed her and none of this is your fault. Wherever she is, she knows it. She knows you love her and will find her." Not sure she'd gotten through to him, Belle shook him again. "Listen to me! Raine's going to need you when we find her. You can't fall apart!" He opened his mouth, but she wasn't finished. "No one had any clue his release date had been moved up, certainly not the detectives working her case, otherwise they'd have been standing at the jailhouse entrance the second he walked out. Hell, even her attorney didn't know, and he called immediately upon getting the news. Unfortunately, it was too late."

What Belle said was true. Jess was leading the officers to the cabin when Gordon had called. "You're too damn late, Hanson! He's got her!" He'd yelled, needing someone to take his anger out on; Gordon was it. "You promised her! You promised to call as soon as he walked out of jail!"

"Dear God, Jess, I just found out not five minutes ago. I checked with Detectives Green and Collins and they weren't aware he'd been released early, either. I don't know what happened, but I'm sure as hell going to find out and rip some new assholes. That was one of the plea bargain stipulations. She was supposed to know ahead of time when he was walking out of that jail."

"Well, it sure as hell didn't work out that way, did it? Somebody royally screwed-up!" He'd yelled sarcastically.

Gordon couldn't blame Jess for being furious. In his place he'd be ready to kill the bastard and there wasn't a doubt in his mind that Jess was about to go gunning for Addison.

Reining in his temper, Jess knew Gordon didn't deserve the tongue-lashing. The assholes who'd let Addison out did. "Gordon. Damn it! I'm sorry."

"Don't apologize. Just find her." Gordon had looked at a worried Molly as she cuddled their baby daughter against her chest. "And Jess, when you do, take care of him. That would be the best gift you could ever give your wife."

"Count on it." There'd been no mistaking the unspoken message. Apparently, they were two of a kind when it came to their women.

"What I can't figure out is how he knew she was here. He had to have help on the outside." Belle mused.

"Probably the same ones that cut Cora's tire and break line. They didn't get cut by themselves." Reaching for his phone, he ignored her look of surprise. So, Cooper hadn't told her. He'd explain later. "Gordon, Andrews had to have help finding Raine. Check the jail's visitor roster for someone other than that S.O.B.'s folks and secretary. I bet you'll find them."

"Already on it, Jess. Green and Collins are headed to the jail as we speak, and Michaels' man is meeting them with warrants. Here's another thing. Addison's folks claim they don't know where he's at. They only know that he was taking a little vacation to clear his head before going back to work."

"Yeah, he's on vacation, all right, and when I get my hands on him he'll be on one permanently, six-feet under." Jess's gut screamed Addison and his accomplice were both here and when he found them they'd both pay. First, he'd give them a taste of the special punishment Addison was so fond of dishing out. Then, he'd put a bullet between their eyes.

Helpless and heart aching, he watched Cooper from the open doorway work the scene. Standing idle for even a moment while Addison could be doing God only knows what to her was eating him alive, but Belle was right. In order to find Raine he had to get a grip on his emotions, otherwise he'd be no good to her.

"I missed something. All week long I've had the feeling someone was watching us, but when I checked I never saw one damn thing."

"Your intuition was alerting you something was going to happen." She nodded to the cell phone still clutched in his hand. "I gather Raine's attorney and the police have their heads together."

"Yeah," he concurred, "they believe someone helped him, too. And you could be right about intuition. Raine's been really skittish the last few days thinking someone was lurking around. Now, we know it was true. Someone tracked her here and spied on her for that scumbag. Gordon's working that end." In frustration, he kicked a porch post. "Son of a bitch! Where the hell is she?"

Not about to let him lose control, Belle gripped his tensely muscled arm. "Jess, listen to me. Call Cora. She needs to know what's happening here. The girls don't need to be here. It'd only scare them to death. I'm sure Inez will keep them and knowing Cora, she'll be right here in the thick of things. While you call, I'll fix a thermos of coffee for us." At his questioning look she smiled gently, the breeze gently ruffling her dark curls. "You didn't think we'd let you go off on your own did you? We saw that gun tucked inside your waistband. You're liable to shoot first and ask questions later. It's not up for discussion. We're going with you." Her tone brooked no argument.

As it happened Cora and the McCullens were just pulling into their driveway when her cell rang. Seeing the number, she grinned. No doubt mom and dad were chomping at the bit to see the girls. "Hello . . ."

Jess's terse tone cut her off. "Cora, don't say anything, just listen. When you get to town I need you to leave the girls with Inez and get home quick."

No elaboration was needed. Cora knew what had happened. Addison had found them. Her throat closed around the panic, but her voice was calm. "We're just pulling into the driveway. I'm sure Inez and Hank won't mind keeping the girls for a while." She shook her head at Inez's inquiring look.

Seeing through the cheerful façade, Inez realized something was dreadfully wrong. "Tell him we'll keep the girls however long he needs." Then she and Hank swiftly ushered the girls into the house.

Cora, white-faced and trembling, was sliding behind the wheel when Inez returned. "It's Raine's ex-husband. He's got her." She said shakily, "Oh my poor little girl. Inez, you can't imagine what that monster's capable of. He nearly killed her the last time he got his hands on her. This time he'll do it for sure. I need to get home. Maybe there's something I can do to help."

"Get going and don't worry about the girls. They'll be just fine." Through the open window Inez squeezed Cora's hand. "We'll be praying for you all."

Watching Cora speed away, Inez keyed in Cory's number. Seeing "Mom" on the caller ID, Cory knew the reason for the call. "You've heard."

"We'd just got home when Jess called. Cora's on her way home and the girls are with us. I know you're probably out searching so I won't keep you. But I'd appreciate it if you'd keep us in the loop."

"I will, and mom, if they need anything I'd appreciate you taking care of it."

"Count on it. I love you, sweetie, you take care, too. That ex-husband is a loose cannon."

"I love you, too, and I promise to be careful." Disconnecting, Cory smiled. She had the best mom and dad in the whole world.

Less than five minutes later Cora careened into the driveway missing a green and white sheriff's unit by a hair's breadth. She was barely stopped before she was racing up the hill.

Still not allowed inside, Jess was pacing the porch when he saw her swiftly moving form. Meeting her halfway down the stone path he gathered her in his outstretched arms. "What happened? And how on earth did he find her way out here?"

"We don't know yet." His voice was husky, "As for how he found her, we're positive someone was helping him. Cora, I just missed her." Grim-faced, he explained about the van and the possibility she'd been in it. "I think the guy driving the van looked familiar."

"I know what he looks like, and I know where there's a picture of him." She was heading for the cordoned-off cabin.

Running after the sprinting woman, he yelled. "Cora, the police have it taped off! It's a crime scene! You can't go in there!"

"There'll be another crime if they don't let me get that picture! I'd hate to have to hurt somebody." She yelled back but kept right on running. Just let someone stop her! She'll punch their lights out!

Cooper, squatting down examining tracks in the snow, found Raine's cell phone at the same instant Cora ducked under the yellow tape. Starting after her, he dropped it in his pocket. "Cora, you can't go in there. It's a crime scene." Attempting to hold her back, she shook him off.

"There's a picture of Raine's ex-husband in there and I intend to get it with or without your permission." Quick as a rabbit she darted through the door before he could stop her.

"Let her get the picture, Coop." Jess ordered tersely.

Through the open doorway they watched Cora enter Katy's former room. Moments later Cora returned; the picture in one hand and a large envelope in the other. "Here," she thrust a glossy eight-by-ten at Jess. "Katy brought it with her when we left Phoenix. I guess the poor little mite knew something was wrong even back then. She's kept it hidden all this time. I'm thinking she didn't want her mom to know she had it, but Raine did." Several times they'd secretly watched Katy take the photo from her hiding place.

Jess stared at the handsome man in the photo. No wonder the guy in the van seemed familiar. He had pictures in his file of Addison. And he *had* been driving the van. His stomach twisted painfully knowing Raine had been in that van when he'd passed it. "That's him." A new round of recriminations rocketed through him. "Why didn't I turn around and following him?"

Cooper took the photo. "You have a scanner?" Jess nodded. "Then let's get copies made to hand out and we'll get this to the other agencies so they know what he looks like." Cooper was already running down the hill.

Reaching the cabin, before going inside, Cora pulled Jess aside and handed him the envelope. "You need to see just what Addison's capable of doing. You saw Raine *after* she'd had a few weeks to heal. This is what she looked like the night he attacked her. They were taken at the hospital."

Sliding the photos out, Jess's face blanched even grayer. Unable to believe what he was seeing, horror closed over him. His stomach curled so harshly he thought he'd be sick. The badly beaten woman in the pictures hardly resembled Raine.

"My God, this doesn't even resemble her," he whispered hoarsely. In the first photo her swollen and battered face was beyond anything he'd ever seen. Even her lips, split and bruised were swollen twice their normal size. As for her beautiful eyes, they were nearly swollen shut and the whites were bloody. It was a wonder she'd been able to see at all.

Other photos showed the bloody welts covering her body and the imprints obviously made by shoes. Mind-numbing fury consumed Jess. They had to find her before she suffered through the same agony, or worse. "Addison Andrews is a dead man!" he growled.

The fierce reaction snagged Belle's attention. Joining them, she peered around Jess's shoulder. "Dear God!" She gasped, swaying a bit seeing the horrific images. In an instant she was transported back to the night she'd been savagely attacked.

"Easy, baby," Cooper, coming up behind her and seeing the photos, held her steady, knowing they reminded her of her own attack. "Come on." Keeping her firmly by his side, he headed for Jess's office. After faxing Addison's picture to the sheriff's office and other agencies, he made copies to take with them. By the time he was finished, though still white as a sheet, Belle had pulled herself together. She finished filling the thermoses while Cora, figuring they wouldn't think about eating, threw a care package together.

"I've got to do something useful while you're gone. I just can't sit around twiddling my thumbs. Isn't there anything I can do to help?"

Thinking for a moment, Jess hit upon what he wanted her to do. "Think you could watch the security tapes to see if anything's on them that I missed?"

"You bet I can, and if he's on them I'll recognize him right away. Just show me how to work the machine." Sitting in front of the bank of security monitors, Cora watched the cameras scan the various areas surrounding the cabins, the stables, and the perimeter of the property. It didn't go amiss that despite all the security measures, Addison had somehow slipped by them.

Flipping a switch on a blank monitor, Jess showed her how to operate the machine then handed her the tapes. "If I see anything I'll call you. Now, go find our girl." She hugged him but didn't let him go. She'd been holding back a vital piece of information. In case Raine hadn't already told him, he needed to prepare himself for what else Addison might do to her.

"Jess," her flat tone chilled him. "There's something else you should know. Maybe Raine already told you. Anyway, remember the incident Katy talked about at Thanksgiving when she stayed with Addison while Raine went to the doctor?" A curtain of dread rose inside him. He wasn't sure he wanted to hear what

Cora was about to impart. "Well, you see, she went to the doctor because one night a few weeks earlier Addison had come home drunk, choked her into unconsciousness and . . . well you can figure out the rest of it." The dawning horror turned Jess's face from gray to mottled red. Okay . . . Raine hadn't mentioned this. "She was late with her monthly and thought she might be pregnant from that night. Addison had found her stash of birth control pills she'd hidden and threw them away. Of course, she paid for that, too. She didn't want to be pregnant and fortunately wasn't. Anyway, I just thought you should know what else he's capable of doing to her."

Just how evil could the man be? "Let's pray he doesn't, but it won't make a difference to me. I love that woman with all my heart and no matter what happens that won't change. You don't have to worry about me turning away from her."

Joining Cooper and Belle, the deadly look in his eyes left questions flying around in their heads which both refrained from asking.

# CHAPTER THIRTY-ONE

**HEADING TOWARD THE** area the van was last seen, they were all well-aware that time was of the greatest essence, especially considering Addison's state of mind. Cooper felt Jess's intent gaze on him and they shared a grim gaze. Both were thinking the same thing: The longer it took, the slimmer the chances of finding her alive. At least they had this one lead. That was something.

Late afternoon sun streamed warm through the windshield. Outside it was turning colder. Their warm spell was over. Typical Missouri weather. Wherever she was, Jess just hoped it was some place warm.

Pondering the thought processes of the vengeance-filled man, those horrifying images flickered through his head like a slideshow while Cora's confiding words played round and round like a record. Clinching his fists, he wished with all his might they were around Addison's neck. Just then his phone broke the silence. "Yeah!" He barked. "Oh, Cora, I didn't mean to snap at you."

Listening to the one-sided conversation, Cooper kept glancing between Jess and the blacktop road ahead. Had she found something? Looking in the rear-view mirror, he met Belle's troubled gaze. Knowing she was extremely aware of just how much damage raging fists could inflict and seeing those pictures of Raine had upset her, he gave her a reassuring smile.

"Damn it!" Jess exclaimed. "How'd I miss it? You did good Cora. Now we definitely know Addison has her and we also have proof he had help." Disconnecting, Jess related what she'd found. "She's got Addison on a tape from this morning. He's coming and going from the woods across the road from the cabins, probably parked on the old logging road. It shows him entering the cabin then leaving a while later carrying something over his shoulder." They knew who Addison had been carrying. A momentary silence filled the vehicle as each prayed they'd find her in time. "Cora spotted the helpers, too. One vandalized her SUV while the other actually broke into the cabin." Danger had walked right through their front door, and they hadn't even known it. Talk about scary!

For hours and hours and miles and miles they drove the back roads littering the countryside while the police radio crackled with communication, but nothing pertained to Raine. They stopped at every open business showing Addison's picture, but no one recognized him. It went unspoken that he could be holding her in any vacant building off the beaten path.

It was going on five in the morning when Cooper suggested returning to the house to regroup. "Shifts are changing soon, and I want everyone up to speed." After that we'll head back out." Jess didn't want to stop but Cooper, being the professional, he trusted him.

While the others were out combing the countryside Cora had fallen back on the one thing that would keep her sane — cooking. After finding Addison and his accomplices on the tapes she'd needed more to do. With Jess's place the command post, until Raine was found, there'd be round-the-clock officers and volunteers needing food and plenty of coffee to keep them going. So, she started cooking and feeding. When the neighbors saw all the police activity, they came to find out what was going on. Apprised of the situation, they pitched in with food and drink and coordinated cell numbers then set off in groups to join the search.

When the three walked through the door their faces grim and wearing exhaustion like a second skin, she got busy filling mugs with steaming hot coffee. Three pairs of tired but inquisitive eyes watched her lace each mug with generous amounts of brandy. "Don't argue. Drink it!"

Without a word they obeyed. Jess felt the heat all the way to his belly. Draining it, he refilled his mug, minus the brandy. Needing a few minutes alone, he slipped away to their bedroom. The lingering scent of Raine's flowery perfume wafted around him. Wearily, he eased into the old rocking chair, the ratty one she'd fallen in love with on their honeymoon and spent hours bringing it back to gleaming life. Stroking the newly varnished wood as though stroking her hand, he bleakly wondered if she'd ever rock in it again. Would she get to lull their babies to sleep in it? An ache so painfully deep made him groan. Scrubbing his hands over his whisker-roughened face, he shoved the dark thoughts away. Time was wasting. He had to get back out searching, but thought a quick shower would help rid the desolate exhaustion.

Fifteen minutes later he strode into the kitchen. Showered, shaved, and dressed in fresh jeans and the sweatshirt he'd picked up on their honeymoon. He was braced for whatever the day brought. Refilling his mug from the coffee urn, he nodded at Cooper and Belle. "Go shower. It'll perk you up."

"And I'll have breakfast ready by the time you get back." Cora said. And it was. "Get to eating." She ordered, nodding at the table laden with scrambled eggs, bacon, sausage, fried potatoes, and biscuits. "You need all the strength you can get. You've gone without sleep all night. But your body needs its fuel. Now eat!" She repeated the order.

Cooper, the first to finish, still needed more caffeine and refilled his mug. "I'll check in with the office again. Maybe something new has turned up in in the last little while." When Cooper shook his head, a sense of hopelessness filled Jess then he quickly shook it off. He wasn't giving up.

As the first steaks of dawn appeared he called Gordon. He'd insisted on being kept in the loop no matter what the time, day or night, news or no news. As though the phone was glued to his ear, Gordon demanded immediately. "Tell me you've found her."

"I wish. We've been all over the area they were last seen. It's like they've vanished into thin air. No one's seen Addison or the van."

Gordon heard the underlying fear. "Don't give up hope, Jess. Someone's seen something. They just don't realize it yet." Then he told Jess of the numerous visits Addison had from what turned out to be a private investigator.

"That's one of his spies." Jess concluded.

"You win the jackpot. There's a sign-in record of him being there right after you and Raine got married." And no doubt he'd delivered Addison right to their doorstep.

Disconnecting, Jess filled them in on what he'd learned. Cooper studied him over the rim of his mug. The man was barely keeping it together. "We have the manpower, and if it takes searching every nook, cranny, and haystack until we find her, that's what we'll do. We may not have much, but the search is ongoing."

"I'm trying to stay positive, but Addison's completely lost it. It's as though they've disappeared off the face of the earth." Jess slipped on his coat. "I've got to take care of the horses. When I'm finished let's head back out to the roads off I-67 again. I just can't help feeling he's still in that area."

Driving up to the stables, he passed the cabin. Yellow crime scene tape cordoned it off. "Andrews, you are a dead man." He vowed with murderous venom.

Approaching the coral, as though knowing something was wrong, the two horses made their way somberly to him. Stroking their velvety noses, he spoke softly. "Don't you worry. I promise I'll bring her back home." A feeling that had nothing to do with desire but deep abiding love for Raine welled inside him as thoughts of the last time they'd been in the stable together swirled through his mind. She'd come wearing that long coat with not a stitch on underneath, a tender smile touched his mouth. She'd given him one hell of a surprise that day. Quickly his smile faded as he worried that he'd never see her alive again. Hot tears burned his tired eyes. Damn it, he vowed angrily, he would find her! And nothing or no one was going to stop him!

# Chapter Thirty-Two

**LOCKED IN THE** dark cellar, Raine had no concept of time as she drifted in and out of consciousness. However, with each moment of lucidness, her mind became clearer. During those bouts of wakefulness she worked at the ropes, but despite how much stretching and straining, the knots didn't budge. Her wrists and ankles were rubbed raw from straining against them. She might be trussed-up like a Christmas goose, but she refused to die in this hellhole if she could help it! All she needed was one of the ropes to loosen a bit and she'd damn well get free and call Jess. That's if Addison hadn't discovered the phone in her pocket.

A sudden scraping noise interrupted her efforts sending a burst of hope through her that it was Jess. Frowning, she remembered he didn't know where she was. Hopelessness knotted her throat knowing Addison was back to punish her again, for the third time. How much more could she withstand?

A wide shaft of light illuminated the darkness when the cellar doors opened. From her peripheral vision Raine watched him approach, a club clutched in his hand. *So help me, if I get my hands on it I won't hesitate to kill him.*

Having a good night's sleep and hearty breakfast, Addison was primed for action. After the last visit around midnight, he'd slept like a baby knowing she was locked up with no way to escape. He noted the rope burns. *So, the little bitch had been trying to get loose. Good. There was still some fight left in her.*

"Let. Me. Go." She hissed through swollen lips. "You're a sick bastard, Addison! This just proves it."

"Call me whatever, but I have the hammer. I'm the one who decides if, or when, you get loose." Trailing a finger over her bare shoulder, her shudder of revulsion sent his temper soaring. On the drive out he'd vowed she wouldn't goad him into anything he wasn't ready to do. He wanted to toy with her like a cat toys with a mouse. He wanted to see the fear in her eyes before meting out one final bout of punishment. That vow disappeared at her reaction to his touch.

Crouching, Addison sharply tapped the blood-smeared cheek turned toward him. It made her head throb and the cloying scent of his cologne gagged her. "You know, you ought to treat me nicer, especially after everything you've done. I'd have forgiven you a lot of things, but you committed the ultimate sin. You broke your wedding vows. You cheated on me. I saw what you did with him. I watched you doing things with him you never did with me!" Raine tried to turn her head but he grabbed her hair, forcing her to face him. "Look at me when I'm talking to you!" He thundered.

"Go to hell!" She screamed as he brutally twisted his fingers in her hair.

"I will, but you'll get there first. You cheated on me, now you have to pay." The grip on her hair was suddenly gone and the swooshing sound of the belt leaving the loops filled the air. He was going to beat her again. The thought was barely formed before the belt bit into her already injured flesh.

Lost in a swirling vortex of agony, the torture went on and on before sheer exhaustion made Addison stop. Standing over her, gasping for breath and dripping sweat, a sadistic thrill hummed under his skin. He didn't feel a bit sorry for her. She'd asked for it and with a renewed burst of energy he delivered several more lashes.

This time when he stopped Addison made the mistake of getting in her face. Despite the agony coursing through her, she spit at him, hitting him squarely in the face. His reaction was to slam his fist into the side of her head. "Don't you ever spit on me again!" He raged, punching her again and again.

Yet that didn't stop another mouthful of spittle flying from her mouth. "I'll spit on you anytime I want, you slimy pig! You make my skin crawl!"

The taunts inflamed him even more and he started pacing and threatening a litany of more abuse he was going to heap on her. Closing her eyes, Raine blocked out the sight him while praying that Jess would come, yet in the next breath hoping he wouldn't. Addison would kill him, too, and that couldn't happen. The girls would need him, especially if Addison left her here to die. And that's what the stark-raving lunatic swore to do. And trussed up as she was, she was helpless to stop him.

Eyes still closed, Raine didn't see Addison grab the club off the floor. The first blow sent explosions of pain roaring through her head. The next one sailed her into darkness. Blessedly unconscious, she didn't feel the belt's biting blows on her anymore.

# Chapter Thirty-Three

**RETURNING TO THE** house, Jess found Cooper and Belle waiting on him. Though they noted his red-rimmed eyes, neither mentioned it. As they started out the door Cooper's phone sounded and several anxious eyes stared at it. "Cooper." It was the dispatcher. "Give me some good news, Dale."

"I sure hope it is, Coop. We just got a tip. Don't know if it's anything to do with Ms. Harper's disappearance but Cory Dugan and Scott Walker are checking it out."

"What's the tip?" Hope rose inside Cooper.

"About midnight a couple of kids were parked out near the old Parker place, off Plankton Road, that's the area we've been focusing on. Anyway, they saw something strange. Said they saw a white van leaving the place. Funny thing is, Cooper, I know for a fact the Parker place has sat empty for years. I thought you'd want it checked out."

"You bet, and Dale," Cooper was curious, "why'd they wait until this morning to call in what they saw?"

"I was hoping you'd ask. Seems they weren't supposed to be out there, so they didn't say anything. I suppose they didn't want to get into hot water with their folks. Anyway, it wasn't until the boy saw the morning news that he realized they might know something. That's when he told his dad where they'd been and about seeing the van the police are searching for. The dad called us immediately. I've already alerted everyone. "

"That's good." Cooper snapped his fingers. "Dale! Tell everyone to go silent. If it is him, we don't want to alert him."

He didn't have to add there was no telling what Addison might do to Raine if he heard them and panicked. That is, if she was still alive, he thought bleakly. Disconnecting, he locked eyes with Jess. Clearly the man had reached the end of his rope and only prayed the news he was about to impart would end up good news.

"What?" Jess demanded. "What's going on? Have they found her?"

"Come on, "I'll tell you on the way." Rushing out the door, Cooper jumped in the SUV. Jess was right on his heels with Belle a step behind him. The doors were barely shut before Cooper was squealing tires on the pavement.

"There's been a sighting of a white van leaving an old abandon farm in the vicinity we've been searching. A couple kids out parking saw it." He gave Jess an encouraging smile. "Let's go see what we have. It just might be the break we've been waiting for." Flipping the sirens on, Cooper wanted to make the trip as fast as he could.

During the eight minutes and two seconds it took to make the drive, Jess wavered between praying Raine was alive and planning Addison's execution. If he'd harmed one hair on her head he'd make damn sure the scumbag ate a bullet. Cooper's fast clip at the exit and silenced sirens snapped him back to reality. He saw both sides of the county road teaming with emergency vehicles. Roadblocks were set up a mile in all directions from the Parker place. An aura of urgency clung thick as a heavy coat of fog. Given the multitude of law enforcement agencies in on the hunt, Addison didn't stand a snowball's chance in hell of getting away, that is, if this wasn't a false alarm.

They were approaching the mud-rutted lane leading to the house when the police radio suddenly crackled. A deputy was reporting a white van on the move. "It's pulling out of a shed."

Cooper gave orders to stay out of sight. "Let him come to you. She may be in the van so don't shoot unless he does." Throwing the SUV into park, Cooper jumped out. "Stay here."

He ordered Belle when she opened her door. Jess was already out. No way in hell, she thought, getting out anyway.

Leaving the darkness of the shed, a jubilant Addison blinked against the brilliant sunlight and shoved on sunglasses. Having accomplished his mission, nothing stood in his way to freedom. He'd gotten a plane ticket using a fake ID to a country without extradition so the feds could never touch him. His greatest satisfaction was that no one would find her until it was way too late. She'd pay the ultimate price for the troubles she'd caused him. As he drove the bumpy road his gloating laughter filled the van. "Oh Raine, baby-doll, they'll never find you. You're as good as dead."

Caught up in congratulating himself, Addison was oblivious to the officers hiding on either side of the road, their weapons trained on him. But then a shiny glint tipped him off. Cursing, he floored the van rounding a curve only to find a squad car blocking the lane. Vowing nobody was stopping him, Addison smashed into the car, knocking it sideways enough to get past it. However, his efforts proved fruitless when he ran over stop-strips. With the tires punctured the van's momentum slowed and the moment it finally stopped it looked like swarms of bees flocking to honey as officers surrounded it shouting for Addison to get out.

But Addison wasn't ready to give up. He grabbed the pistol off the passenger seat and exited the van his finger continuously pulled the trigger until it was empty. Thankfully, out of all the bullets Addison fired, a single one winged the nearest deputy in the shoulder, the impact staggered him, but he regained his balance quick enough to fire back. A trained sharpshooter, the round he got off was a lot more accurate than Addison's wild shots. Dead-on, it struck Addison squarely in the heart. There was a quick flash of stunned surprise on his face before Raine's tormentor collapsed. He was dead before he ever hit the ground.

Seeing Addison bail out and start shooting, Jess broke into a dead run toward the van, his own gun drawn. Having no qualms about bringing the bastard down, he took aim, but the deputy took the pleasure away from him, shooting Addison first. Not wasting another second, he shoved the gun back in his waistband and raced to the van to see if Raine was in it. Not finding her he headed for the farmhouse.

A couple of officers stayed with Addison's body while the rest fanned out to search across the property. Cooper and Belle followed Jess inside the ramshackle building. The smell of ages old grime and mustiness assailed them. Jess took the second floor while they scoured the first. "She's not here." He yelled from the second floor.

"She's not down here, either. Maybe he took her someplace else." Belle suggested.

"No." Intuition screamed she was nearby. Practically jumping the stairs to the first floor, he tore outside and began pacing around the hardscrabble yard and shouting her name. Suddenly he stopped, closed his eyes, and concentrated hard. *She's here. I can feel her.* Opening them again, he took a fresh look around and that's when he spotted the ground-level doors. A root cellar! In that moment his heart jumped with excitement. Was she locked in the pitch blackness of it? Drawing nearer, he noticed the shiny padlock and knew they'd found her.

He pointed to the ground. "She's in there! I know it! It's a root cellar and the doors are fastened with a new padlock." Looking around, Jess found a large rock to beat it off. He could've shot it off but feared Raine might be near the doors.

After several blows it gave way with a loud crack. He and Cooper hefted the doors open. A shaft of daylight lit Jess's way down the cellar's creaky steps. The space was dank with the musky scent of earth. Blinking in the sudden glare of Cooper's flashlight his gaze fell on the old metal bedstead. And Raine.

Intense relief turned his legs rubbery, but the relief was replaced with a blinding fury seeing her stripped bare and bound to the bed. "Dear God in heaven!" He whispered hoarsely. If Andrews wasn't already dead he'd march right back out there and shoot him again. "She's down here!" He yelled. "We need an ambulance!"

He checked for a pulse. She was alive, but what a mess. Given the bleeding and oozing welts, Addison had obviously resorted to his favorite punishment. Swiftly untying her Jess gently examined her head, finding several bleeding lumps. Besides the whippings, the S.O.B. had struck her in the head. Wiping his fingers on the old mattress, Cora's confiding words crossed his mind and he prayed that hadn't happened.

"Raine, baby, can you hear me? It's me, Jess." Maybe it was better she was out of it otherwise she'd be in agony. Hearing the steps creak, he called out. "Wait a second." Slipping off his jacket, he gently draped it over her. No matter what, she'd be mortified if anyone saw her this way. "Okay."

"Is she . . ." Belle choked out, catching sight of Raine.

"No," he quickly assured her, "she's unconscious. Jesus! He really messed her up." It worried him she hadn't responded to him yet. Just how bad were her head injuries? Then she moaned. "Hey baby." His voice was low and gentle.

"Jess?" A whimper passed through swollen lips. *I must be dreaming*, she thought, even as more layers of darkness lifted.

"Hey sweetheart, it's me. You're safe now." It *was* Jess and not a dream!

"You found me." Tears trickled down her cheeks, smearing the blood on them, "I prayed you'd come." Then panic rushed over her. "He'll be back. He leaves then comes back and hurts me some more." Rising up, Jess caught a glimpse of the front of her. Addison had left his savagery everywhere. In that moment he wanted a do-over. *He* wanted the honor of killing him!

"Baby, Addison can't hurt you anymore." Touching the hand nearest him, her fingers were swollen, the nails ragged and encrusted with blood, proof his brave girl had put up a fight. "He won't every hurt you again, sweetheart," he repeated, "he's dead." Jess felt, more than heard, her whispered, "Yes!"

"The ambulance is here Jess," Cooper called.

The EMTs expressions spoke volumes seeing how bad a shape Raine was in. They'd seen a lot of domestic abuse injuries but what had been done to this woman was incomprehensible.

If the scumbag wasn't already dead they'd each like to have a go at him. Since Raine's back was the worst, she remained on her stomach when put on the stretcher. A carefully draped sheet replaced Jess's jacket.

Catching a glimpse of the damage Addison had inflicted left Belle sick and shivering with memories of her own attack. Seeing it, Cooper gathered her to him.

When they loaded Raine into the ambulance, Jess, not about to leave her side, climbed in too. As the EMT closed the door, he was thinking, *Buddy, I'd do the same thing in your shoes.*

With every jostle Raine groaned, which in turn had Jess demanding she be given something for the pain. "I can't," the EMT attending her explained, "she has to wait until we reach the hospital. Believe me, I wish I could ease her misery a bit. I promise we'll be at the hospital in a few minutes."

"Jess." There was trickle of blood at the corner of her mouth. He dabbed it away with a section of white sheet. "Don't let him take Katy. You have to keep him away from her. Please promise me."

Obviously, she didn't remember him telling her Addison was dead. "Baby, Addison can't get Katy, or ever hurt you again. He can't hurt anyone ever again. He's dead. He wounded a deputy and the deputy managed to shoot him."

It took a moment, but at last comprehension dawned on her that Addison was truly dead. At that moment, a billion-pound anchor holding her down lifted and she floated off into the darkness.

While Jess went with Raine, Cooper made sure the scene was taken care of. Belle called Cora to let her know Raine had been found and which hospital she'd been taken to. Cora in turn called Inez.

"That's wonderful news. You head for the hospital. The girls are doing fine. We're going to church, and I'll make sure they have a visit from the Easter Bunny. If they ask why they're not going home yet I'll come up with something."

Cory and her partner, Scott Walker, arrived at the hospital first. They'd been taking the statements of the teenagers who'd spotted the van when news she'd been found reached them.

At the hospital, Raine was rushed into triage while an irate Jess, demanding to stay with her, was hustled to the waiting room. Cory met him in the doorway and shoved a very large, very hot cup of coffee in his hand. "Drink it!" She ordered.

"I don't want any damn coffee! I want to stay with my wife!" He grizzled.

"Well, they don't want you in there!" She gritted through her teeth right back and then softened it with a grin. "The doctors need to check her out thoroughly, Jess. Give them time to do that. Now, drink the damn coffee. You need it."

Still grousing, he tilted the cup, took a slug of the strong black brew, and nearly spewed it out, shooting her with a killing look. "What the hell are you trying to do, poison me? There's sugar in it. I hate sugar in my coffee."

"Yeah, well . . . like I said, you need it. It'll perk up your system. You've had a shock, too, and barely been hanging in there since all this started." Sipping her own coffee she looked at her partner. "Scott, why don't you head on home and get some rest. I'll catch a ride back with Cooper and Belle."

Nodding, he turned to Jess. "My prayers were answered that you'd find her." Simple words, yet so profound followed, "If that were my wife, I'd want to kill the bastard."

Jess hugged the other man. "That's exactly what I wanted to do but the deputy beat me to it."

Alone, they sat in silence. "Do you realize if those kids hadn't spotted the van we might never have found her?" Cory mused aloud drawing an agonized groan from Jess. Her consoling hand touched his. "God, Jess. I'm sorry."

"It's okay. I was thinking the same thing. She was right, you know. Addison was determined to make her pay and was wily enough to use that early release to catch us flat-footed." The hand holding the coffee trembled. "I think I died a thousand deaths finding her gone and the place torn up."

Taking a sip of the sugary coffee, he continued. "I'm just thankful Cora and the girls weren't there. They might have been hurt and Addison could have made off with both Raine and Katy."

"But that didn't happen. I think fate was working in your favor when they went to Branson with my folks."

Just then Cooper and Belle rushed into the waiting room. "Any word yet?" Both demanded at the same time.

"No. Not one damn word!" Jess groused. "You'd think they'd know we're worried to death and give us some news."

"Patience," Belle schooled. Taking his cup, she sipped then screwed up her face. "Ewe . . . that's awful! It's sweet. You don't drink sweet coffee."

"That's what I told her," he gave Cory an, 'I told you so look,' "but smarty-pants seemed to think I needed the sugar, something about me being in shock."

"She's right." Belle handed the coffee back, ordering. "Drink it!"

Cory smirked an, 'I told you so,' right back at him while thinking how good it felt to tease after the hellish hours they'd suffered through.

Twenty minutes later Cora rushed in going straight to Jess. "How is she?"

Hugging her tight, he said. "We don't know yet. She's still being examined."

"I wished I'd been there when you found them. I'd have liked to shoot some punishment into the monster, too. At least he can't ever hurt her again. I just hope the fires of hell are burning hot when he reaches there." She said succinctly, a sentiment shared by all.

# CHAPTER THIRTY-FOUR

**TIME DRAGGED BY** as they waited. In between his many trips to the nurse's station demanding word of Raine's condition, Jess updated Gordon and Molly that she'd been found and Addison was dead. "We're at the hospital now. He hurt her pretty bad, Gordon."

"Jess, she'll be just fine. Thank God this nightmare is finally over. As far as Addison . . ." Gordon trailed off.

Jess got Gordon's unspoken sentiment. "I feel the same way." He concurred. "When I know more, I'll call back."

Hospital sounds, — the soft squish of rubber-soled shoes on the glossy tile, the rattle of medicine carts, ambulance sirens wailing, filled the air around him. Jess tuned it all out as he willed the automatic doors to open and the doctor come out to tell him she would be all right.

While the women sat in shared silence, Cooper touched base with his department and the agencies that had helped search for Raine. The county coroner was handling Addison's body, taking it to the morgue for the time being until his next of kin, that being his mother and father, could be notified. Sticking his hand in his jacket he encountered the cell phone he'd found back at the cabin. In all the excitement he'd forgotten about it. Maybe it belonged to Raine's ex-husband. He started to look then tucked it away again when he was interrupted by a call.

Jess was about to harass the nurses again when those automatic doors opened and a white-coated doctor strode through them. Tall and erect, Jess pegged him for his mid-forties. Rugged and rangy, he should have been on horseback riding the range instead of in a hospital ER. He even dressed the part for beneath the open white coat was a western shirt with pearl snaps, crisp jeans, and highly polished cowboy boots. From the stormy look on his face he was not a happy cowboy. Jess's stomach plunged as though free-falling from a plane.

"Mr. Harper?" Jess nodded. Instantly the stormy look transformed into a huge smile. "Mr. Harper, I'm Dr. Chris Kincaid. I'm tending your wife." Wanting to ease the husband's obvious worry, Dr. Kincaid got right down to business. "First off, she's going to be fine. That's one tough woman, but I think you already knew that." Jess nodded again. "I've gone over her with a fine-tooth comb and though she's been through hell, with time, and a lot of TLC, she'll be back to her old self before you know it." Given his first impression of Jess Harper, he was positive the man would be giving his wife plenty of TLC. They'd practically had to hog-tie him to keep him out of the ER.

"She'll be moving pretty slowly for a while given the fractured ribs she suffered. There's some trauma to her kidneys, too, and she passing blood. With the medication she's been given it will go away." Jess swore violently and Dr. Kincaid empathized with him. "She told me about the prior injuries to them complements of the same man. Given the double-whammy I think she should see a kidney specialist." His gaze fell on the others. *That badly battered woman sure had a lot of people who cared about her. As for her husband, the man still had blood in his eye for the animal that had hurt her.* "She's concussed and has one hell of a headache. We did a CAT scan, and everything looks fine."

Jess could only nod in abject relief as the doctor gave him a long, measured look. Most times the doctor kept his opinions to himself, but not this time. "She shared some details of other attacks while they were married. I probably should keep my opinions to myself, but personally I'm glad the S.O.B.'s dead. If that were my wife . . ." anger radiated from him as he trailed off. "Anyway, I'm keeping her over-night for observation. If I think she's well enough in the morning, I'll release her to go home."

A question hung heavy in the air that Jess couldn't put into words, but he thought Dr. Kincaid a mind reader when he said, "And, he didn't rape her. She didn't think, so but being unconscious several times she wanted to be sure and insisted on being examined."

A chorus of pent-up breaths filled the room. Apparently, it had been an unspoken shared concern. Expelling the deepest breath he'd ever held, Jess figured it was a good thing he was already sitting or he'd have ended up on the floor in a weak heap.

"The rest of her wounds have been cleaned and a soothing antibiotic cream put on them. She's on pain meds that will have her dozing off and on and I'll also make sure she has some when she's released. That old wive's tale of no pain, no gain, is for the birds. She'll heal much faster if the discomfort is kept to a minimum. We're getting ready to move her to a private room. I'll have a nurse come get you on the way." He hesitated, adding. "I don't guess I have to tell you again your wife is one very lucky woman." Then he was gone.

A while later Jess stood over his lucky woman. Someone had attempted to remove the blood from her hair, but traces remained. It pained him seeing how messed up her face was, and another bout of rage engulfed him. *Just be grateful she's alive and Addison's the one dead.* Watching the slight rise and fall of her chest he leaned down and lightly touched his lips to her swollen ones. "Sleep, sweetheart. I'll be right here when you wake up." He thought he detected a glimmer of a smile but just as quickly it was gone.

Reluctant to leave them, it was late evening before the others finally left. Cora, leaving her SUV for Jess, rode home with the others. Staring into the starry night, she gave a thankful prayer. Having been there the first go-round, this time could have ended up a lot worse. The doctor was right. Raine was a strong woman and she had a strong man to help her heal.

As for the strong man, Jess didn't budge from her side as he held her hand and kept vigil. She'd definitely be sore for a long while to come and there'd probably be more scarring, but it was the image of the bruised imprint of Addison's hand on her breast that made Jess ache to put *his* mark on the sadistic monster.

But the monster had been slain. He couldn't hurt her anymore. Yeah, but no thanks to him, he swallowed a double-dose of guilt. It was his fault Addison had gotten his hands on her.

Caressing the back of her hand, he contemplated the concern Dr. Kincaid had about her kidneys. He wasn't a doctor, but he knew enough that if they were severely damaged, she could be affected for the rest of her life, especially when it came to having babies. But that was a bridge they'd cross later. If they never had any of their own, he didn't care, as long as he had her. Gradually his eyes grew heavy as exhaustion finally claimed him.

Odd noises penetrated Raine's drug-induced sleep. Opening her eyes was a major feat but she finally managed it. Moving her head, a dull thudding filled her head. Jess was in the chair beside her, his head bent, his chin nearly resting on his chest, yet in sleep he clung tightly to her hand. A rush of love filled her. "Jess," she whispered his name, lightly squeezing his hand.

Immediately his eyes shot open. He surged to his feet. "Hi, pretty lady." He whispered, kissing her forehead.

"Pretty beat up you mean." Her eyelids drooped then slowly opened again.

"You'll always be beautiful to me. How do you feel?" Careful not to jar her, he perched on the edge of the bed. Smoothing a strand of silky hair from across one blackened eye, he envisioned Addison's fists slamming into her face and his stomach lurched like a boat in a storm. "Are you in pain, sweetheart? Do you need the nurse?"

"No," she sighed softly, "I'm floating pretty toasty right now, but you look exhausted." She smiled and grimaced. "Why don't you curl up here beside me? There's room for both of us." Though the pain was excruciating, she scooted over, groaning with the effort.

"I might hurt you." A gentle finger stroked her bruised cheek. "I'm fine in the chair."

"I'll feel a lot better if you're here with me. I need you to hold me." And he wanted to hold her, beg her forgiveness for not protecting her from Addison. Both needing the reassurance that the nightmare was finally over.

Toeing off his boots, he slipped beneath the covers. As soon as his arms slipped around her a blissful sigh slipped from her. The steady beat of his heart beneath her ear was a soothing balm. It was the best medicine she could ever have asked for. Peacefully resting in his arms, her eyes drifted closed. Jess assumed she'd fallen back to sleep but that wasn't the case. Raine was thinking about how *his* mind worked. She knew he was beating himself up for Addison kidnapping her. It was her responsibility to stop the gigantic guilt trip and make him understand what happened wasn't his fault.

"You need to stop blaming yourself for what happened," she admonished softly. *The woman is a mind-reader*, he thought. "I'd hoped he'd leave me alone once he got out, but that was foolish thinking. Addison was determined to get revenge for all the wrongs he imagined I'd done him and nothing, or no one, was going to stop him." She decided now wasn't the time to confess her fool-hardiness in baiting Addison.

"But I let you down," he said roughly. "If I hadn't left you alone he might have decided not to chance it. And to make it worse, I missed you by bare minutes. I even passed the van you were in. If I'd known that I'd have followed you."

"No!" She replied vehemently. "If you'd confronted him, he'd have killed you. This is how it was supposed to end. And I refuse to listen to any more talk about you blaming yourself!"

Jess chuckled. Even under the influence of pain meds she was a bossy little thing. Reaching into his shirt pocket he removed the wedding rings Addison had torn from her finger. "Let's see if they'll go on."

"You found them," she sighed happily. "He was so furious I thought he'd thrown them away."

Carefully, Jess slipped them onto her swollen finger then gently kissed her injured hand. "I love you, baby, with all my heart."

A profound peace she hadn't experienced in years stole through her. Just as her eyes drifted shut a horrible thought jolted her into wakefulness. "Oh God, Jess, he had pictures of us! He tried to make something dirty and vile out of our love for each other. We've got to find them! The last I remember, they were on the floor of the cabin. No one can ever see those pictures!"

"Shush. It's all right. It's okay." He reassured her. "No one will ever see them. They're locked in the safe until we can destroy them." Upset as she was now he debated telling her what they'd found at the motel Addison had holed-up in. Knowing she'd rather know everything he looked in her eyes and continued, "Honey, the coroner found a motel key in Addison's pocket. Cooper's there now," he hesitated, "there was a darkroom set up to develop all the pictures taken." Raine moaned in mortal embarrassment. "Don't worry. Cooper's got the negatives. Nobody will see them, and we'll burn them right along with the pictures."

It was just too much for her emotionally battered mind. Heartrending sobs tore out of her. After being held prisoner by a madman, suffering the unimaginable tortures he'd inflicted, she needed to get it out of her system. Cradling her closer, her pain became his and his own eyes burned with tears. Finally, her sobs lessened to sniffles and after a time she went limp against him in an exhausted sleep. Jess wasn't far behind her. A while later a nurse stepped into the room to check on her patient and smiled seeing the big man curled protectively around her. After the ordeal they'd been through this was the best kind of medicine anyone could give her.

Later, a slight noise woke Raine. Disoriented, it took a moment to remember where she was. Ignoring the dull throbbing pain from her abused body, she studied her dozing husband. Deep grooves of exhaustion bracketed his mouth. She trailed her hand down the side of his unshaven cheek. The poor guy had been through hell, too.

"How come you're not sleeping?" His voice was raspy, his eyes remained closed but the arm cradling her tightened a bit.

"Something woke me. I've just been lying here admiring my real-life hero."

"I like the sound of that, but I wasn't the only one who was there for you, babe. It took a whole bunch of people starting with the trucker who saw Addison exit the interstate, to the officers, our neighbors, and the kids out parking that saw him leaving the farm where he had you. I hope they didn't get too much grief for being out there. I owe them big time.

As soon you're up and about we'll go thank them personally. Now, pretty lady, how about trying to sleep a little more? If you're a good girl maybe we can talk the doc into springing you from here. I bet I know two little munchkins chomping at the bit to see their mommy."

"Umm . . ." her brow furrowed. "What day is it?" The element of time was hazy. When he said Monday she couldn't believe it. "When did you find me? And how long did he have me?"

"Not quite twenty-four hours. Addison grabbed you Saturday and we found you Sunday morning. Again, if I'd been a few minutes sooner he wouldn't have gotten away with you at all," guilt coating his words.

"Stop blaming yourself! There was no way of stopping him. He'd have blasted through a concrete wall to get at me. At least the only person hurt was the deputy he shot. Do you know how he's doing?"

Jess wasn't surprised she didn't include herself. "Yeah, luckily it was only a flesh wound. I swear it was like a scene right out of an old mobster movie when Addison bailed out of the van guns blazing."

Raine gave him a swollen, wide-eyed look. "And just where were you and your gun?"

"Headed straight for the b . . . ," he stopped abruptly. "How the hell did you know I had a gun?"

"I know you, Mr. Harper. Someone took something that belonged to you and you were getting it back, even if you had to use deadly force."

"You're right about one thing, Mrs. Harper. You're my woman and I don't care if that sounds macho, sexist, or whatever the hell you want to call it! No one takes my woman, my kids, nothing, and gets away with it!" Possessive arrogance mixed with left over fear spilled into his voice.

This time it was Raine who soothed her agitated husband. "Hey! Hey! It's all over and I'm right here with you. No one will ever take me away from you again. I promise." Beneath her hand his heart thudded strong and steady.

"They damn well better not even try!" He bit out succinctly. "Those hours you were gone were a living hell. Knowing Addison had you about drove me nuts! Thank goodness for Cooper, Belle, and Cora. They kept me from going berserk.

Cooper and Belle helped me search for you and Cora kept everybody fueled up with food and coffee. Plus, she studied the surveillance tapes and found Addison slipping in and taking you. She also found his spies. Come to find out one was a private investigator hired to track you down. The guy sure picked the wrong person to work for. As for the other, he was covered from head to toe. There's no way to identify him."

No wonder she'd felt someone was watching her. "What do you mean he picked the wrong person to work for?" She asked despite guessing the answer.

"He's dead. His body was in the adjoining motel room stuffed in a trunk. If I had to guess I'd say he knew too much so Addison got rid of him."

What a destructive path Addison had left in his wake. But Addison was dead, just like his spy. Should she feel sad on Katy's behalf that her father was dead? Absolutely not! Addison hadn't been a father to Katy in a long time.

It finally registered, Jess had said it was Monday. "Oh no, we missed Easter. What about the girls? Do you know how they spent it?"

"Yes, we missed it, and yes, I know how they spent the day. Inez took care of everything including picking Ethel up from the airport. The girls went to Easter service at church and were visited by the Easter Bunny. Cora found their baskets we'd hidden and gave them to Inez."

"We really have some very good friends, don't we?" She sighed.

"I can't imagine any better ones." He kissed her battered cheek. "Now, snuggle in here and close those raccoon eyes of yours." He grunted when she elbowed him. "I'll let you get away with that for now." He teased, spooning against her.

# Chapter Thirty-Five

**IT WAS MID-MORNING** before Dr. Kincaid made an appearance. Examining her, he poked and prodded while expecting the little gasps she couldn't hold back. Satisfied, he released her but issued several restrictions. No — lifting or carrying anything over a pound, drink lots of water, and with a stern look at Jess, no intimacy until she is up to it. Both flushed a deep crimson. Lastly, he wanted to see her in his office in a few days.

When Mrs. Harper showed up for her check-up he'd recommend a colleague who just happened to be an OBGYN. It appeared she wasn't aware she was pregnant. That she hadn't miscarried was a miracle.

Arriving home, you'd have thought they were celebrities given the welcoming crowd. Their two little angels were front and center. As Jess hoisted them up to kiss mommy, he locked eyes with her. Unspoken, they shared the same thought — explaining Addison's death to Katy.

"Careful girls, mom had an accident. We don't want to squeeze her too tight." Setting them down again, the girls glowered at Cooper as they dashed inside.

Eyeing everyone gathered around her, emotion knotted Raine's throat. "Thank you," tears of gratitude blurred her blackened eyes, "Thank every blessed one of you for being here for us."

"That's what families do, honey." Inez gently patted her arm. Hank added. "We take care of our own."

"They're right. You and the munchkin have been our family for a long time," Ethel gently hug her, "and now we have Jess and Kathy, too."

"We have a little surprise for you two." Cora said as she hugged her carefully. There wasn't a place that wasn't either black and blue or scraped and split. "Actually, it was the munchkins' idea. Since you couldn't be here for Easter they wanted to have another one when you two got home."

Raine beamed. "We sure do have two very special kids."

"You bet we do." Jess glanced around. "And just where did they run off to, anyway?"

Crossing her arms over her chest, Cora shot Cooper an exasperated look. "They're guarding their Easter baskets. Seems they caught Cooper scoping out the goodies and they're sure he's going to eat all their candy. They even wanted me to arrest him."

Cooper loved teasing the little girls. He'd make a great dad, Jess thought, even as he glared at him. "Cooper, leave my kids' candy alone! Get your own kids and eat their candy!"

Grinning mischievously, Cooper threw up his hands. "Hey, old buddy. I'm working real hard on getting a kid of my own. Just ask Belle. Honey, tell Jess how hard I've been working morning, noon, and night. Belle!" Cooper called to his quickly retreating wife. "How come your face is so red? Hey! Where're you going? Belle! Tell him I'm working overtime on making a baby!" The slamming of the screen door was her answer while everyone laughed.

Jess slapped him on the back. "Just keep practicing, old buddy. You'll get it right." Raine just rolled her swollen eyes at the two grown men. "Come on, let's go find our girls." Slipping a protective arm around her, they slowly walked inside followed by the others.

The girls *were* guarding their Easter baskets. Sitting on the loveseat with the baskets between them, they watched mommy walking very slowly with daddy helping her.

"How did you get your boo-boos, mommy?" Katy asked.

Settling Raine on the sofa, Jess sat beside her then gathered a girl on each knee. Too little to be told the entire truth, he explained that mommy had been in an accident but would get better with lots of love. They gently kissed the boo-boos on her face but it was her colorful eyes they were fascinated with. Both wanted their eyes painted black and purple just like mommy. That made Jess laugh with relish while Raine gave them an emphatic, "I don't think so!"

A while later, noticing her wilting, Jess insisted Raine take a pain pill and rest. The girls trailed behind them to the bedroom. If mommy was napping then they were, too. Ever careful not to jostle her, they snuggled beside her on the king-size bed, and still not trusting Cooper, kept a firm grasp on their Easter baskets.

Observing them, Jess was envious. He wanted to cuddle up next to mommy, too. Seeing the look, she mouthed, "later."

Grinning in understanding, he sat on the edge of the bed. "Can you girls take good care of mommy while daddy takes a shower?"

"Yes, daddy," Katy answered, poking a malted-chocolate egg between his lips. He cheeked the candy and kissed her shining hair. His eyes connected with Raine's. Katy was right. He was her daddy. Of course, she'd have to be told about Addison, but that would wait until later.

She must have dozed off, because the sound of laughter roused her. Following the sounds she headed for the kitchen, arriving as Jess and Cooper came through the door from putting things right at the cabin so Cora and Ethel could stay there. Seeing her, he moved to her side and slipped a supporting arm around her waist.

"You really don't have to do this," she flashed a cheeky grin then grimaced when it hurt, "but I like it. I could get used to all this pampering. You better be careful, Jess Harper, you're creating a monster."

"As long as you're my monster, I don't care. Besides, the doctor said you have to take it easy." He sat down beside her at the table. "As far as I'm concerned, you deserve a lot of pampering."

Wise woman that she was, Raine read between the lines. He was still in the throes of guilt. But he'd been a victim, too. Leaning into him she whispered, "Okay, but you do know that includes dressing and undressing me as well as bathing me. Sure you can handle it?"

His broad shoulders shaking with laughter gave her his answer. So did the lips that kissed the crook of her neck. The fire smoldering in his eyes made her forget any discomfort she was in. "It sure is going to be a long couple of weeks." She grumbled for his ears only. This time his laughter was carefree, a sign he was getting back to his old self.

With everyone gathered round the large table, Jess joined hands with her to say the belated Easter blessing: "Dear Lord, we give thanks to You this day, for the prayers You've answered in returning our loved one safely to our family, and for the gift of Your life. We bless this food in Your name. Amen." Around the table everyone echoed Jess.

# EPILOGUE

**STANDING IN THE** warm sunshine, Raine and Jess admired the newly completed additions to their home. Life had certainly been hectic since her abduction and Addison's death. Besides wanting to get the new addition finished, they'd also wanted to get out from under all the evilness associated with Addison. So as soon as she'd been fit to travel they'd driven to Phoenix.

With Gordon and Molly's help, they'd gone through everything and save for a few things, the rest went to a battered women's shelter. As for the construction company, when they'd divorced, Addison apparently hadn't thought to change his will, so at his death it was Raine's to do with as she pleased. Raine sold it to a competitor despite his parents' protest and the proceeds went into a college fund for the girls.

No one attended Addison's funeral. After what he'd put her through she'd have been a hypocrite to go. Glad he was dead, and not feeling a bit guilty, she'd have climbed up on his grave and danced the Charleston. After all, hadn't he left her to die locked in that cellar? Had it not been for those kids out parking she'd have never been found. The thought still sent icy chills racing through her.

What really shocked her was Addison's folks' requesting a visit with their granddaughter. If not for their insinuations Katy wasn't Addison's, she might have agreed. Instead, she informed them that if they wanted news of Katy they should maintain contact with her attorney. After what they'd said and done in the past, Katy didn't need contact with them until they proved their sincerity.

In explaining Addison's death to Katy, they'd been truthful to a certain point telling her daddy had gone to heaven. Raine knew better though. *Anyone as evil as Addison has no place in heaven. I'm betting he's giving the devil a run for his money.*

Old enough to understand death and the finality of it, Katy had cried for a while then held her arms out to Jess. "I want my good daddy to hold me." Wrapping her in his protective arms, he assured her. "I'll always be a good daddy, Katy-bug."

As for Kathy, fate worked in their favor. Her father decided it was in her best interests to be adopted into a loving family. Ironically within days of signing away his rights they received two messages: That he'd died in a fight with another inmate and that her mother had been found dead of a drug overdose. Kathy, just as Katy, wanted her good mommy and daddy to hold her as she grieved for her loss. It was an emotional time having two grieving children in the house but surrounded by all the love, their pain was easing.

Cora remained with them instead of returning to Phoenix. She had a life with her surrogate family and besides that she'd met a gentleman at church. The arrangement suited both sisters just fine and they were happy visiting back and forth.

Slipping an arm around Jess's waist, Raine hid a grin. She'd just come from her checkup regarding her kidneys, plus another doctors' appointment she hadn't mentioned to Jess. "It's beautiful and the girls are over the moon having the playroom."

"Yeah, they were pretty insistent on it. I thought they'd stage a protest when I said they couldn't have it." A dreamy look appeared in his eyes. "Can you imagine if we had any boys? We'd have to add a whole other floor. It'd be his and hers everything." Gazing at the house, he didn't see her grin grow bigger.

"Actually," she was thinking maybe he should be sitting down, "you might want to get started on that other floor." She announced, then waited for his reaction.

It took a moment for her words to sink in, then his head whipped around and he gaped at her like she'd sprouted two heads and eight eyes. "What?" He barked at her idiotic suggestion. "We just finished enlarging the place. Why on earth would we need to add another . . ." gradually realization dawned and the biggest smile spread across his face.

Lifting her off her feet, he swung her around. "We're having a baby? You're sure? When? And here I thought you had a flu bug." Sobering, he set her gently on her feet. "Is your body up to it? You know Dr. Kincaid's worried about your kidneys." Eyes that could pull her into their very depth were filled with worry. The very thought of anything happening to her scared the hell out of him. After all, he'd come so close to losing her only a few short weeks ago.

Breathless, she answered each question separately. "Yes! Yes, I'm sure! And we're due in about six months. It must have happened on our honeymoon. Dr. Kincaid says both kidneys are healing nicely so my pregnancy shouldn't be too much of a strain on them. He promised to keep a very close watch on me. He and my OB are just amazed I didn't miscarry during Addison's beatings."

At her first checkup Dr. Kincaid had told her she was pregnant. "I was hesitant about doing any scans, so we tried making sure you were shielded. I thought about mentioning it then, but you two had enough to deal with, plus I didn't see anything wrong. However, you should start seeing an OBGYN to monitor everything baby-wise." Wanting to make sure everything was okay before making her announcement, she'd kept mum. This was her second OBGYN visit in as many weeks.

Jess swore a blue streak. "If that had happened, I'd for sure shot him deader than he already is."

Ranie didn't doubt him. But Addison was no longer a threat. He wasn't going to taint their joyous news. "But it didn't happen, so forget Addison. He doesn't play a part in our lives anymore."

Happily claiming her lips, his body immediately stirred with desire. The woman could stir him right out of his jeans. No wonder she was pregnant. "You taste like cherry cool-aid. Now back to what the doctor said."

"I passed a snow-cone stand in town and just had to have one. It was me and a whole pack of little kids in line. I didn't think I'd ever get my hands on it." She giggled lightheartedly. "Now you know why I've had those cravings. Anyway, Dr. Kincaid wants us to be extra cautious even though he says I'm strong and healthy and should have no problems."

"Then we'll do everything to make sure you and the baby are all right. We don't want anything unexpected or any surprises to pop up."

"Well, actually . . ." There was one more *ginormous* surprise. "There is one more little surprise." He gave her quizzical look. "You know that baseball team we joked about? Well . . . we've got a darn good start on it." Placing his hand over her slightly rounded tummy, she thought for a man who knew her body quite well he'd missed the thickening of it. "There are three in here."

Incredulous, his eyes grew huge and his jaw hit the ground with a resounding thud. "Thr . . . ?" He croaked. "Three. We have three in there?" His large hand pressed against his babies, a tidal wave of testosterone inflated his ego by leaps and bound. "Hot damn, woman am I good or what!" *I guess he thinks he did it all by himself,* she mused as he planted a kiss that left her fanning herself when he finally let her go. Whipping out his cell he keyed some numbers. "Ha! Michaels, I beat you and your twins. I'm having triplets!"

Raine rolled her eyes as his exultant laughter filled the air then he flipped the phone closed and hauled her back into his arms. This time it was a kiss filled with undying love, an intimacy that belonged to only the two of them and a promise of a lifetime of love.

However, when he lifted his mouth his expression turned formidable. "Now I have a little surprise for you. In all the excitement of Addison making off with you, Cooper found this." From his pocket he withdrew a familiar looking phone. "And to *my* surprise it's chock full of messages to and from Addison. You've been a very bad girl and I'm thinking you need to be punished."

Guilty surprise reddened her face and she started sputtering. "Jess . . . honey . . . I can explain . . ." was as far as she got before his mouth claimed hers again. Well, if this was his idea of punishment she was going to keep on being bad!

# ABOUT THE AUTHOR

Tina swears she was bitten by the writing bug probably further back than she can remember, attributing it to the tales and antics she recalls as a youngster growing up amongst a whole passel of aunts, uncles and cousin. Now with her own family there are even more stories to inspire ideas, even collaborating with granddaughter Harmony for a poetry contest and finishing second.

Though a Missouri girl, a graduate of East Central College in Union Missouri with a degree in Criminal Justice, she, her husband Tom and family have resided on the Florida Gulf Coast for twenty-five years, arriving the same month that Hurricane Andrew. Among the many hats she wears is office manager at a local law firm and now has donned a new one with the plunge into the literary world with her first release of You'll Come to Me.

Besides her love of travel and history, Gatlinburg Tennessee being one of her favorite places to go, Tina loves family vacations and reunions, doing genealogy, reading, crocheting, baseball and soccer. A lover and spoiler of animals she unabashedly admits her little Morkie Marshmallow absolutely rules the house.

If you enjoyed reading this second book in the

# Dusk *to* Dawn Series

be sure to let the author and publisher know by leaving
your comments on your favorite online bookstore.

Stay connected with Tina on Facebook
and be the first to know about her new
releases and Raine's continuing saga.


Facebook: tinamarienicholsauthor
Website: www.tinamarienichols.com